Praise for Stronger at the Seams

"*Stronger at the Seams* draws us into an emotional journey that cannot fail to touch us all. A normal family life turned upside down by loss and devastating illness, this is a story about listening—listening to your heart, listening to helpful and unhelpful responses, and then unravelling interpretation, understanding, and responding to shared people and experiences. Listening is the glue to life, and Shannon Stocker understands firsthand the importance of wholesome listening. A beautifully written book that I shall certainly be sharing!"

DAME EVELYN GLENNIE—MUSICIAN, SPEAKER, A[

FOUNDER OF THE EVELYN GLENNIE FOUNDAT[

"I went through every possible emotion reading *Stronger at the* [
which feels appropriate both to the young tween/teen experie[
the gut-wrenching medical fears of the main character. No [
tensions, though, I came away with the overwhelming feelir[
and resilience even in, or maybe because of, Twyla's deter[
the face of great adversity."

HEIDI E.Y. STEMPLE, CHILDREN'S BOOK AUTHO[

"From the first page to the last, I was invested in T[
of this beautiful cast of characters. Stocker's cor[
demonstrates the importance of self-advocacy . . . [
It serves as a reminder to us all that grief and pai[
not) be ignored, and we are all feel broken som[

NATALIE WEAVER, [

AND FO[

SHANNON STOCKER

STRONGER AT THE SEAMS

BLINK

BLINK

Stronger at the Seams
Copyright © 2024 by Shannon Stocker

Published in Grand Rapids, Michigan, by Blink.

Requests for information should be addressed to customercare@harpercollins.com.

ISBN 978-0-310-16318-3 (audio)

Library of Congress Cataloging-in-Publication Data

Names: Stocker, Shannon, author.
Title: Stronger at the seams / Shannon Stocker.
Description: Grand Rapids, Michigan : Blink, 2024. | Audience: Ages 13-18. |
    Summary: "When Twyla begins struggling with health issues the doctors dismiss
    as minor, she finds herself searching for answers on her own, while also dealing
    with friendship fallouts and the lingering effects of her mother's death as she
    navigates her freshman year of high school"— Provided by publisher.
Identifiers: LCCN 2024005613 (print) | LCCN 2024005614 (ebook) | ISBN
    9780310162353 (hardcover) | ISBN 9780310163039 (ebook)
Subjects: CYAC: Sick—Fiction. | Friendship—Fiction. | Grief—Fiction. | Family
    life—Fiction. | High schools—Fiction. | Schools lcgft | BISAC: YOUNG
    ADULT FICTION / Health & Daily Living / Diseases, Illnesses & Injuries |
    YOUNG ADULT FICTION / Family / General (see also headings under Social
    Themes)
Classification: LCC PZ7.1.S7524 St 2024 (print) | LCC PZ7.1.S7524 (ebook) |
    DDC [Fic]—dc23
LC record available at https://lccn.loc.gov/2024005613
LC ebook record available at https://lccn.loc.gov/2024005614

Blink titles may be purchased in bulk for educational, business, fundraising, or sales
promotional use. For information, please email SpecialMarkets@Zondervan.com.

Cover Design and illustration: Ellen Duda
Interior Design: Denise Froehlich

Printed in the United States of America

24 25 26 27 28 LBC 5 4 3 2 1

If the floor has crumbled beneath you,
or the darkness swallowed you whole.
If you've ever felt broken
or fractured
or cracked,
with your life spinning out of control . . .
Then these pages are yours for the turning.
This window is yours to gaze through.
You're not solo.
I see you.
Together, let's heal.
Sweet reader . . . this book is for you.

And for Greg, Cassidy, and Tye—my golden seams.

Chapter 1

UNGLORY

My stomach roiled as the sickly-sweet smell of sugar filled the car. Usually, I liked ice cream as much as any other fourteen-year-old. But today, the thought of it made me want to puke. Wolfie slurped at the melting scoop around the edges of his cone.

Ugh.

"Twy?" Dad squinted at me through the rearview mirror. "First, you don't want a treat. Now, you're making that face. *Again.* Seriously . . . are you okay?"

I gripped the field hockey stick in my lap until my knuckles blanched. For someone who didn't like to talk about his feelings, he sure seemed nosey about mine lately. This was the third time he'd asked me how I felt since we left Brain Freeze. Of course, I didn't *really* feel fine. My stomach hadn't felt right for a week, with random nausea spells seeming to strike out of nowhere. But there was absolutely no way I was about to admit that and risk being pulled from the summer field hockey tournament. I'd worked too hard, for too long. And too much was on the line. If I sat on the sidelines because of some stupid upset stomach, I'd never make varsity next year. Besides . . . this was *our* year to win. I could feel it in my bones.

"I'm fine, Dad." I pretended to be engrossed by the oaks whizzing by on my favorite twisty bypass. Curtains of trees lined one side of the road, allowing an occasional view of a distant creek hidden beyond, and steep rock rose from the road in jagged crags on the other side. In the winter, icicles formed on the rock, thick

1

and long like massive stalactites. When we were little, Dad did this funny voice every time we passed the icicles, yodeling as Icicle Bill for thirty hysterical seconds. I wished Icicle Bill were here now instead of Prying Dad.

From the corner of my eye, I could see Dad studying me in the rearview mirror.

"In the fall, this street will be gorgeous, don't you think? With all those oranges and yellows . . ." I trailed off, as if deep in thought. I stole a glance at him to check if he bought it.

Dad raised one brow. I sighed.

"I just . . . I didn't want to eat right before the game, okay? Sugar doesn't sit well when I have to run."

Dad's eyes narrowed.

"Hey, Twy, know what?" Wolfie lapped the salted caramel now puddling between his fingers, completely oblivious to the weirdness in the car. "Eating ice cream can make your body temperature *rise*. Did you know that?"

I always marveled at the crazy facts my little brother tucked into his brain. Wolfie licked from the base of his palm all the way up to the top of the ice cream scoop. "Wait. It makes your body . . . *warmer?*" I asked.

"Mm-hmm. And did you know it takes twelve pounds of milk to make just one container of ice cream?"

I smirked. "But what *size* container?" For sure, that question would get him. No fifth grader committed that kind of information to memory. Not even . . .

"A gallon," Wolfie said. "And did you know vanilla is the most popular flavor? I mean, whoever answered vanilla to that question never had salted caramel chocolate chunk, that's for sure. Not that I don't like vanilla, but it's not even close to being the best flavor. Maybe it's just the most popular because of cake." His teeth crunched into the cone.

I tilted my head. "Because of . . . cake?"

Sugary bits flew from his mouth as he answered. "Yah. Caush eh goesh well wif vanilla."

"Ewww . . . Wolfie! You're spitting on me!"

"Wolfie! Please don't get food in the car, or I'll never let you eat in here again." Despite Dad's stern tone, Wolfie threw his head back and laughed silently, mouth wide open.

So gross.

My stomach spun again, and Mom's words echoed through my mind: "Everything happens for a reason, Twyla." It had been five years since she'd died, but in that moment, it was like she was right there next to me, running her long, trim fingers through her slick, black hair, whispering into my ear. Mom loved mottos: *You are what you eat. Be yourself—everyone else is already taken. Don't sweat the small stuff.* She had a million of them, but "everything happens for a reason" was her favorite.

Sometimes, it made a lot of sense to me. If you tripped, it was probably because you weren't paying attention to the world around you. If you failed a test, maybe you needed to study harder. If it rained, the trees or the flowers probably needed the water. But then there were other times I couldn't find a reason at all, no matter how hard I tried. Like, why was my friggin' stomach bugging me so much lately?

Dad's voice pulled me from my pensiveness. "Hey, guys, wanna hear a joke?" He grinned, and Wolfie and I exchanged a "here comes another bad Dad joke" glance.

"What's brown and sticky?" Yup. Another bad Dad joke.

He didn't wait for us to guess. "A stick." He laughed. "Get it?" He turned the steering wheel with one hand and slapped his knee with the other.

Wolfie spit out even more cone through fits of giggles. Ugh.

My phone dinged.

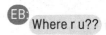

EB: Where r u??

Emilia and I always met in the parking lot ten minutes before warm-up, walked to the field together, then claimed the left end of the bench for our water bottles. I checked the time: exactly twelve minutes before warm-up. My fingers tapped at the keyboard.

Me: Chill, girl. Pulling in now.

Our car rolled into the big, crowded parking lot. People carrying collapsible chairs and sun umbrellas trudged toward the fields in the distance, coolers and toddlers in tow. I peered up through the window and shaded my eyes. Cumulus clouds covered enough of the sky that I knew we wouldn't roast too badly. Cumulus were my favorite. During the day, they provided the best shade. But when they floated in the sky at sunset, it looked almost like you could poke a stick through them, take a bite, and they'd melt on your tongue. But today, they just looked like cotton balls. Fluffy, beautiful, shade-casting cotton balls.

It was our last game before the summer tournament. We'd won every single one that summer, but some had been super close . . . and the Red Eagles were also undefeated. Whoever won today would get top seeding in the tournament. We'd not only have to play our best individual games, we couldn't afford to be selfish. Everyone would have to be willing to pass.

Even Lindy.

Yeah. Like that's gonna happen.

My mom used to quote basketball legend Michael Jordan. She'd say, "Talent wins games, but teamwork and intelligence win championships." I frowned.

If you were here, you'd know what to say, I thought. *Even to Lindy.*

But Mom wasn't here. Dad meant well, but he never knew how to handle girl drama. Anytime I tried to talk to him about stuff like that, he suddenly remembered some work obligation or had to go to the bathroom.

I ticked through a mental checklist, knee bouncing with each emphasized syllable.

Bubble ponytail. *Check.*

Shin guards. *Check.*

Blue sleeves. *Check.*

Mouth guard. *Check.*

Face shield. *Check.*

Stick. *Check.*

Rub my favorite snow globe for good luck.

Ohhhh . . . crap.

Emilia believed with everything in her that if I failed to rub my snow globe, we were sure to go down in a blaze of . . . whatever the opposite of glory is. Unglory? Yeah.

A blaze of unglory.

For as long as I could remember, Emilia had been driven by superstitious beliefs. When we were little, I'd thought it was just the way she'd been raised. In her house, crystals and gemstones hung from strings or sat in shiny white bowls on counters. Incense burned constantly, banishing negative energy. A variety of Native rituals had been a part of her family's history for generations, passed down from her great-great-grandmother, the first shaman in their lineage. She'd died long ago, and the traditions now belonged to Emilia's mother, also a spiritual healer. But as I got older, I came to realize that superstition and spirituality were two very different things. Emilia's mother knew more about medicinal herbs, reiki, and acupuncture than anyone I'd probably ever meet in my life. Her practice was based in things like love, gratitude, forgiveness, and compassion. Emilia's superstitions, on the other hand, seemed to come from a place of fear. A desire to control things.

Like me, our other best friend, Anna, didn't really buy into Emilia's superstitions, but she and I also didn't see any harm in playing along if they made Emilia feel better. After all, we each had our own quirks when it came to handling things—Anna preferred to quietly observe from a corner and chewed her nails, while I liked to research things ad nauseum. Maybe that's why we'd always gotten along so well—I never questioned their quirks, and they never questioned mine.

Which, ultimately, was why I'd rubbed the snow globe before every game that summer. Every game except this one. Nausea had struck while doing my ponytail, and then Dad was yelling that we were going to be late.

Doubt nipped at my brain, but then reason sank in. No. I did *not* need a snow globe to win. I needed to play hard. *And* smart.

Dad scanned the lot until he saw an open spot by a sprawling oak. He always tried to find shade so the leather seats didn't burn the backs of our legs when we got back in. The Kentucky sun didn't blister us like Florida rays, but it could still be pretty fiery. I barely remembered the old ranch house we used to live in, before Mom had been recruited to Louisville as an exotic vet. She'd been good with horses, so the move made sense, and I knew exotics were her favorite. She'd studied at Busch Gardens, operating on lions and birthing baby giraffes. Her stories had mesmerized me. A picture still hung on the wall of Dad's bedroom, with Mom all scrubbed in and grinning over an anesthetized gorilla. But even though she'd spent most of her post–Busch Gardens time with puppies, kitties, and horses, the truth was that she never turned away any animal that limped or slithered through her door. Snakes, squirrels, turtles . . . she'd helped them all.

The tires rolled up onto the lawn as shadows crawled from the front of the car into the back. When it stopped, sun shone on only the driver's seat.

Typical Dad.

As soon as we got out, Emilia bolted toward our car. I smiled at the blondes waving, princess-like, from the stands: Anna and her mother, Dr. Rose. Whenever anyone got injured, we knew we could always rely on Dr. Rose. Even though she was a kids' brain doctor (or *pediatric neurologist*, if you want to get technical), she once braced someone's broken wrist right there on the field with a folded newspaper, a towel, and an Ace bandage from her car. Ever since then, some of the teammates started calling her Dr. MacGyver, like the TV dude who always got out of a jam with whatever supplies he could find. But to me, she was still just Mama Rose.

Anna hopped down the stands and jogged our way.

Dad turned to me, hands outstretched, one palm up and one down. "Ready?"

A few of the girls from the varsity team wandered by, glancing our direction. I hesitated, wondering if they'd think our handshake was stupid.

Dad's grin faded. "Oh. You don't . . . Do you . . . Should we skip it this time . . . ?"

Conflicted, I dropped my eyes to the ground. "Maybe," I mumbled. Dad withdrew his hands.

"Hey," he said. I looked up.

"Go get 'em, Twilight." He winked. I breathed a sigh of relief and winked back.

My parents started calling me "Twilight" when I became obsessed with the meaning of names and realized my name also meant my favorite time of day: That moment just after sunrise, or just before sunset, when the world glows in vibrant shades of orange, red, pink, and gold. That one brief moment when everything falls still but the croaking bullfrogs, the chirping crickets, and the whisper of the wind.

It's magical.

I once googled the reason the sky seems to burst into flames at twilight, and I even learned a bit about "scattering"—how short wavelengths of light, like blues and violets, are more scattered by air molecules than other colors in the spectrum. Then, when the sun is low on the horizon and has to pass through more of the atmosphere, those same short wavelengths are scattered away from your eyes. But the other colors—the oranges, yellows, and reds—those can still be seen. At first, I wanted to learn as much as I could about the phenomenon . . . but something about decoding the beauty of that time of day felt wrong to me. So I closed my laptop and never looked back.

But of course, my name isn't Twilight. It's Twyla, like the dancer, Twyla Tharp. My parents met in college, when Dad was the pianist for all the soloists. He said Mom had the most angelic voice he'd ever heard . . . but it was when he first saw her dance that he knew he was a goner.

"She skimmed the floor like a dragonfly on water," he'd say. His words always made her smile. "Light, airy, delicate, and yet . . . unpredictable." Then they'd laugh.

I missed that laugh.

When I closed my eyes and listened hard, I could still hear it . . . tinkling like a soprano wind chime in the breeze. But the further we got from That Day . . . the more it seemed to fade.

The more *she* seemed to fade.

"Twy! You coming? It's *time*, girl!" Emilia's thick black ponytail bounced between her strong shoulders. Her stick cut back and forth through the grass, like she was dribbling past a defender. I envied the way her already-gorgeous skin bronzed in the summer.

Mine just freckled and burned, like Dad's.

Anna trailed behind her, laughing. "No way you guys will lose with those kinds of moves, Em," she said.

Emilia winked at her.

"Wait!" My hand flew to my shoulder, naked without my stick bag. "I forgot my—"

Dad thrust the long, turquoise bag toward me.

"Thanks!" I said, tossing the bag over my shoulder.

"Hey . . . !" Wolfie had been hanging from the branch of a nearby tree, but as soon as he saw my friends, he hopped down and bolted our way.

"Hi, buddy!" Emilia tousled his hair. Anna hugged him.

"Did you know there are no left-handed hockey sticks?" he asked.

"I didn't know that! I wonder why," Emilia said.

"'Cause they lead to injureeeeees," Wolfie said.

"Well, well, well . . ." Lindy's drawl curdled my blood. "If it ain't Wolfman, the little Mistah Know-It-All."

Why did we have to play for the same team?

Emilia waltzed toward Lindy until her face was so close, she must've been able to smell Lindy's minty-fresh breath.

"Well," Emilia spat, "I guess next to you, who knows nothing, everybody's a know-it-all." She leaned in one more inch, clenching her teeth and mocking Lindy's tone to perfection. *"Ain't* they?"

"GIRLS!" Coach Givens motioned to us. Her voice cut the tension. "GAME TIME! Let's GO!"

Lindy's shoulder whacked Emilia's as she huffed past. Anna grabbed Emilia's arm before she could explode.

"She's not worth it," Anna whispered. At barely five feet tall, Anna's command of situations always surprised me a little. She opened her arms to invite us both in for a mini huddle.

"The best revenge is to win, *despite* her," she said. "You two are the strongest players on this team. When she goes low . . ."

"We go high!" Our voices rang in unison. Anna always knew she could pull Emilia from any level of frustration with a Michelle Obama quote. Emilia adored powerful, compassionate women in politics. We always joked that her high school superlative would probably be "Most likely to change the world," while Anna's would probably be "Most likely to hold the world's hand."

We were still trying to figure out mine.

Emilia and I sprinted toward the field as Anna ran back to the stands. Suddenly, my stomach heaved. I clutched my waist with one hand and cupped the other over my mouth, willing myself not to vomit.

"Twy! You okay?" Emilia stopped dead in her tracks.

I dropped down to a crouch and yanked my shoelace. "I'll catch up," I said. "Gotta tie my shoe."

If Emilia noticed anything weird, she didn't let on. She nodded and took off.

I retied my shoe and threw my bag back over my shoulder, willing the wave of nausea to pass. Then I looked to the sky.

For once, I thought, *I don't care what the reason is.*

Please just help me get through this game.

Chapter 2

CRAP! CRAP! CRAP!

The team gathered around Coach Givens. "Okay, listen up. My forwards are Lindy, Twyla, and Erin. Offensive midfielders are Emilia and Danielle. Defensive midfielders . . ." As Coach rattled off the rest of the usual starters, I looked to the stands. Dad waved, while Wolfie sat beside him, face buried in an iPad.

"Now," Coach said, "two laps around the pitch, girls. GO!"

I took off with the rest of my team, half expecting to feel poorly again—but all I felt was sweat dripping down my nose and excitement pounding through my veins. By the time we hit the pitch and took positions, I felt like myself again.

The whistle blew.

CRACK! Danielle's stick smacked the ball cross-field to Emilia, who drove it past first one then two defenders, on toward the goal. She passed to Erin, who didn't have a shot . . . so Erin hit it back to Emilia.

"LINDY IS OPEN, FOR GOODNESS' SAKE!" A familiar voice shrieked from the stands, startling Emilia long enough for a defender to steal the ball. I glared at Lindy's mom, but it only took Danielle about five seconds to steal it back. She hit it to Lindy, but another defender's stick knocked it off course.

Straight toward me.

Instinct took over. I spotted my target, pulled back my stick, and swung.

Just as the ball sank into the net, another wave of nausea steamrolled me. I raised my stick to indicate I'd been the one to score the goal and walked back to the bench, hand across my stomach.

"Nice shot," Coach said. Her eyes scanned my hand. "You okay?" She kept her voice level, but the undercurrent of concern was impossible to miss.

Although Ms. Givens had only been coaching me for a few weeks, she'd lived next door to me long enough to recognize when something was wrong. In fact, for the last few summers, she'd been the go-to mom on our street for scraped knees, headaches, and upset stomachs. I usually found solace in her comfort when I was down and out . . . but she'd pull me if she thought I might be sick. And I did *not* want to be pulled.

"Just need some water." I avoided eye contact with her.

But as I continued to play, each turn of my head brought yet another wave. Eventually, my pace slowed, and balls started rolling past me. I didn't even hear the whistle blow.

"Twy! Coach is calling you!" Emilia pointed toward the bench. Clouds parted and the skin on the back of my neck boiled as I jogged to the sidelines. Coach handed me my water bottle and a wet cloth.

"Here," she said. "Drink."

I did as I was told, praying the water would help.

"Take a seat," Coach commanded. She shot me a stern look, brows stitched together, and I knew better than to argue. "Caise, you're in at forward."

My butt hit the bench. Hard. I tried to shake off the worry, but Mom's words rang through my ears.

Everything happens for a reason, Twyla.

So why? Was I fighting some kind of virus? No way this was all because of a dumb superstition. Was I dehydrated? Had I been getting horrible sleep? My elbows pressed dents into my knees as I focused on the game. Whatever the reason, I'd figure it out later.

"COME ON, DRAGONS!" I shouted.

Caise and Erin each took two strong shots, but the Eagles defense was an iron wall. Then, right before the halftime whistle, Lindy drove toward the net. Just as she seemed ready to shoot, a defender stole the ball and drove it all the way back to our goal.

The Eagles scored.

"WHAT are you THINKING, LINDY? HOW could you let HER steal from YOU?"

As Lindy's mom screamed from the stands, Coach Givens glared and balled her hands into fists. Lindy threw her stick onto the turf.

I glanced at Dad in the stands—arms crossed and head down. It looked like he'd fallen asleep.

Well, I thought, *at least he never yells at me like that.*

When the halftime whistle blew, I filled my lungs and stood. Emilia gave me a weak thumbs-up and tilted her head. She mouthed, *You okay?* I nodded.

"Coach? I drank some water. I'm better now," I lied.

"Okay," she said. She gathered the team in a huddle. "Girls, you're holding strong against tough competitors. I know you're getting tired and the sun is hot. Hydrate, use your cooling towels, and take this time to recharge. When we go back in, I want Twyla, Erin, and Caise at forward. Emilia and Lindy, you'll be offensive midfield. Then I want—"

"Ummm . . . Coach?" Lindy's usually confident voice faltered. "You said you wanted me at midfield. Didn't you mean . . . forward?"

"No, Lindy, I want you at midfield starting the second half, behind Twyla. You'll do great there."

"But—"

"Lindy . . ." Coach Givens shot her a warning look. "I'm the coach in this game. And don't let me see you throw your stick again, or you'll find yourself on the bench."

When the whistle blew, Coach clapped her hands twice. "Okay, Dragons. Hit the pitch!"

The second half delivered constant, heart-pounding, back-and-forth action. Each time one team seemed about ready to score, the other team's defense would step up, or a goalie would make a spectacular save. Finally, with only three minutes left in the game, the fastest Red Eagle dribbled straight through all our defenders. The slender forward chipped the ball perfectly into the upper corner of the net, and we found ourselves down, two-one. Coach called a time-out.

"Girls." She closed her eyes for a moment, releasing a slow breath. "To get top seeding in the tournament, we have to win this game." Coach opened her eyes, glancing purposefully from player to player.

"Can we do this?"

"We can do this," everyone mumbled. Lindy's steely eyes remained glued to her cleats.

"I said, CAN. WE. DO. THIS?" Coach's mouth smiled, but her eyes glared at Lindy. When everyone chanted back, louder this time, Lindy mouthed the words.

As I trotted back to the field, a few vultures circled overhead. I couldn't help but wonder what had died.

We took our positions. When the whistle blew, Emilia dribbled past three Eagles before finding Erin open. Erin took a shot, but with forty-five seconds left, the ball hit an Eagle on the cleats, pausing the play. When the whistle blew again, Erin hit the ball back to Danielle, who faked out the defender and smacked the ball to Lindy. I found my opening and posted by the goal. Lindy locked eyes with me . . .

And made a run for the goal.

Herself.

"GOOOO, LINDY! TAKE IT! ALL THE WAY DOWN!!!" Her mother's shrill screech could be heard above every other parent in the stands. Only Coach Givens's voice cut through it.

"LINDY! TWYLA IS OPEN!"

Lindy's jaw clenched, and she set off at a run. I glanced at the clock.

Twelve seconds.

She sprinted straight toward their largest player, then at the last second, dodged to the right.

Nine seconds.

About ten feet away, Erin's defender bolted toward Lindy, freeing Erin for a shot. But Lindy didn't pass. Head down, she dribbled forward.

Six seconds.

Erin's defender closed in. I stood in front of the open net and screamed, "LINDY!"

It was the faintest of glares, but I could see it.

She was not going to pass to me. She would *never* pass to me.

Lindy raised her stick, poised to shoot . . .

Just as the buzzer went off.

Game over. Just like that . . . we'd lost.

Crap.

Crap! Crap! Crap!

In the stands, Dad's head snapped up. We locked eyes and he gave me a questioning thumbs-up. Nearby, Wolfie spun in quick, tight circles until he was so dizzy he crashed into a trash can. I shook my head. Dad shrugged.

Even though it was Lindy who had hogged the ball, my stomach knotted. Why wasn't I able to stay strong throughout the game? Why the heck was I so nauseous? Was I doing something wrong?

Ultimately . . . had we lost the game because of *me*?

Chapter 3

My Mother, the Tree

Crickets.

The whole car ride home . . . silence. Emilia and Anna had both dinged my phone, but for once, I didn't feel like texting. I had no interest in small talk, and Dad never played the radio in the car anymore. Music used to be everywhere, all the time, but that was before Mom died. Even Wolfie was silent now, though that was just because he was stuck in a video game trance. So I listened to the hum of the tires, Mario's muffled theme song in Wolfie's earbuds, and an occasional honk in the distance. When we finally pulled into our driveway, I almost jumped out before we stopped.

"Whoa, Twy, let me park first," Dad said. "Wolfie, don't you think you've had enough technology? Let's do something else, kiddo."

"I'm going for a walk," I announced. Dad turned to face me.

"To the willow?"

I nodded, waiting for his approval.

"You've been going there a lot lately. And it's almost time to eat," he said. "I'd really like your help setting the table."

"I won't stay long. And I'll help set the table when I get back," I promised. When he didn't say anything right away, I added, "You know I like visiting her when I've had a bad day."

Dad's forehead drew together. He pinched the bridge of his nose.

When Mom died, Dad had turned her into a tree. Well, not

like, wave a magic wand and *poof!* you're a tree. But he'd found this cool company, where you could put almost any kind of tree in a special urn that held dirt, plant food, and someone's ashes. Dad had chosen a young weeping willow for Mom, then planted it by the creek in our backyard. He'd said it looked graceful and elegant, like her. At only five years old, Wolfie had been too young to have an opinion about it. But me? I thought it was perfect. And sad. Perfectly sad, maybe. Like how a red-orange sunset sometimes bleeds into the deep, black sky before the night swallows it whole. Now, at over twenty feet tall, the willow's branches had a way of drooping and swaying in the wind like it understood exactly how I felt. And having a tree mixed with Mom's ashes somehow made it feel like she was still with us. But of course, I also liked its meaning.

The name Willow means "freedom." It's better to think of Mom as free than . . .

Well, it's just better.

"Dad?" I prompted.

Dad sighed, releasing the bridge of his nose. "Okay, Twy. But please be home in time for dinner."

Just the thought of food spun my stomach.

"I will," I said.

Dad turned back to Wolfie, tapping his knee. Wolfie plucked out his earbuds and raised his eyebrows in question.

"Off," Dad said.

"Can I finish this level? Please? I'm almost done. Please, please, please?" Dad's head thumped gently against the headrest.

"Fine."

We all got out, and I followed Dad into the house, dropping my field hockey bag and phone onto a mountain of raincoats, unopened school supplies, and shoes in the mudroom. I pulled sneakers on and snagged my journal from the kitchen table. Mama Rose had bought it for me, saying, "Journaling helps you process hard feelings." I'd never really thought of myself as much of a writer, but I *did* feel better after pouring emotions onto a page. You could always tell how I felt just by looking at my handwriting. When it was loopy, I was usually writing about my friends or getting an A. When it was jagged, I'd probably had a bad day.

Today was a jagged kind of day.

I flew through the backyard and disappeared into a familiar maze of oaks and maples. Boulders and puddles would've hindered another person, but by now, I could run this path blindfolded. Finally, the weeping willow appeared ahead, just beyond the slope where Wolfie and I used to play when we were younger.

The slope where Mom's leaves now tickled the ground and her roots sipped creek water.

The thought made my heart both swell and break at the same time.

Of course, my favorite time to visit the tree had always been twilight. The sun peeked through the trees and made the creek look like it was filled with diamonds. When I closed my eyes, the rushing water sounded like rain on a tin roof. It almost felt like the woods were crying with me.

I kicked off my shoes, stuffed my socks inside, and waded toward a fallen bald cypress that stretched from the opposite bank almost all the way to our willow. The cool water, comforting and familiar, settled my stomach and eased my anxiety. Crayfish darted away from my feet, and tadpoles dug deep into the silt for safety. I loved the smell of our woods in the summer. Like a dogwood dipped in moss. I hopped onto the cypress and hugged my knees to my chest, cradling my journal in between. A centipede scurried this way and that, as if it couldn't decide which ridge might lead to its next meal. I knew better than to touch it, though. Years ago, Dad had taught me that although it didn't happen often, centipedes could sting. Dad loved his creepy crawlies as much as Mom loved her furballs. I stretched my legs, careful not to disrupt the centipede, and opened my journal.

Dear Mom,

I'm at your tree again today. Lots of animals are scurrying around. That should make you happy.

I wonder if you can feel me here.

Today sucked, Mom. We lost our game, and now we won't get top seeding in the tournament. It's our first loss of the summer. ☹ Coach was nice about it, but I still can't help but wonder if I'll be stuck on JV throughout high school. Lindy didn't want to pass to me, and then she didn't get to the goal in time . . . but somehow, I feel like it was my fault. Like I should've been doing something different.

I wish you were here to tell me what to do. Or what NOT to do. You always seemed so sure of yourself.

Remember how you always used to say, "Everything happens for a reason"? Well . . . I'm worried that we lost today because I was nauseous. If the team finds out I played when I wasn't 100%, would everyone hate me? And would Emilia be mad if she found out I didn't rub my snow globe for good luck? I know that's not why we lost . . . but would she?

I just feel like I let everyone down.

But I also wonder . . . why have I been feeling so bad lately? And why did I have to feel so sick today, of all days? I tried to do everything right. Did I eat too much? Not enough? Should I have hydrated more? What is going on with me?

I believe everything happens for a reason, Mom. I do.
I just wish I knew what it was.
I miss you.

Love,
Twyla

By the time I closed my journal, the centipede had disappeared. I looked all around to be sure I hadn't squished it by accident, but it was nowhere to be seen. I just hoped it hadn't fallen into the water trying to avoid the intruder on its log.

The sun still floated pretty high in the sky, but my internal alarm clock blared at me. Dad expected me back now. I could feel it.

I dipped first one foot, then the other, into the cool water, and stood. When my feet moved quickly, silt stirred like a tornado and all the critters scattered. But when I eased forward, like the centipede, the water remained crystal clear. I scanned the creek for my favorite finds—red-eared sliders or painted turtles. Today brought no such luck.

Figures.

But just as I waded back to the bank, something caught my eye. There, wiggling at the bottom of the slope where Wolfie and I used to play, was an eastern box turtle.

Upside down.

His little legs kicked wildly, like he thought he was racing the fastest hare alive. I felt pretty sure he was a boy because of the dip in his belly, or plastron, Mom had taught me to look for. But I knew for sure when I bent down to examine him. The bright orange-and-black patterns on his shell looked like one of the Navajo tapestries that hung in Emilia's house. And his eyes? They shone red as the coneflowers in Mama Rose's garden.

"Don't be scared, little guy. I'll help you," I whispered.

As soon as I stretched toward him, he sucked himself back inside his shell.

"Awww . . . I'm sorry, buddy."

I flipped him right side up and stepped back to hide in the shadows of the willow. Within a few minutes, he popped himself back out and toddled away.

As if nothing had ever happened.

Breathless, I watched until I could no longer see him through the trees. And then I looked back at the place where I'd found him, and I wondered, *How the heck did he get upside down?*

What could possibly be the reason for *that*?

Chapter 4

THE SNOW GLOBE

Instead of flakes, tiny stars floated around a crescent moon when I shook my favorite snow globe. The motion eased my anxiety from the mini fight I'd had with Dad when I'd gotten back.

"You're late." Dad's tone was annoyed. Which annoyed me.

"Sorry." I'd avoided his gaze as I traipsed through the kitchen. "I'm not hungry. Going upstairs."

"You have to eat, Twyla."

"Not right now, Dad."

"If not now, when?"

"I don't know. Later, okay?" The words had come out angrier than I'd intended, but I just didn't have it in me to explain something I didn't entirely understand myself. I just knew I definitely didn't want to eat. So I'd stormed upstairs to my room, leaving Dad and Wolfie slack-jawed. Even though I hadn't planned my entrance that way, it had had the intended outcome: they'd left me alone all evening.

With my shirt, I'd polished the glass sphere that sat atop a shiny silver base engraved with the words GODSPEED, LITTLE TWYLA. When I turned the key, a metal cylinder with pegs revolved inside, while comblike teeth plucked out a melody. One of Mom's friends from college crafted music boxes, so he'd created this one to play "Godspeed" at her request. I shook it again, memories swirling like the stars.

I'd was only five when she gave it to me. We'd just moved from

22

Florida, and my squishy collection had somehow gotten lost in the process. I'd been crying on the floor, face pressed into my palms, when I felt the warmth of Mom's hand against my back. I looked up, meeting her deep-brown eyes with my sad baby blues, and she wrapped me in a hug, rocking me gently.

"I have just the thing to make you feel better," she said. "I was saving it for the right moment, but . . . I think that moment is now."

I remember watching her disappear into her room, wondering if I should follow. But instead, I closed my eyes, listening to Dad humming with Wolfie in the living room. Eventually, Mom placed something heavy yet obviously fragile in my lap.

"I had it made just for you," she said. When she unrolled the treasure, I gasped. It wasn't like those little plastic ones I'd seen in Florida tourist shops, with chipped paint and plain white flakes inside. This one had glass, and real silver, and a real Swarovski crystal star hanging from the top of a glittery crescent moon. And it was more than just a snow globe . . . it was a music box too. When Mom turned the key, our special melody plinked. Surprised, I sucked in my breath and ran my fingers over the engraving on the base:

GODSPEED, LITTLE TWYLA

As Mom had explained it, *Godspeed* was something people said when they wanted to wish someone well on a journey. But it was also the song she'd sung to me every single night, from the day I was born until That Day. The original lyrics were written for a boy, but Mom had changed them when singing to me.

Now, sitting on the floor of my bedroom, I touched the words delicately, savoring the memory like the sweetest, rarest candy. I turned the key on the side of the music box and listened. When the house was quiet enough, like it was right then, I could still hear my mom's voice, singing along.

Godspeed, little girl.
Sweet dreams . . .

Over the last couple of years, though, her voice had begun to fade from my memory. I sometimes found myself straining to listen, until it would finally crystalize in my head. I wondered if time would eventually swallow her voice whole, like the night sky swallows sunsets. I pressed my eyes, forcing the thought away.

Ever so gently, I shook the globe again. Stars spiraled around the moon and swirled to the top. Then, when I stopped shaking it, they floated back down, like leaves on a windy autumn day. The movement calmed me.

"Twyla?" Wolfie's voice broke me from my trance. I sighed.

"What do you want, Wolfie?"

Wolfie mistakenly took my response as an invitation to enter. "Did you know that sliced grapes catch on fire when cooking them in the microwave?" I glared at the Weird but True book clutched in his fist.

"Not right now, Wolfie," I said.

With his free hand, he pulled my phone from his pocket and tossed it onto the bed beside me. "Here. You left this downstairs. Did you know that refried beans are only fried once? And did you know crocodiles—"

"Wolfie, I mean it. Not right now."

"Crocodiles can go two years without food. TWO WHOLE YEARS! I thought it was crazy that lions could go two weeks without food until I read—"

"WOLFIE!" I yelled. "I am NOT in the mood for weird facts!"

Wolfie's eyes widened. "Oh. Okay," he said. "Well, you wanna read a book with me? Wanna read Keeper of the Lost Cities together? I'll let you read one of them to me. However long you want. And I won't even complain."

Typically, I would've jumped at a free pass to share my favorite series with Wolfie. He hadn't fallen in love with books yet the way I had when I was his age. I was convinced he'd be enthralled with Sophie Foster if just given the chance. But tonight was not the night.

"I think I just wanna go to bed, Wolfie."

"Well do you wanna . . ."

"ARE YOU NOT LISTENING?" It was like a flame had suddenly reached the end of a wick on a stick of cartoon dynamite. "Oh my GOSH! Is your head clogged? I do NOT want to do ANYTHING but think about why we lost the game today, okay? OKAY?"

Wolfie recoiled, his lower lip quivering. Then, suddenly, his brow furrowed.

"Why do you always need a reason for *everything*, huh? Did you ever think that maybe sometimes, things just *happen*?!"

I felt like he'd slapped me. My teeth clenched.

"Get out," I hissed.

"FINE! I don't wanna be in here with you *anyway*!" He stomped out of my room. I started to yell, but my phone dinged.

Anna.

> **AR:** Hey. I'm sorry you guys lost today. Maybe a sleepover would help?

Almost immediately, another ding. This time, it was Emilia.

> **EB:** Name the place. I'll bring the party.

My fingers tapped quickly.

> **ME:** My place? After the tourney? I think we did E's last time.

From down the hall, I heard Wolfie's door slam shut. He never closed his door.

A pang of guilt washed over me. Wolfie only wanted to be with me. I knew that. Although he rarely knew when he, himself, was pushing someone's buttons, he always seemed to sense when others were upset. Like a fly to light, he was drawn toward sad people, always looking to exchange weird facts for a smile. I shouldn't have yelled at him.

Sigh.

I knelt down and slid a box out from beneath my bed. I rewrapped my snow globe in Mom's soft *Wicked* shirt with a picture of Elphaba, gently placed it in the box, then carefully slid it back under my bed.

The hall floorboards creaked under my feet as I tiptoed to Wolfie's room. I knocked.

"Wolfie?" When he didn't answer, I turned the knob and peeked inside. Wolfie sat on the floor, his back turned toward me. Nugget, our fat, orange tabby, purred in a puddle at his feet. Wolfie fiddled with a pile of rocks stacked beside him. Many were flat, in a variety of reddish, yellowish, and blackish shades, but a few were bigger. More . . . rockish.

"What kinds of rocks are those?" I asked. Wolfie plucked a reddish one out and cradled it in his hands, rotating away from me as I walked toward him.

"Shale," he muttered.

I reached for a yellowish one and he pushed my hand away.

"Don't touch it," he snapped. "They break easy." I pointed at a big gray rock with lots of little white pieces in it.

"What about that one? Does it break easily too?"

Wolfie snorted. "No, stupid. That's called an IG-NE-OUS rock." He pronounced each syllable like Dad used to play staccato piano notes. Suddenly, his eyes flew open wide and a smile crept across his face. "Know what it's made from?" he asked.

I shook my head and grinned. If only all arguments could be fixed with rocks.

"It's made from lava!"

"Nuh-uh!"

Wolfie swung to face me, the quick movement annoying the orange tabby puddle. Nugget flattened his ears and jumped on the bed. "They are, I swear! And see this?" He handed me a whitish one that sparkled in the light. "This one is quartz." He said the word *quartz* gently—like it, too, could break. One side of his mouth twisted up, he tilted his head, and then he offered me the treasure. I turned it over in my hands.

"How do you know what they're all called?" I asked.

"YouTube." Wolfie shrugged. "You can find anything on YouTube."

Wolfie stretched, then climbed into bed. His Pokémon pajama pants were about two inches too short. I made a mental note to remind Dad to buy him new ones.

The mattress sank under my weight as I sat next to my little brother.

"Wolfie, do you know what your name means?" I tucked the sheets tightly around his body, like a mummy. Wolfie yawned and shook his head.

"*Wolf* means . . . well, wolf," I said. "But *gang* means 'path' or 'journey.' So together, your name means 'path of the wolf.' Isn't that cool?" Wolfie shrugged. For a kid who liked weird facts so much, he sure didn't seem to care much about the meaning of names.

"And do you know who you're named after?"

Wolfie shook his head. I lay down next to him so our foreheads almost touched.

"Do you remember when Dad used to play 'A Little Night Music' and 'Turkish March' on the piano?"

Wolfie scrunched up his face, and then his eyes flew open. "Are those the really fast songs?" he asked. "I loved the fast ones."

"Mm-hmm, they are. Remember how we would dance around like crazy?"

Wolfie laughed, nodding. "And remember how Dad watched *us* while his fingers went do-da-do-da-loo-da-loo, all over the place?"

I knew exactly what he meant. Dad never had to look at the keys when he played. It was like his fingers just knew.

"Well, those songs were written by Dad's favorite composer. His name was Wolfgang Amadeus Mozart. You're named after him!"

Wolfie smiled. "I didn't know that," he said. But then, the corners of his mouth turned down. "I miss when Dad used to play music for us. Piano and guitar."

My shoulders drooped under the weight of my brother's sadness. "I do too, Wolfie."

"Remember when he'd sing that song from *Toy Story*?" he asked.

"'You've Got a Friend in Me'?"

"Yeah, that one." Wolfie sighed. "Why do you think Dad won't play anymore?"

"I don't know," I sighed back. "But I'm sure there's a reason."

Wolfie fiddled with his comforter. "Twy? Will you sing me a song?"

I wrapped my arm around my little brother and combed his hair with my fingers like Mom used to do to me.

Wolfie's eyes closed as I sang, imagining dragons flying over vast oceans, fish nipping at moonbeams, and lost boys sailing past pirate ships in the night.

It took no time for Wolfie's breathing to turn to the slow, even breaths that come with sleep. I kissed his forehead, tiptoed to the door, and turned out the light.

"Twyla?" Wolfie's sleepy voice drifted through the dark.

"Yes, buddy?"

"Can you remember Mama's voice whenever you want to?"

I closed my eyes, the memory washing over me, fast and furious. *Do you like the snow globe, baby?*

I love it, Mama. I promise I'll keep it safe forever and ever.

Tears caught in my throat and, for a minute, I couldn't say anything for fear they'd break me. Somewhere outside, an owl hooted. The moon hung low in the sky, casting gentle beams of light through Wolfie's window. I swallowed the lump in my throat.

"I can," I admitted.

Wolfie sighed. "I wish I could too," he said. His words felt more wistful than heartbroken, but nonetheless, they crushed me. I responded the only way I knew how.

"I love you, Wolfie."

But he didn't answer.

He was already sound asleep.

As I crawled back into my own bed later that night, I thought about the field hockey game and what Wolfie had said.

Maybe, things just happen.

I shook my head. No . . . he was wrong. With everything in me, I *knew* he had to be wrong. Nothing just happened. There was a reason for everything. A reason we'd lost. A reason I'd felt sick.

Now I just had to figure out what it was.

Chapter 5
LUCKY

"I don't see anything wrong with his pajamas." Dad gesticulated, flapping his arms up and down in Wolfie's direction. Wolfie leaned over his plate and stuck his tongue through the center of a donut. He lifted it up, tongue still in the middle, the glaze gluing the doughy ring to his face. He laughed like a madman and the donut dropped to the floor.

"Well, I need clothes for school too," I said, ignoring my brother.

"You have clothes."

"Not clothes I'm excited about." I scrolled through my phone, hoping Emilia or Anna might've responded to my shopping invitation by now. Where *were* they?

"Well, I'm not excited about the idea of going shopping," Dad countered. I raised my eyebrows. At his core, Dad was both practical and fun-loving. But when it came to malls, his practical side always won. I pocketed my phone and switched back to my first tactic.

"Wolfie, stand up," I commanded. He did, and I pointed at his exposed ankles and the super-high hemline. Dad shrugged, obviously unimpressed, so I told Wolfie to put his arms up in the air. His belly button winked at us. "See?" I said.

"Who wants orange juice?" Dad asked. Wolfie kept one hand raised. Dad high-fived him.

"Seriously?" I asked, incredulous. Wolfie looked ridiculous, and I desperately needed a new outfit for the first day of school, no matter how much they hated to shop. That morning, I'd flipped through everything in my closet and pawed through all my drawers. Nothing looked right. I'd never really cared about clothes before, but I was a freshman now. And being the lowest on the social ladder, I'd be an easy target if I didn't up my game. Why couldn't Dad understand that?

An idea struck.

"Welllll . . ." I drew out the word, enjoying the idea that I was about to make both of them very, very uncomfortable. They smiled smugly at each other.

"If it's not enough to know that Wolfie's pajamas are way too small, maybe it'll be enough to know my *bra* doesn't fit . . ."

Dad's eyes grew wide and he pretended to fly a tiny flag. "Okay! Okay! Wolfie, go get dressed. We're going shopping." Wolfie groaned.

Through the kitchen window, I could see my field hockey coach—and soon-to-be teacher—washing her silver Toyota Prius in the driveway next door.

"Meet you guys outside!" I sang.

When the screen door slammed shut behind me, Ms. Givens's head snapped up. She waved her sponge, soap bubbles flying everywhere. "Coming out to help?" she asked.

"Isn't that what Elliott's for?" I teased. At the sound of my voice, Felix's head popped up and his feathered, golden tail thumped the concrete. He released a tennis ball from his front paws, grabbed it between his teeth, and hobbled my way. When he dropped it at my feet, I tossed it into their front yard. It always surprised me how quickly he could move on three legs.

"Elliott's still at summer camp," she said. Then she jutted her chin toward Felix. "You know, he only seems to want to play ball with the two of you anymore."

I grinned. Felix had been special to me since we'd first moved.

It was Mom who had saved his life one summer day, much like this one, eight years ago. Elliott and I had been cartwheeling through the sprinkler, grown-ups sipping brightly colored drinks from tall glasses with tiny paper umbrellas, when we'd heard the screech of tires followed immediately by Felix's high-pitched, anguished yelp. And then, all hell broke loose. Mom immediately went into vet mode, rushing into the street to analyze the situation with Mr. and Mrs. Givens hot on her heels. Wolfie, only a toddler then, had burst into tears the moment Mom ran off, so Dad scooped him up to soothe him. I remember Elliott's face, a mix of sprinkler drops and tears staining his sun-kissed cheeks. His blond hair spiked out in every direction, and his chest jerked with the effort of holding back sobs. I hadn't known what to say, so I just stood there with him, sharing his sadness, until his dad rushed back to let us know Felix and my mom were on the way to the hospital.

After the accident, I'd wondered how Felix would get around with only three legs. But Mom had been right.

"Animals aren't like people," she'd said. "When they lose a limb, they don't sit around feeling sorry for themselves. They figure out a new way of doing things, and then they just *do* it. As someone once said, 'A bird sitting on a tree is never afraid of the branch breaking, because her trust is not on the branch but on her own wings.' Watch. You'll see."

She'd been right. Within no time, three-legged Felix jumped and ran and played just like four-legged Felix had. Over the years, I'd even taught him to catch a ball midair. I'd throw it underhand, just high enough that he had a little time to run. Then he'd launch himself up with that one good hind leg and snatch the ball from the sky with his teeth.

It was a beautiful thing.

"Hey, are you excited for AP Biology?" Ms. Givens grinned at me, deep dimples digging into her cheeks. "I hear your teacher slash field hockey coach slash neighbor is pretty amazing."

I laughed. Although we hadn't formally gotten our schedules yet, Ms. Givens was the only one teaching ninth graders AP Biology this year, a fact that delighted me. Not only would I have her as my coach for my favorite sport, she'd also be teaching my favorite subject. "I am excited," I said. "Are you excited to have your son as a student?"

She nodded, pensive. "Actually, yeah. I am!" Quickly, she broke from her thoughts and studied me. "How are you feeling? I've been worried about you."

My hand subconsciously shot to my stomach. The nausea hadn't returned since the game. "Fine," I said, truthfully. "I think I just need to be better about hydrating."

Felix dropped a slobbery ball at my feet. I tossed it back into the yard.

"So." Ms. Givens squeezed the sponge, waving bubbles my way again. "What do you say? Wanna help me with—"

At that moment, our garage door creaked open. "You know, I'd love to help. Really." My voice dripped false sincerity as I walked backward toward our car. "Washing cars in ninety-degree temperatures is one of my favorite things, truly. But Wolfie needs new pajamas, so . . ."

"Back-to-school shopping, huh? Well, ask your dad to grab an extra pack of field hockey balls for me if you go to a sporting goods store!"

Felix barked as I hopped into the car. I grinned, remembering how I'd looked up his name the day of the accident. *Felix* meant "lucky." At the time, I'd seen it as a sign from the universe that he was going to be okay—and that he was lucky my mom was his neighbor. But over the years, I'd started to wonder.

Maybe *we* were the lucky ones to live next door to them.

Chapter 6

LETTING GO

Yes?

I texted Emilia and Anna a picture of a light-green crop top with an emerald snake that wound its way along the right side up and over one shoulder.

Super cute, Emilia shot back.

Love the snake, Anna added.

Unfortunately, my friends had been unable to meet us at the mall due to family plans, so it was up to me to convince Dad that his definition of "stylish" had parted ways with the rest of the world decades earlier. So far, he had rejected every back-to-school shirt of my choosing. I was beginning to feel like he'd never like anything. "What about this one?" I asked, eyes pleading.

Wolfie ran as fast as he could around a circular clothing rack, touching every shirt in his path. I hoped his fingers weren't sticky. Dad wrinkled his nose.

"Mmmm . . . I'm not crazy about it," he said.

"But it has a snake on it. You love snakes!"

"I do, but that's not a snake. That's a shirt. Why don't you get a dress? You used to love wearing dresses on the first day of school."

"Maybe when I was ten," I huffed. "I'm in high school now."

Dad sighed. "You don't say."

A burst of laughter caught my attention and I turned to see a girl about my age collecting clothes. Her mom trailed behind her, arms loaded with a variety of tops, skirts, and jeans. The girl plucked a red, ribbed-knit crop top from the rack and placed it on her mother's head. They laughed again. I furrowed my brow and moved to the next rack. Dad followed me, leaving Wolfie to run in circles.

"Oh! How about this?" I held up a baby blue top with a square-cut neckline, layered flutter sleeves, and a short, smocked bodice. "This is super cute!"

"Mmmm . . . I don't know, Twilight." Dad took a few steps toward a nearby table display, unfolding a plain white shirt with a retro Pac-Man on it. "How about this one?"

My eyes became tempered slits. "Seriously?"

Dad looked down at the shirt. "What's wrong with it?"

I sighed, shaking my baby blue shirt at him. "What's wrong with this one?"

Dad balled up the Pac-Man shirt and threw it back onto the display table. He half leaned, half fell into a chair against the wall. "Well, for one, it's not even a whole shirt. Where's the rest of it?"

My mouth dropped. "It's a half shirt, Dad. That's a thing now. I could layer them over tanks and stuff. Everyone wears them."

"Everyone meaning *who*, Twyla?"

"Everyone meaning *everyone*, Dad." My tone matched his a little too closely, and I knew I was treading disrespectful waters. But I also knew he was choosing shirts that no ninth-grade girl would be caught dead in. I grabbed another one, a purple corset crop top with spaghetti straps that he'd undoubtedly hate. "And this one?" I challenged.

Dad clenched his jaw. "No, Twyla."

I pulled a low-cut, black tube top with fringe at the bottom, one even the giggling girl wouldn't have stacked on her mother. I dangled it, daring my father to deny me again.

"Over my dead body."

The old, familiar words were said reflexively, but they still stung.

"Mom used to say that," I hissed.

Dad closed his eyes and pinched the bridge of his nose. Any mention of Mom drew tears, and I could tell he was fighting them now. Ever since she'd died, it was like he'd locked her memory away, never to be retrieved or discussed. He rarely visited her tree. It was almost like in *his* world, That Day never happened. I usually tried not to push that button, because I knew how much it hurt him. But in that moment, I didn't care. He wasn't listening at all.

A moment later, Dad's head snapped up, as if he suddenly remembered that he'd left the oven on. He looked sharply to the right.

"Wolfie?" he called. I followed his eyes back to the rack where my brother had just been racing in circles. He wasn't there.

Dad jumped from the chair, panic spreading over his face. "Where's your brother?" he asked. "He was just here a second ago!"

"I . . . I don't know. Wolfie? WOLFIE?"

I dropped my clothes and ran after Dad, checking for feet beneath rack after rack after rack, calling for my brother. A few stray customers stopped shopping to watch us, but no one offered to help. My heart thudded against my chest, bile rising in my throat. What if he'd wandered off and was lost? Or worse yet . . . what if someone had taken him . . .

"Excuse me?" The woman I'd seen earlier called to us and waved her hand in circular motions, indicating that we should go to her. She stood by the dressing room next to a bench with a stack of clothes that looked like it was about to topple over. Without asking questions, we both raced toward her, almost knocking over a statuesque, perfectly coiffed perfume girl in the aisle.

"I think your son is in the dressing room," she whispered. Without thinking, Dad began to rush inside until I held my hand to his chest.

"It's the women's dressing room, Dad," I said. "I'll get him."

Dad's panicked eyes filled with tears. He nodded at me, and the woman lifted the stack of clothes so he could sit on the bench. "I'll just . . . I'll go join my daughter," she said. She offered us both a sympathetic smile before disappearing into the dressing room. Dad collapsed on the bench and cradled his face with his hands. I started to follow the woman inside but turned to touch Dad's knee instead.

"Are you okay?" I asked.

Dad nodded but didn't look up.

It wasn't hard to find the stall my brother occupied, as he'd left the door wide open. Inside the tiny room, he spun in circles on a bench, admiring his reflection in the mirror directly opposite him. "Look, Twyla!"

He turned to face me, beaming. There he stood, wearing nothing but Mario boxer briefs and a plain white tee with a retro Pac-Man on it.

"You look great, buddy," I said. "Why don't you put your pants back on, and we'll go show Dad?"

When we left the dressing room, Dad's face was still buried in his hands. I cleared my throat.

Dad looked up, his forehead creased and his cheeks wet . . . but he opened his arms and engulfed Wolfie in a hug. "You scared me, Wolfie," he whispered. Gently, Dad pushed back to look Wolfie in his eyes. "You can't run off like that. I don't mind if you want to try something on, but you have to tell me first, okay?"

Wolfie nodded. "Do you like my shirt?" he asked. "Did you know that Pac-Man was originally called 'Puckman'? I don't know why. And it was inspired by pizza! That's why he's round and his mouth looks like a missing piece."

Dad pulled Wolfie back into a hug, but his eyes found mine over Wolfie's shoulder. They were tender. Sad. He opened one arm, motioning for me to join them. I did.

After a few moments, Dad said, "Wolfie, why don't you go back in and change into your own shirt. Okay?"

"Can I get this one?" he asked. Dad nodded, and Wolfie took off back into the dressing room, singing the Pac-Man theme, "Bup,

bup, bup, bup, ba-da-la-da, bup, bup, bup, bup, ba-da-la-da," at the top of his lungs. Dad sighed.

"Why don't you go back and get that snake shirt, Twy. And the blue one with those . . . fluffy sleeves."

"Flutter sleeves," I corrected.

"Whatever," he said. Dad took my hands and his eyes held mine. For a moment, we both just stood there. Frozen. When he spoke again, his posture softened into a slight hunch.

"When your mom died, I knew there would be times like this," Dad said. I froze, holding my breath, fearful that if I moved or said anything, I'd break the magic of the moment. When he continued speaking, his voice was quiet. Pained.

"I knew there'd be times when I'd fall short. When I'd be in architect mode, just trying to make things work the way they always have." He filled his lungs, then let the breath out slowly. "But that's not how kids work. They change. *You're* changing. I . . . I guess that scares me a little . . ."

Again, the tears came, but this time they were different. More . . . regretful, maybe?

"I always thought your mom would be here to help you—to help *me*—navigate these changes. I never thought I'd have to do this alone." He shook his head. "You're growing up so fast, and . . . I don't always know what I'm doing, Twilight. But I'm trying."

This time, when he looked at me, I saw him. The dad who used to play "You've Got a Friend in Me" on guitar, over and over, until his fingers were too sore to press the strings for one more second. The dad who took us for endless walks in Florida, teaching us how to catch lizards the right way, so they wouldn't lose their tails.

The dad who was trying his best to raise me and my brother. Alone.

I kissed his forehead. "I'm sorry I got snappy," I said.

"Me too." His half smile was tired, but grateful. "Now," he said. "Go grab your new shirts, before we lose your brother again."

Chapter 7

TOURNAMENT TIME

This time, Dad offered his hands before we got out of the car. "Front, back, slip, slap, goooooooo DRAGONS!" He batted at my bubble ponytail as I exited through the passenger door.

We arrived early for the tournament—Emilia and Coach Givens were the only two who'd beaten us there, but other cars quickly poured into the lot. The sun burned down, with no cumulus clouds in sight. No *any* clouds in sight. Before we'd left, Dad had tried to give me California Baby sunscreen, which always made me look like a ghost. As if I wasn't already pale enough.

"Can I use a different brand, please? You can't even see my freckles with this one."

"Since when do you care about seeing your freckles?"

"Dad . . . please?"

He'd skewed his head at me, but then silently retrieved a different bottle from the hall closet.

After a few days of feeling fairly normal, my stomach had begun twisting again the night before the game. I'd barely touched dinner but had gotten away without eating by blaming it on tournament nerves. That said, it hadn't felt like "just nerves" to me. For the first time since the last game, I'd felt this weird combination of being full, despite not eating since breakfast, and queasy. Like, I-couldn't-eat-another-bite, mixed with don't-make-me-eat-that-or-I-might-throw-up-on-you. But I also knew we had a big game to play, and stress could definitely make my stomach churn.

I'd even looked it up to be sure, and Dr. Google had confirmed: "Anxiety can cause nausea and other gastrointestinal problems."

Luckily, I had not been suffering from those "other" gastrointestinal problems.

"Hey!" Wolfie bounced on his feet while we walked, like his shoes had tiny trampolines in them. "Did you know the Chinese softshell turtle can pee out of its mouth?" I scrunched my nose, and Emilia playfully nudged him.

"That's cool, Wolfie!" she said. "Did you learn that from your Weird but True books?"

"Nope." He popped his *p* at the end of the word. "I saw a video on YouTube. They have such cute, little pointy noses!" Wolfie strung out each syllable, and the way his voice went up an octave when he said "cute, little pointy noses" made me want to hug him. He chattered on.

"They live in salty water, which isn't really good for them, so they don't actually drink anything at all. Isn't that cool? They just suck stuff up, swish it around, and spit out pee, and they can do that for like one hundred minutes! I wish I had a Chinese softshell turtle. I'd keep it in my room, or maybe in the bathtub. Yeah— probably in the bathtub, where it would have lots of room to swim and pee out of its mouth. And I'd bring it to school and show everybody!"

As much as I loved turtles, this one did not sound like it would make a very good pet to me.

"Hi, girls! Twyla, have you been drinking plenty of water today?" Coach tilted her head. I saluted her.

"Yes, ma'am!" I lied, patting the full bottle weighing down my field hockey bag. "Ready to play!"

"You sure?" she asked. Her eyes scanned me up and down. "You look puny. And maybe a little pale." With perfect timing, Anna sprinted over from the stands and threw her arm around my shoulder, hugging me sideways.

"Blame the sunscreen," I mumbled. My eyes darted around to be sure Dad wasn't nearby to hear me. I forced a laugh, and Anna side-eyed me. No *way* I wasn't going to play today.

"Hiya, Cooooach." Lindy's voice sliced the air behind me, just before she forced her way between me and Anna. "Will you *pleeeease* tell Elliott that I said hello?" She stretched out the word *please* like slime.

Since when was *she* friends with Elliott?

"Sure will, as soon as he gets back from camp," Coach said.

"Awww," Lindy purred. "When will that be?"

"Just before school starts," Coach said. I rolled my eyes.

By now, nearly the whole team had arrived. Coach put two fingers in her mouth and whistled. "Two laps, team!"

Lindy sashayed away and Emilia tugged at Anna and me.

"Will you pleeeeeeeeeeeeeeease tell Elliott that I said hello?" Emilia's impression of Lindy was so spot-on that I choked on my water. Anna mimed sticking her finger down her throat.

"Boys are dumb," Anna said.

"I don't know." Emilia sighed. "I think they're kinda interesting. Like geodes. The outside might be dirty and rough, but the inside's still shiny." She smiled wistfully at the sky, like Rapunzel at the floating lanterns.

Anna pretended to stick her finger down her throat again. I laughed.

"We'd better start running," I said to Emilia. "This tournament's sudden death . . . so we have to play all three." I channeled my inner coach. "But in order to do that . . ."

". . . we have to keep winning." Predictably, Emilia finished my thought.

"So . . . can we do this?" I grinned at my girls.

"We can do this!" Emilia and Anna shouted.

"Well, you can do this." Anna shrugged. I hugged her.

"Not without our greatest fan, we can't."

Anna grinned, then blew a kiss and ran back to sit in the stands with Mama Rose, who pushed her purple glasses up her pointy nose and waved.

Since we weren't the top seed, we had to play a tougher team in our first game. Thankfully, though, my nausea eased up, and our team came out on top, three to one. The second game was closer, but we still won, one-nothing. Fast and unstoppable, Emilia had scored our only goal. Lindy's mom spent the rest of the game having a conniption in the stands.

"LINDY! What are you DOING? There was no one at the GOAL! SHOOT, for goodness' sake! Are you gonna leave the scoring up to everyone else? SHOOOOOT!" When Lindy gave her mother a thumbs-up, Emilia and I rolled our eyes.

We weren't surprised to learn we'd be facing the Red Eagles again for the tournament championship game, but it made us all antsy. Everyone's towels rotated quickly between the large, blue Igloo cooler filled with ice water, to hot, sweaty foreheads and necks. But as the first half began, a rush of adrenaline coursed through the team. Defenders blocked more shots. Passers hit balls farther. And shooters took better aim. Unfortunately, the Red Eagles were equally infused with renewed energy.

By halftime, the score stood even, zero to zero.

Beads of sweat covered my body. Wet bangs and rogue strands of ponytail hair clung to my face and neck. For nearly three hours, I'd managed to suppress the gnawing churn in my stomach. The burn in my throat. But trying to convince myself that I felt fine was becoming increasingly difficult as fatigue set in. *The nausea isn't that bad*, I told myself. *I just need to drink more.* But with every sip of water, with every swing of my stick, with every minute of play . . . it worsened. At halftime, I had to spit out a bite of granola bar for fear I'd lose the small amount of water I'd been able to keep down since our final game began. I glanced at the clock.

Twenty-five more minutes.

You can do this, Twy.

"Okay, girls, we're holding firm . . . but we don't want to go to a shootout, right?"

"Right!" we all chanted.

"Caise, remember to keep your stick down. Erin, watch your position—and don't let number six break free. Lindy, when you don't have a shot, pass the ball. I need you to trust your teammates." Coach Givens clapped her hands. "Water, everyone."

I picked up my thermos and dumped its contents over my head. *Well*, I thought, *that's one way to hydrate.*

When the buzzer indicated halftime was over, I shook out my arms and legs, rolled my head, and jogged back to my position. My feet felt like they were filled with cement.

Twenty-one arduous, sluggish minutes later, with no goals scored for either team, Coach called a time-out.

"Girls, do you want to win this game?" she asked. Everyone nodded, like a storefront of bobbleheads. "Okay, then. Hear me out. How much time is left on the clock?"

"Three minutes and fifty-six seconds," Lindy said.

"Exactly," Coach replied. "You girls can do anything for four minutes. *Only four minutes.* I want to see the best from you. The best you have to offer. To me, to your team, to yourselves. I believe in you girls. Can we do this?"

"We can do this." The team's staggered, half-hearted chant sounded as fatigued as I felt.

"Not good enough," she said. Then, with fierce determination, Coach yelled loud enough that I was sure she could be heard from the top row of the stands. "CAN WE DO THIS?"

I looked from one teammate to the next. Exhaustion burned every player's cheeks, just like mine. Sweat dripped from every nose, just like mine. And hope filled every heart . . .

Just like mine.

"WE CAN DO THIS!" This time, we shouted in unison.

I ran back onto the field, a second wind hitting as the nausea released its grip. *Maybe*, I thought, *we really can do this!*

With all sticks down and every player prepared to pounce, the whistle blew. Electricity sparked as the ball volleyed between our teams like it was being handled by two tennis pros at Wimbledon. When one player's concentration intensified, so did their defender's. Determination and drive were palpable. Then, with thirty seconds left, I saw a chance to steal, and I took it. Immediately, I whacked the ball to Emilia, who flew past two defenders. She then passed it to Erin, who shot it straight between number six's legs. To Lindy.

"GOOOO, LINDY! SHOOT!" Her mom's shrill voice raised the hairs on my neck. Both Caise and I were open . . . but Lindy ran with it. Again.

She charged toward the net like a bull toward a red cape, ignoring Coach Givens's impassioned pleas to pass. She dodged first one Red Eagle, then a second. No doubt about it, she was fast.

But number six was faster.

Lindy didn't see Six coming up behind her. And she didn't see her stick stretch out. Suddenly, the ball was just gone.

And headed straight toward our goal.

Their passing was perfection. Unpredictable and precise. You could almost hear our hearts break when the ball swooshed into our net.

With twenty-two seconds left, Coach called our last time-out.

"Lindy, I want you at mid. Emilia, you're at forward. Go tie this game, girls."

"But *Coach* . . ."

Coach Givens's glare cut Lindy short. The whistle blew and we all jogged back onto the field. But when my stick hit the turf, my stomach lurched.

No, no, no, I thought. *Don't throw up, Twy. Don't. Throw. Up.*

I shook my head, breaths quick. Twenty-two seconds. I could do anything for twenty-two seconds.

Couldn't I?

As if she could read my mind, Emilia nodded at me.

Yes. I could.

The whistle blew. Quickly, Emilia dribbled the ball past two Eagles. When she hit a wall of defenders, she passed to Erin, who then passed back to Emilia. I posted by the goal. With seconds left, Emilia whacked the ball straight toward me. I pulled back my stick . . . and the ball disappeared.

I swung reflexively, chipping the turf. Stunned, I craned my neck to see who'd stolen it. Everyone was staring directly to my left.

At the ball.

The buzzer sounded, ending the tournament. It had rolled right past me, and I hadn't even seen it.

We'd lost. Again. And this time, there was no doubt.

It was all because of me.

Chapter 8

MORE THAN NAUSEA

Whack!

"Owwww! What the heck, Em?" I rubbed my temple and glared at my friend, whose soft, downy pillow felt like an anvil against my head. My lukewarm peanut butter ball milkshake sloshed against the lid, almost falling from my hand. "You're gonna make me spill," I whined.

"Trying to knock you out of that trance. Were you even *listening*? Anna likes a *dude*!" Emilia swung her pillow again, but this time I saw it coming. I threw my free hand in front of the feathered weapon and ripped it from Emilia's grasp. Glaring at her, I placed my milkshake on my dresser, out of harm's way. It was making me feel like crap anyway.

"That is not at all what I said," Anna countered, cool and even. She stole the pillow from me and chucked it at Emilia's head in one swift motion. "I just thought it was strange that Malik was there today. He never comes to games." Anna snagged her plastic sundae spoon from the empty bowl on my desk and chewed on the end.

"But you wouldn't have *noticed* him there if you didn't *like* him," Emilia teased. Anna shook her head.

"Projecting much?" Anna asked. "Just because *you* notice *all* the boys . . ."

Whack! Emilia smacked Anna and rotated full circle, pillow extended from both arms. She was about to hit me again when I ducked, but she kept turning, apparently intent on making contact with my head.

"Emilia, stop! What is wrong with you?" My hand flew up between us to serve as a barrier.

Whack!

"No," she said, her tone suddenly falling flat. "What is wrong with *you*? You've been mega weird today. For a while, actually."

"I have not," I protested. Emilia motioned to Anna, who hugged me and put her head on my shoulder.

"Ummm . . . yeah. You kinda have," Anna said. She twisted a blond lock.

Emilia waltzed over to my dresser and picked up my full milkshake cup, shaking it back and forth just a bit, accusingly. "Then why aren't you drinking this? I finished mine like an hour ago!"

Anna sat up and stuck her hand out, silently demanding my milkshake. Emilia gave it to her, and she took a gulp. Then, as if realizing it had been made with dung beetles, she held it away from her body. "Wait . . . you're not sick, are you?"

I shook my head, shoulders tense. "I don't think so."

She shrugged and took another gulp.

Emilia flopped onto her sleeping bag on the floor, arms crossed. "Come on, Twy. What's going on?"

Defensively, I wrapped my arms around myself. "I don't know, guys. I'm just not feeling great lately."

Anna swallowed what was in her mouth, looked into the cup as if she'd find the mystery of life inside, then put it back on my dresser and pushed it all the way against the wall.

"So . . . you might be sick?"

My head flopped side to side, caught somewhere between a nod and a shake. "I don't think so. I've been a little nauseous lately, but it's been going on for a while now. And it hasn't been consistent. I googled it, and most stomach viruses last one to ten days. I should be better by now, if that was the problem."

Emilia waved her finger, clucking. "I have this cousin, and she throws up before every period. I bet that's what's wrong with you."

"But I'm not on my period," I protested.

Anna plopped down in a beanbag. "Mom says some people get nauseous when they ovulate. Maybe that's you?"

"I bet that's you," Emilia said. "I mean, you don't have any other symptoms, right?"

My mouth opened, then snapped shut again. Today, I'd completely whiffed on the ball. Was that a symptom?

A symptom of lameness, maybe.

"No," I finally said. "No other symptoms. I just . . . I can't help but wonder why I played so poorly today."

"Awwww, Twy!" Anna patted a spot on the beanbag, and I sat. She wrapped an arm around my shoulder. "You played great today!"

But even as she said the words, I knew they weren't true. And when Emilia averted her eyes, I knew she knew too. I squeezed Anna's hand.

"Thanks, Anna. I just can't help but feel like I'm doing *something* wrong."

Emilia's head snapped up.

"Wait a minute . . ." Her eyes narrowed at me as her sentence stalled, and my throat tightened.

"Did you rub your snow globe before the game, Twyla?"

I crossed my arms over my chest and glared at Emilia. But I nodded, feeling a twinge of guilt for the half-truth.

"I know you wore your ponytail, and you obviously had the right sleeves on. Did you change anything between all the other games we won and the ones we lost? Like, did you use a new shampoo or something?"

"No, Emilia." I couldn't help but roll my eyes. "We didn't lose the game because I used a new shampoo." Frustration took over, and I spat the next words without thinking. "That's just stupid."

Emilia looked like I'd punched her, and Anna's jaw dropped. I backtracked, lifting my hands defensively.

"Not stupid. I'm sorry. But . . . you seem kinda fixated on the snow globe and ponytail and whatnot," I said.

"You're the one who always wants to find a reason for everything," she grumbled.

The small amount of milkshake I'd ingested felt like it was curdling in my stomach. For a moment, we all sat there in silence, waiting for someone else to break the tension.

"Maybe . . ." Anna's voice halted, and both Emilia and I watched her chew her cheek. "Maybe someone *else* changed their tape color . . .?"

Emilia snapped her fingers twice in approval.

"Or maybe someone's stick was cracked."

"Or maybe they didn't tie their shoelaces . . ." Anna prodded.

"Or maybe they didn't wash their pinnie . . ." Emilia added.

Reflux burned my throat as my stomach twisted.

"Or maybe their favorite candle burned out . . ."

"Or maybe someone's dog died."

Anna's eyes grew wide. "Dark, but okay. Or maybe someone lied about something . . ."

"Or maybe Lindy's mother—"

"IS A BONA FIDE WITCH, and NOT the reason we lost the game today!" The words erupted from me, hotter and angrier than I'd intended. In response, the room seemed to darken at the edges, spinning slowly at first, and then faster . . . faster. . . . faster. My hand flew to my mouth, and I dashed to the bathroom, barely making it to the toilet in time.

Footsteps pounded across the floor in my direction. I hugged the toilet as milkshake came up in violent, acidic bursts. Emilia touched my back, but the heat of her hand made the room spin again. I shrugged her away.

"I'm gonna get your dad," she whispered. The pungent smell

of vomit stung my nose, but I couldn't move. My mouth watered between violent heaves as I heard Emilia rush back down the hallway.

I didn't know why I was sick. And in that moment, I didn't even care.

All I wanted was my mother.

Within seconds, my father was at my side. "Twilight?" I couldn't stop heaving long enough to answer.

"Girls, I think it's time to call your parents to come get you," he said.

For a moment, no one said anything. The only sound was my retching, echoing through the bathroom corridor. Then my dad, trying to soothe.

"She'll be okay, girls."

Feet, shuffling.

"Feel better soon, Twy." Emilia sounded like she might cry.

"We love you," Anna whispered.

I held up one hand to indicate that I'd heard them, then clutched the toilet seat again.

When it was just me and Dad, he said, "Do we need to go to the ER?"

"Please . . . no," I moaned. I heard the clunk of his back falling against the bathroom door behind me.

"Okay," he said. "But I'm taking you to a doctor tomorrow."

I held a hand up once more, then folded both together on the toilet seat and rested my forehead on the makeshift pillow. I tried to do the math in my fuzzy head. We had less than two weeks before school started. I could not miss the beginning of high school. Everyone would get into their routines and I'd be left out. Or worse yet, I'd fall behind in classes and be unable to recover. I'd never gotten anything but As before, and now I had AP classes. Those were precious college credits I did *not* want to waste. I *had* to get better.

Maybe, between me, Dad, and the doctor, we could figure out what was wrong. Then, maybe, everything would be okay.

Yes. That was it. We were going to figure this out.

We had to.

Chapter 9

NURSE SHAR-PEI AND DR. BUZZ

I'd vomited all night long, so Dad had insisted on going to the ER as soon as Ms. Givens could come over to watch Wolfie in the morning. I hadn't wanted to go, but in the end, his insistence had been stronger than my resistance.

My hand throbbed where the third needle had finally found its target. Bandages mostly hid growing bruises on both arms from the first two misses. I prodded them tenderly, wondering how long they'd last. Clear liquid dripped from an IV bag into my vein, and I curled myself around a vomit basin.

I'm gonna look like I've been in a fight, I thought. *Great timing. Just . . . great.*

"How long has she been vomiting?" My nurse appeared to be about ninety, with a tight bun and heavy foundation caked over cavernous wrinkles. Her husky voice carried the bored undertone of Roz from *Monsters, Inc.* I half expected her to call my father Wazowski. With rows of loose skin overtaking her chin, she reminded me of an old shar-pei. A grumpy, old shar-pei. She stared straight ahead at the monitor, waiting for Dad's reply.

"I'm . . . I'm not sure." Dad had been pacing but stopped to study me. Like the answer was written across my forehead or something. "I think it started around nine o'clock last night . . ."

"And it's been constant since then?"

Dad sank into a chair beside my bed. I avoided his gaze. He nodded.

Nurse Shar-Pei gave me the stink eye over her black, cat-eye glasses. "She looks pretty dehydrated to me," she barked.

Dad's head drooped.

"Any other symptoms? Fever? Diarrhea? Constipation? Pain?"

Dad touched my leg. When I met his eyes, he raised his brows at me. I shook my head.

"No. She says no. But her appetite hasn't been great lately," he said.

"For how long?"

I closed my eyes and pretended not to hear them.

"Ummm . . . a couple weeks, maybe?" Dad mumbled.

"Any remarkable family history?"

My eyes flew open. Dad shifted in his chair.

"I . . . I have high blood pressure. Her younger brother's healthy." Dad's hands wrung together as if the room was sub-zero.

"And her mother?" Nurse Shar-Pei yawned.

I froze.

Dad closed his eyes, stretching his neck first toward one shoulder, then switching sides. With his arms crossed, he leaned against the counter and gazed at the ceiling. His hair looked grayer than I'd remembered. He looked like he was afraid to speak. Almost like he was hiding something.

"Her mother passed away five years ago," he said.

"From what?" Nurse Shar-Pei croaked.

Something flashed in Dad's eyes. Fear? But if so . . . why?

"She was in an accident," he muttered.

Before the nurse could ask another question, the door slid open and a white-coated, pimple-faced guy in Buzz Lightyear scrubs strolled into the room. He barely looked old enough to be Wolfie's babysitter, let alone a doctor. The blood pressure cuff whirred, strangling my arm.

"Someone's tummy is upset, I hear!" Was he trying to do a Mickey Mouse impression? I raised my eyebrows at him.

"I think . . ." The doctor glanced at the chart in his hands. "Tonya's going to be just fine," he chirped.

"Her name is Twyla," Dad said. "What did the X-ray show? And her bloodwork?"

"Ah, yes. Her bloodwork all looks great. Tonya—I mean, Twyla—lie down on your back for me, will you please?" he squeaked. He sounded like he'd been inhaling helium.

I did as I was told and fixed my eyes on the flickering incandescent lighting in the ceiling. Everyone probably looked sick under these lights. Dr. Mickey-Buzz pushed on my stomach, and I groaned.

"Are you tender here?" he asked. I nodded. Of course I was tender. I'd been vomiting all night. After a healthy dose of pushing, prodding, and hammering, he proceeded to ask a slew of overly enthusiastic questions about my bowel habits.

"Well, Ton— Twyla, I know you feel icky, but I think you're gonna be okeydokey! I'm going to prescribe you some *Mir-a-lax*. It looks like you might have a little bit of hard poopy right here"—he poked my stomach—"in the descending colon, which is just another name for the large *in-tes-tine*. I'm also going to ask you to drink some PediaSure, and you'll be right as rain in a few days!" I wrinkled my nose like he'd just farted.

"Wait—you think I'm throwing up because I'm . . . constipated?"

"Yuppers!" he chirped. "Let's looksie." He turned a computer monitor to face me, clicking a few keys until an X-ray of my abdomen appeared.

"This line of bones, in the back, is your spine. And see this? That's your pelvis. All around this area in the middle, those are your squishy-wishy *in-tes-tines*! And these dark pockets there . . ." Dr. Buzz frowned at me. "That's poopy."

I resisted the urge to smack him.

"But I'm not constipated," I insisted. "I'm pooping every morning." I winced as Nurse Shar-Pei yanked the IV from the back of my hand and applied pressure with gauze.

"Well, sometimes you can be constipated and still pooping every morning. Isn't that funny?" He smiled at my dad, who looked as pained as I felt, though I wasn't sure if it was for the same reason. The doctor walked back to the sliding doors.

"The nurse will give you your discharge papers. But as for me, I must be off . . ." He turned back dramatically to face us. "To infinity and beyond!"

I raised my eyebrows at Dad, and a smile tugged at the corner of his lips. Nurse Shar-Pei thrust papers toward his chest, then swept out after Dr. Buzz. For a moment, Dad and I stared at each other, slack-jawed.

Then we both burst out laughing. Dad inhaled deeply, then blew out slowly.

"How you feelin', Twilight?" He walked over and cupped his hand over mine.

"A little better," I said. "The fluids helped, I think. I don't feel nauseous anymore. But my hand hurts." I rubbed my finger gingerly over the bandage. Dad nodded.

"She wasn't the gentlest nurse, was she? But at least we know the problem, and it's an easy one to fix. I think we even have some Miralax at home."

His words sat in my stomach, heavy, like a pound of bubblegum.

An easy one to fix. Something about it just felt wrong.

"Dad, I'm not so sure I'm constipated . . ." My voice faltered when my father turned to face me again. Fatigue blanketed him, weighing down his eyes and his shoulders. He sighed.

"I know he was strange, Twy. But he's the doctor. If he says this is the problem, don't you think we should listen to him?"

I looked at my feet. "I guess so," I said.

When Dad turned to leave, I swung my legs off the bed. Cradling my sore hand, I followed him out of the ER. Sometimes, when Dad asked questions, he really wanted to know my answer.

But somehow, I got the impression that this was *not* one of those times.

GEODES

Once, when I was little, I decided I pretty much hated anything with fiber in it: beans, apples, almonds, bananas, sweet potatoes, just about every vegetable . . . and at the same time, for some weird reason, I also waged war on water. Before long, I was as clogged as a pug's nose. Nothing passed through me. Nothing. As a result, Mom spooned Miralax into my mouth, and the wretched medicine caused such severe cramps that I cried for two days straight. It finally cleaned me out, but it left me with a memory I never wanted to repeat.

Still, Dr. Buzz insisted I was constipated, even if I was pooping normally (which I knew I was). So, essentially, I had no way of knowing whether the loon was right or wrong without complying. I'd tried to have another lovely conversation about crapping with Dad on the way home from the hospital, but it hadn't gone well.

"Honestly, Dad, I'm not trying to be difficult. But I'm pooping fine."

"He said you can be constipated anyway," Dad retorted.

"Have you ever been constipated and still pooping fine?"

Dad scrunched his face in thought. "I don't know, to be honest. But I'm sure it's possible."

"Have you ever taken Miralax when you were pooping fine?"

Dad shrugged. "You're saying 'pooping fine' a lot."

"But have you?"

"You're taking Miralax, Twyla."

I glared at him. "Did *Mom* ever take Miralax when she was pooping fine?"

Dad's jaw tightened at my question, tilting up slightly, his eyes set into a firm stare forward.

After a painfully quiet stretch of five minutes that felt like five hours, he'd finally muttered, "Please. Don't fight this. Neither one of us wants to argue."

He'd been right about that part. When I'd gotten home, I'd googled images of X-rays with constipated abdomens, and I swore they had many more "dark pockets" than mine did. But I also read from multiple sources that constipation could, in fact, cause nausea and vomiting. A few articles even confirmed that it could be present even if someone pooped every day. Several times a day, in fact. And—for me, this was the biggie—it could lead to a decreased appetite. Even I couldn't argue with the fact that my appetite had been poor lately.

So, over the course of the next week, I took loathsome liquid. "Pooping fine" turned into "pooping loosely with horrible cramps all the time." I hated every dose. But my nausea *did* eventually wane. And, at the end of seven days, with squeaky clean pipes, I was finally allowed to stop taking it. By the time high school started, I was convinced that my spinning stomach was a thing of the past . . . first-day jitters aside.

The parking lot buzzed as Dad pulled into Springfield Elementary. Every year, he insisted on driving us the first day, just like a billion other people. Smiling parents shot photos of clingy kindergartners with bow ties and dresses, and fifth graders zoomed around on familiar turf.

"You ready for your last year of elementary school, Wolfie?" I asked.

Wolfie shoved a mini blueberry muffin into his mouth and nodded. He dropped the plastic wrap on the floor. I picked it up and tucked it into my pocket.

"Then what are the seven continents?" I asked.

"Ummm . . ." He swallowed hard. "North America, South America, Asia, Africa . . ."

"Mm-hmm," I said.

"Antarctica, ummm . . . Australia, and . . .". Wolfie screwed his face up.

"One more," I encouraged.

"And . . . Wisconsin?" he said. I burst out laughing. Wolfie pouted.

"I'm guessing that's not right?" he asked.

"Time to hop out," Dad said.

Wolfie opened the car door but turned his body to face me. "What's the last one?" he asked.

"Europe," I whispered. He smacked his forehead with his hand and groaned.

"Love you, buddy. Have a great first day!" I winked. Wolfie threw on his backpack, waved, and disappeared into the school.

Soon, Dad wound through twisty roads, past tennis courts and the football field where field hockey played home games. A pitch-black track encircled the bright-green turf with freshly painted lines, and my heart skipped a beat.

"You ready for high school?" Dad asked. I grinned and nodded. "What are you most excited about?" he asked.

"Field hockey!" I announced. He gave me a "you know that's not what I meant" look, and I held up my hand. "AP Biology," I conceded.

"Your first college credit," he said. Our Kia rolled to a stop at the end of the carpool line, about ten cars away from the front doors.

"You think you're gonna scare me?" I poked his shoulder, scanning the crowd for familiar heads. "I'm going to college in only *four years*. Who's scared now?"

Dad laughed.

Unlike middle school, kids wound their way through the cars

here, crossing the street helter-skelter. In the parking lot, a group of girls leaned against a Lexus, laughing and flipping long locks over their shoulders. A brunette who looked old enough to legally drink passed a tube of lipstick to a friend, who applied it and smacked her lips together.

I ran my fingers across my bare lips. Why didn't I think about makeup? Would all the other girls be wearing lipstick? I kicked the toe of my sneaker into the floorboard, then looked back toward the girls in the parking lot.

One pair of cowboy boots, several pairs of ankle booties, and even one girl in strappy heels. Not a sneaker in sight.

Great, I thought.

Mom would've thought about makeup and nice shoes.

I caught sight of Emilia and Anna loitering by the front door. They looked like they were sharing a joke. FOMO panged my heart.

"I'm gonna just jump out here, okay? Bye!" Before Dad could protest, I darted out of the car and jogged to meet my friends, who were now doubled over with laughter.

"Hey, guys . . ."

Anna looked up, wiping a tear. "Hey, Twy!" She pointed over my shoulder. "Your dad—he's waving . . ."

"Well, well, well. Fancy seein' you here, Twyla." At the sound of Lindy's drawl, Emilia's lip half twisted into a snarl. Lindy flipped her perfectly curled chestnut locks behind her shoulders. Apparently, she'd gotten the memo about high school. Lindy's hazel eyes were framed by perfect cat-eye liner, the blush on her cheeks just pink enough to give the impression she'd just returned from the beach. She was dressed head to toe in off-white: a form-fitting tank on top, a slitted satin maxi skirt on the bottom, with matching knee-high stiletto boots. An open-knit sweater hung loose, baring both her shoulders, and she clutched a trendy beige hobo bag in one of her mean little hands.

Lindy smirked. "I didn't think you'd have the, shall we say, *stomach* to show up today, hmmm?" My jaw dropped, and I dug my nails into my palms.

Emilia cupped her hand around my fist and stepped forward.

"Lindy, your hair, it's so . . . perfect." Emilia's words came steady. She wound a strand of Lindy's hair around her finger and flicked it away. "But tell me . . . how do you manage to style it so your horns don't show?"

Lindy's eyes flashed fire. She spun on her heels and huffed away.

More to myself than anyone else, I mumbled, "How did she know?"

Emilia brushed her hands together, as if swiping away crumbs. "Does it matter?" she said. I shook my head. Part of me had always been envious of the way Emilia stood her ground. Nothing, and no one, shook her. Her name meant "strength," so it suited her perfectly. But part of me was also just grateful that she was my friend. I never wanted to be on her bad side.

Ever.

Anna, on the other hand, hated rocking the boat even more than I did—though that was sort of perfect for her too, since her name meant "gracious." I always loved it when names and people came together serendipitously.

"So." Emilia turned to Anna. "You have Ms. Craft first period too, right?"

"Yup! For English," Anna said.

"That's not fair." I pouted, though I'd already memorized both their schedules. "I don't get to be with you guys," I said.

"That's because you're a smarty-pants," Emilia said. "You're in *AP Biology.*"

I rolled my eyes. "Hey!" I clapped my hands together, then opened my arms wide toward my friends. "What about this weekend? Can we do a back-to-school night at the Vogel house? I hate that we never got to finish our sleepover."

Emilia wrapped both her hands around one of mine and said, "I wish I could, but we're having dinner at Uncle Tyee's on Friday, and Mom wanted us to have family time on Saturday."

"We're doing family time too," Anna said. "But hey . . . at least we all have choir together!" She sang the last two words with her arms spread wide to the sky.

We pushed through the front doors and a clear student divide greeted us in the halls. Nervous freshmen fiddled with new lockers and searched for room numbers, while senior cliques flocked together. Sophomores and juniors wandered around like middle children, some with steady steps and chins held high, others watching bored feet that carried them to class. If I was being honest, I had to admit that I probably felt more freshman-y than most.

We passed the office immediately on our right. Through the glass window, I noticed a sign on a door that read "Nurse Julie." I stopped and cocked my head. Emilia and Anna stopped with me.

"Hey," I said. "How do you think Lindy knew about my stomach problems? Have you guys heard anybody talking about me?"

Emilia scoffed. "Are you kidding? We literally just walked in the door, Twy."

"Hi, Twyla." A shy, baritone voice caught me by surprise. It was both familiar yet new. Emilia and Anna's eyes grew wide before I turned.

Elliott.

He'd sprouted about a foot over the summer, and his arms and shoulders seemed to have grown muscles. Gone were the gangly legs that barely held up pull-on athletic shorts. In their place were toned runner's legs, and he now wore a pair of khaki, belted shorts and a lime linen button-up shirt with loafers and no socks. His short, layered hair had been replaced by a longer, styled cut, with bangs that swooped over his sea-green eyes. I felt my face go red.

"Elliott? I mean . . . of course you're . . . I mean . . . how was camp?"

Stupid mouth.

Emilia grinned. Anna chewed her thumbnail.

"Good," he said. He stuffed his hands into his pockets. "Are you in AP Bio first period?"

Emilia snorted behind me. I stepped on her toe.

"Yeah," I said. "Your mom is teaching."

O. M. G. I. Sound. So. Dumb.

He nodded, then jerked his chin to flick his bangs out of his eyes. They seemed greener than they'd been before. Did puberty change eye color?

Emilia grabbed Anna by the hand and tugged her in the opposite direction. "We have English. Language arts. LA. Which is called English in high school. We have to go. Bye, Twy."

They both did a decent job hiding their amusement until Emilia turned around and yelled, "See? Geode." Then, they burst into fits of giggles. I glared at them.

Elliott gave me a crooked smile and my stomach did a weird, twisty thing. "Geode?" he asked.

"I have no idea what they're talking about," I mumbled. "Wanna find our room?"

We waited awkwardly for the other to move, then both started walking at the same time. Our shoulders bumped.

"Sorry," he said. Elliott held his hand out in front of him, motioning toward our classroom. "After you."

I started to move, then halted. This was still the boy who had grown up next door. Whose dog my mom had saved. Who caught salamanders in the creek and played in the sprinkler with me. I didn't want puberty to change that.

"Elliott, are you nervous about being a freshman?" I watched the floor as we walked. "I'm nervous."

He gave a tiny laugh that was almost like a hiccup. When I looked up, he smiled at me and shrugged. My stomach jumped.

"Isn't everyone?" he said.

"Well . . . welcome home, Elliott." Lindy stepped between us, batting her lashes. "See ya in class." She flipped her hair behind her, sashaying through the door. Her hips swung hypnotically, like one of Emilia's crystal pendulums. Elliott followed on her heels.

I gritted my teeth.

Apparently not everyone, I thought.

Chapter 11

AP BIOLOGY

Black lab tables sat in rows with two chairs per table. Each table had a number taped to it, starting with one and going up to twelve. Kids were scattered about, with only one person at several tables and a few already in pairs. I'd started making a beeline toward Erin, who was solo, when Coach—*Ms.* Givens—stopped me. Her tidy field hockey ponytail had been replaced by a wavy down-do, and instead of sportswear, she donned a pink, pinstripe pantsuit and a copper top that matched her tan. I'd always thought she was pretty, but now she looked so . . . teacherish. She shoved an upside-down hat toward me.

"Pick a number," she said.

"Pick a . . . what?" Elliott asked.

"Seats are assigned so there's no fighting over lab partners," she answered. "Table numbers will be random. Twyla . . . pick first."

Glancing around the room, I realized that the only number I did not want was six. Lindy sat at table six, her chair positioned in the middle so whoever she was partnered with would get a fraction of the space she did. She filed her nails, watching everyone draw numbers like a snapping turtle ready to attack its next meal. When I stretched my hand into the hat, she stopped filing.

"Eleven," I said. Lindy smirked and resumed filing.

Ms. Givens pointed to an empty table toward the back of the room, right next to a window. Perfect. I set my backpack on the floor just as Ms. Givens echoed me from the moment before.

"Eleven," she said. "Go join Twyla, Elliott."

Elliott's eyes met mine, and the room suddenly felt too warm. I busied myself with my pencil pouch as he navigated toward me.

Lindy cleared her throat. "Um, Ms. Givens? Can I *puh-lease* switch with *Twah-la*? My doctor thinks I should sit by a window whenever possible because . . ."

"What was your number, Lindy?"

"Six," Lindy mumbled.

"Then you'll stay at table six," Ms. Givens instructed. Lindy crossed her arms and slouched in her chair.

"I think Lindy likes you almost as much as she dislikes me," I whispered to Elliott. He laughed.

Had he always had those freckles?

The rest of the empty seats quickly filled, with a small, lost-looking redhead squeezing into the unfortunate chair beside Lindy.

Ms. Givens whistled just like she did in practice. "Welcome back to school, everyone! And welcome to AP Biology. I am Ms. Givens, your teacher, and there's a lot to learn this year." She wrote her name in purple on the board, then spun on her heels to face us. "On your desks, you should each have a copy of this year's syllabus. You'll see that unit one is about the chemical properties that make life possible. In units two and three, you'll increase your cellular knowledge, and in unit four, you'll learn about cell cycles, communication, and division. But it is units five and six, more than any others, that intrigue most people. As a result, I like to sprinkle little genetics experiments here and there throughout the year, to keep everyone interested.

"So. Let's begin with a show of hands. Who got a sunburn this summer?"

I glanced sideways at Elliott, who didn't look like he'd be raising his hand. His bronzed skin matched his mother's. Why didn't *I* ever tan like that? The redhead next to Lindy, whom I didn't recognize, raised her hand an inch, then pulled it back down. Ms. Givens nodded at her.

"Welcome to Springfield High, Samantha. Most of you probably know that fair-skinned people, like Samantha, are more likely to burn. But did you know that your skin tone is also a result of genetics?"

Lindy raised her hand.

"Yes, Lindy?" Ms. Givens said.

"I tan easily," Lindy said. "In fact, I never burn."

Ms. Givens nodded. "Well, you probably have your genetics to thank. That, and perhaps some good sunscreen."

Lindy snorted. "Twyla's the one who *looooves* a good sunscreen," she drawled. I breathed in deeply through my nose, swallowing my irritation.

"That's great!" Ms. Givens said, ignoring the obvious sarcasm in Lindy's voice. "Then everyone should follow Twyla's lead, since sunburns can cause cancer."

Lindy rolled her eyes.

"Now. Have you ever wondered why you share some traits with one parent but not the other? Or how you turned out one way, but a sibling may be totally different? Today, we're going to meet our classmates by examining a genetic quality that some people have and some do not: tongue rolling."

Students everywhere turned to one another, folding and twisting their tongues like floppy acrobats. Elliott and I instinctively faced one another and made loops with our tongues.

"Each person in this classroom inherited two forms of a gene, called alleles, for tongue rolling—one from each parent. If you can roll your tongue, then you have at least one dominant allele." Ms. Givens wrote a capital *T* on the board. "If you cannot roll your tongue, then both your parents gave you recessive alleles." Next, she wrote a lowercase *t* on the board next to the capital *T*.

"So," she continued, "if this tongue-rolling genotype of *Tt* represented your alleles, then which gene would be expressed? In other words, would you be able to roll your tongue or not?"

Lindy's hand shot into the air. "Yes, Lindy?" Ms. Givens asked.

"The *dominant* allele, or ability to roll the tongue, would be *expressed*," she fawned.

"That's correct, Lin—"

"Like this," Lindy interrupted. Then she rolled her tongue for the world to see.

"Okay," Ms. Givens said, "so since you can roll your tongue, Lindy, can you tell me what your genotype would be?"

"Of course," Lindy said. "Big T, little t."

"Well, that could definitely be right," Ms. Givens replied. Lindy beamed. "Or," Ms. Givens said, "it could be wrong. Can only one of your parents roll their tongue?"

Lindy shrank a little in her chair. "Well, I guess I'm not sure."

Ms. Givens nodded. "In that case, you might be big T, little t . . . or you might be big T, big T. Remember, you only need one big T to inherit that dominant trait. Which leads me to today's activity.

"On your desk, by your syllabus, you'll find a sheet of paper with everyone's name in this class. Since today is our first day of school, I want you to meet every other student. Once you do, I want you to write every possible genotype they might have for tongue rolling beside their name. Okay? GO!"

A cacophony of shuffling papers and chattering filled the room. Everyone jumped to their feet, shaking hands with students and rolling (or not rolling) their tongues. But suddenly, I didn't feel like being social.

All I could think was that after school, Lindy could go home and ask both parents whether or not they could roll their tongues. In fact, everyone could, if they wanted to.

But I would never know.

And *that* made me wonder . . .

What else would I never know?

Chapter 12

NOT AGAIN

"*Thai food is* here!" Mama Rose poked her face around the wall beside the basement stairs to announce the arrival of dinner. In doing so, she looked like a floating head. Every time I saw her, I couldn't help but see an older version of Anna. They both had the same long, blond hair, the same heart-shaped face, the same petite, pointy nose. Like her mother, Anna had never needed braces. Their smiles were model-perfect. Besides age, the only major difference between them was that Mama Rose wore glasses, and Anna did not.

"Be right there, Mom!" Anna fiddled with the dials on her new camera, then pointed the lens at me.

"Say cheese," she sang. I put my puzzle pieces back on the table and obliged. Emilia drummed her fingers against the handrail at the base of the stairs.

"Why do you need a big, clunky camera anyway?" she asked. "Doesn't everyone in Photography Club have a camera on their phones?"

Anna turned the lens on Emilia, who first feigned modesty, then strummed an imaginary guitar. Anna snapped. She glanced at the viewfinder and turned a knob.

"Most probably do, but it's not the same. With this, I have better control over aperture, shutter speed, ISO sensitivity, that kind of thing."

Emilia shrugged. "I have no idea what any of those things mean," she admitted.

Anna slid her camera into its case, snapping the lid shut around it. "Well, you don't have to," she said. "*You* have field hockey and Amnesty Club."

Emilia draped one arm over Anna's shoulder and pointed a finger to the sky with the other. "Human rights for all people!" she said.

I laughed, following them up the stairs.

The appetizing aroma of crab rangoon and peanut pad thai enveloped us once we entered the kitchen. We filled our plates with warm, savory dishes, and my stomach growled. Although my appetite hadn't exactly been voracious over the last few weeks, my nausea, thankfully, had waned.

"Hello, girls!" Anna's dad sauntered by, whistling some happy, upbeat melody. He rubbed his balding head like a crystal ball. Buttercup, the Roses' lazy, old golden retriever, flopped down by our feet, patiently waiting for occasional noodle bits to hit the floor.

Mr. Rose reached for a crab rangoon on Anna's plate. Mama Rose slapped his hand.

"Your plate is in the dining room!" she scolded.

Mr. Rose rubbed his fingers, as if she'd really hurt him. He leaned back to glance through the doorway.

"I don't see any crab rangoon on my plate," he pouted. Mama Rose patted his belly.

"You don't need fried food," she teased. "Enjoy your dinner, girls. We'll give you your space." Grabbing a little white box of rice in one hand and a container of panang curry in the other, she followed Mr. Rose into the dining room.

Emilia, Anna, and I sat around the table, catching up on classes, clubs, and gossip. Emilia was enjoying Social Studies most, because Tanner sat next to her. Anna, who had read five books in the last three weeks, was looking forward to the upcoming poetry unit most. And I, of course, was happiest when buried in biology.

"That's just because her lab partner is . . ."

"It's not always about boys, Emilia. I happen to like biology."

"Admit it, Twy. You like him."

"Of course I like him. He's been my friend since I was, like, six."

"You're in denial," she hiss-whispered.

"Are you going to eat your last crab rangoon?" Anna asked me. I shook my head.

"What about the rest of your pad thai?"

Again, I shook my head. She scooped my leftovers onto her plate and dug in. I wondered how she stayed stick thin when she was always consuming my leftovers.

"You didn't eat very well," Emilia said, watching Anna pick my plate clean.

Mama Rose waltzed into the kitchen on the heels of Emilia's words. I stood to rinse my plate, feeling moderately annoyed by the observation.

"I've got it." Mama Rose took the plate from my hands and side-eyed me. "Are you still feeling poorly, honey?"

I shook my head. "Not really. I'm just full." Then, turning back to my friends, I said, "I'm gonna head down to look at the puzzle. See ya down there."

Buttercup followed me downstairs, and I scratched her head while separating edge pieces from center pieces. I wasn't sure what it was about the interaction that had bothered me so much. It was true that I hadn't been eating as much as them, but it wasn't like I was trying to starve myself, either. My appetite was decent, and I ate until I felt full . . . just like everyone else. Who cared if I wasn't shoveling other people's leftovers down my gullet?

Laughter drifted down the stairs, and I wondered what they were talking about.

Boys, probably.

By the time my friends joined me, all the pieces had been pulled into their respective piles. Emilia nodded approvingly and swiped her hands together, as if brushing dirt from her palms.

"So, what are we watching tonight, ladies?" she asked.

"Let's watch an old Disney movie," Anna cooed. "Like *Bambi*!"

I played with a purple corner piece. "Mmmm . . . nah," I said. "Not in the mood for a cartoon."

"*Guardians of the Galaxy*?" Emilia offered.

I scrunched my nose. "Seen it," I said.

"We all have, but it's good!" Emilia countered.

"How about a musical? Like *Les Misérables*? It's a classic . . ." Anna's fingers fluttered, like she was trying to draw me in. "I dreamed a dream in time gone—"

"No, no, and no," I said. The sharpness of my tone seemed to push Anna back into herself, while simultaneously triggering Emilia. Her hands hit her hips.

"Why not?"

Emotions swirled, confusing and tumultuous. I shrugged.

"I'm going to the bathroom," I muttered. I threw the corner piece back onto its pile and climbed the steps, feeling my friends' eyes bore into my back. I knew I sounded unreasonable. Maybe it was the teenage hormones Dad was always bemoaning. Maybe it was because I'd been up late doing homework for the last couple of weeks, and I was tired. Whatever the reason, I felt fragile.

With the bathroom door closed safely behind me, I caught a glimpse of my reflection in the mirror. My face looked more angular than it used to. I touched my cheekbones, more prominent than I remembered them being. My collarbones, too, arched on either side of my neckline. I'd always looked most like Dad. But in that moment, I saw Mom. And that's when it hit me.

Bambi. Guardians of the Galaxy. Les Misérables.

Why? *Why* did the mother have to die in so many movies?

My throat burned, and I felt like a dam was about to burst somewhere inside me. I wasn't angry with my friends. How could I be? It wasn't their fault they hadn't seen the connection. I was angry that I couldn't help *but* see it.

I closed my eyes, listening for her voice.

"Twyla, there's a reason for everything."

So, what is it? I thought. I'd wondered back then, on That Day. And now, in Anna's bathroom . . . I wondered again. *Why?*

I remembered choosing not to view her body in the casket. Even though I knew it wasn't really her anymore. It was just a place where her laughter once lived.

Did I regret that decision now? I couldn't really tell.

I remembered the chapel smelled like a flower garden, with lilies, daffodils, tulips, roses, orchids, hydrangeas . . . every flower I'd ever known. Spray arrangements perched on tripods, others hung in colorful wreaths, and yet others stretched tall from vases. You could hardly see the front of the chapel through the forest of flowers.

I remembered Dad trying to speak from the podium, but ultimately unable. The pain in his chest had been too heavy to carry spoken words.

And I remembered my friends. Me in turquoise, Anna in pink, and Emilia in rainbow stripes. Because Mom would never have wanted everyone in black.

My friends. My beautiful, wonderful friends.

I owed them an explanation.

Centering myself with a deep, slow breath, I headed back downstairs. Emilia and Anna huddled together at the puzzle table, whispering. Anna was shaking her head, forehead furrowed, while Emilia nodded animatedly.

I cleared my throat.

My friends turned, faces etched with worry, and I let the tears come. Anna ran toward me and wrapped me in a hug. Emilia, too, joined our hug-huddle. For several minutes, we stood together on the stairs, my friends wrapping their arms around me in a protective barrier. Finally, Anna spoke.

"You wanna sit on the couch?"

I nodded.

Anna snagged a box of tissues and Emilia got a garbage can. The room was quiet—everyone waiting for me to speak first. I curled myself around a large, fluffy throw pillow and breathed.

"Do you guys remember Mom's funeral?" The words escaped my lips, soft and vulnerable. Although I kept my focus trained on the ceiling, I could feel Emilia's and Anna's eyes on me.

"I do," Anna whispered.

"I remember stealing nuts and pretzels," Emilia said. I smiled.

"Those funeral home workers were so mean," Anna added.

"Maybe they wouldn't have been so mean if we hadn't stolen bowls of snacks," I said. We all laughed a little.

"Remember running around, looking for an exit, with our arms full of silver bowls?" Emilia asked.

"I do! And that poor girl we knocked over in the chaos," Anna added. "I think we gave her a salt shower."

I shrugged. "I felt so, so angry. But then, once we were outside, it all kind of melted away for a minute when we threw that first handful of nuts. The way they ricocheted off that tree was so . . . satisfying."

Emilia giggled. "It was. I remember yelling something like, 'THIS IS FOR THAT STUPID HAIRCUT MY MOM GAVE ME!'"

Anna laughed. "I remember throwing some because of that time when a bunch of kids in our class laughed at me when I fell off the teeter-totter."

"And then I threw a bunch because our little league soccer team had lost a game," Emilia said.

"And then I threw some because I was mad at humidity for frizzing my hair," Anna added, laughter dying down. She sighed. "Geez, that sounds so stupid now."

"No, it doesn't," I said. "None of it sounds stupid. We weren't throwing nuts because of humidity or haircuts or soccer games."

I didn't have to say more than that. We all knew the real reason.

Silence again blanketed the room. When I finally tried to sit up, a familiar rush of nausea washed over me. It was so sudden, so severe, that I jumped to my feet with my left hand outstretched and my right over my mouth. I knew I needed to find a bathroom quickly.

"Twyla?"

"What's wrong?"

"MOM!"

Emilia and Anna both shot up, yelling simultaneously. By the time Mama Rose came downstairs, I'd already thrown up once.

Ever so faintly, Emilia whispered, "Not again."

"Twyla?" This time, it was Mama Rose. Her hand touched my clammy forehead and neck. "You don't feel feverish. Did you vomit any blood, honey? Anything that looks like coffee grounds?"

Coffee grounds? I shook my head. "Just dinner," I managed.

"Anna, please go get Twyla a cool washcloth and a hair tie. Emilia, can you call Mr. Vogel?"

Shuffling and murmuring ensued for the next several minutes until the immediate threat of further vomiting had passed. Mama Rose guided my head onto a blanket that had magically appeared on the floor.

"Can I poke on your belly?"

Somehow, I didn't mind the little-kid talk nearly as much from her. I nodded.

Mama Rose asked me a billion rapid-fire questions while she pushed on my belly and sides. Her voice remained calm. Soothing, almost.

"Does it hurt here? Here?"

"Have you been exposed to anyone who's been sick lately, that you know of?"

"Do you have any lower back pain, sweetie?"

"Any other symptoms of illness?"

"Have you had diarrhea lately? Constipation?"

"Does it hurt when you pee?"

"How about any blood in your urine or stool?"

"Have you felt bloated lately? I mean, other than typical period bloating."

"When's the last time you vomited before this?"

"Have you been able to pass gas lately? Had too much gas?"

After several other questions, more prodding and tapping, and another minor wave of nausea, Mama Rose patted the cool cloth on my forehead.

"I don't think you have appendicitis," she said. "But I'd like you to see your doctor on Monday, okay? I know it sounds counterintuitive, but vomiting can actually be a result of constipation.

I groaned.

"Mr. Vogel is here," Emilia said.

"But I'm feeling better, really . . ." The hard floor had worn its welcome, and I pushed myself to a seated position.

Mama Rose didn't even acknowledge that I was speaking. Just held her hand out to help me stand.

"Bye, Twyla." Anna's voice drifted behind me, sad and sweet.

My heart sank, and Emilia's words rang in my head.

Not again.

Chapter 13

THE SEARCH BEGINS

Hunger jolted me from my sleep. Nugget kneaded the comforter between my knees. His purr rumbled my legs.

"Hey, boy," I said, scratching between his ears. He rolled his head into my palm. Late-morning light poured in between the window blinds, shading the wall in stripes.

And then I remembered.

Movie night.

The vomiting.

Ugh.

Wolfie's heavy steps pounded up the stairs. My door creaked open a smidge.

"Twyla?" he whispered through the crack. "You awake?"

"I'm up," I sighed. "Come on in."

He bounded in like a monkey at a banana bonanza. Nugget skittered away. "Twy! Hey, did you know that even when you're dead, you're still doing something, because you're just lying there? And after you're dead, did you know you can still burp and fart? I got that second part from a book, but that first part I thought up by myself." Wolfie forced a fake burp, and I shook my head.

"No, Wolfie. I didn't know that." He failed to notice my dead-panned tone.

"Yup! Hey! Dad just got back from the store. Brunch will be ready soon!" And just as quickly as he'd appeared, Wolfie vanished again.

Brunch? I glanced at my phone, charging on the air purifier that doubled as a bedside table. It was 11:44. Not as bad as it could've been. But still, I couldn't believe I'd slept away the whole morning.

At least I'm feeling better, I thought.

"Twyla? You coming down?" Dad called.

I stuffed my toes into my slippers and shuffled a few steps until they were all the way on my feet. "Be right there!" I yawned.

"Okay!" Dad answered. "I've got medicine for you!"

My stomach dropped. The night before, Dad had called the doctor on duty after picking me up. The good news was that they said I could just come to the office when it opened on Monday. The bad news? They wanted me to take Miralax.

Again.

I chewed on the inside of my cheek. The whole idea of constipation simply wasn't ringing true to me, but I already knew I couldn't very well argue about taking a medicine the doctors wanted me to take just because their diagnosis "felt wrong." That said, Dr. Buzz had barely even seemed to consider any other possibility. Surely, other explanations were out there.

I padded over to my laptop, flipped it open, and waited for Google to reboot. Then I typed: *What causes nausea or vomiting?*

The first article that popped up was on a site called webmd. com. Surely, if it was good enough for MDs, it was good enough for me. I scanned the list titled "Common Causes":

Motion sickness (nope)

Early stages of pregnancy (OMG, no)

Medication-induced vomiting (not yet, but if Dad made me
    take Miralax again, it might happen)

Intense pain (I *did* feel pain at Anna's, but if that was the
    reason for the nausea, then what caused the pain? And
    I hadn't been hurting like that the other times I'd been
    nauseous, so . . .)

Emotional stress, such as fear (possible, but I'd actually felt *less* stress after talking with my friends—not more)
Food poisoning

I paused, thinking about that last one. Food poisoning. My pulse quickened, and I typed into the Google search bar: *How quickly can food poisoning hit?*

Again, the first source that popped up sounded credible: Johns Hopkins. I'd heard that name before—it was a big hospital. And the website was a dot org, which my dad had taught me was typically more reliable than a dot com. I read on.

Symptoms can start any time from 30 minutes to 3 weeks after eating contaminated food.

Wow . . . pretty vague window of time. I mentally ticked through the timeline of the prior night. We'd eaten at least half an hour before I'd started feeling sick. It was certainly possible. I tapped my chin, then typed: *How long does it take to recover from food poisoning?*

This time, the first blurb that popped up was from Mount Sinai. Another hospital with a dot org address. Credible.

You'll usually recover from the most common types of food poisoning within 12 to 48 hours.

"TWYLA? Are you okay?"

I slapped my laptop shut, relief washing over me. It had been well over twelve hours since I'd gotten sick. Food poisoning. That *had* to be it.

"Yeah, Dad! On my way!"

I skipped the stairs, two at a time, then approached the breakfast table with a smile. "Morning, gentlemen!" I plopped down in front of my eggs and toast. Dad and Wolfie exchanged a suspicious look.

"You seem to be feeling better," Dad said. I sank my teeth into a piece of peanut butter toast drizzled with honey, taking a particularly big bite for effect.

"I am." I held up my finger to indicate I was chewing but had more to say. Dad waited for me to continue. I swallowed, considering my words carefully.

"So. Dad. Before you reject this hypothesis, I'd like you to hear me out."

Dad's eyebrows shot up.

"Please?"

His face relaxed, but his arms remained crossed in front of his chest. Wolfie ran into the living room and began plunking out the beginning of the Mario theme song on the piano.

Ba-da, da, da-da, dum, dum.

Ba-da, da, da-da, dum, dum.

"I was doing some research this morning—on credible sites, like hospital sites—and I feel certain I know what was wrong with me. I had food poisoning."

Again, the eyebrows.

"Why do you think that?"

Ba-da, da, da-da, dum, dum.

"Well, you know I was with Mama Rose last night. She asked me a bunch of questions about bowel habits, urination, pain, who I'd been around, that kind of thing. Ultimately, nothing struck her as terribly unusual, and as you know, she wants me to see the doctor tomorrow. Which I'm going to do, right?"

Ba-da, da, da-da, dum, dum.

Nod.

"Okay. So, I looked good enough to her that she didn't think I had anything big or crazy, like appendicitis. So this morning, I began researching different causes of nausea and vomiting . . . and *yes*, I submit that constipation can cause nausea. *But* . . .

Ba-da, da, da-da, dum, dum.

". . . so can other things."

Ba-da, da, da-da—

"WOLFIE! Can you play any more of that song? That one line is driving me crazy!"

"Dad. Are you listening?"

"Yes, I'm listening."

"Okay. So I looked up other causes of nausea and vomiting, and food poisoning is a common culprit. Symptoms can start within thirty minutes of eating, and then they can resolve again as soon as twelve hours after. The timeline fits, Dad."

Ba-da, da, da-da, dum, dum.

Dad's fingers gripped the countertop behind him.

"Besides, you know Miralax doesn't make me feel well. It causes cramps, really bad ones, and last time I actually felt worse on it . . ."

"And yet, your symptoms improved after you took it for the prescribed amount of time, did they not?"

Ba-da, da, da-da, dum, dum.

"They did, but . . ."

"Did everyone eat different food last night?"

"I . . . well, no, but . . ."

"And you think it's reasonable to assume that you've had food poisoning twice in the last month?"

"More reasonable than constipation," I huffed.

Ba-da, da, da—

"WOLFIE! STOP!"

Dad's voice rang through the kitchen, echoing off the walls as if he'd just shouted into the Grand Canyon. For a moment, the only sound in the house was the padding of Wolfie's socks back into the kitchen and Nugget's piercing mew, demanding food.

Dad pinched the bridge of his nose and sighed. "Twyla, the doctor saw constipation on your X-ray. Please don't argue with me, okay? Your dose of Miralax is on the table. End of conversation."

"But, Dad . . ."

Dad thumped the counter with his fist, causing both Wolfie and me to jump. His eyes remained glued to his hand, which now uncurled itself and spread its fingers wide as he inhaled deeply. "Just take your medicine, Twyla," Dad said, turning back to the eggs on the stovetop. Wolfie stared at his feet.

Without thinking, I poured the Miralax into my napkin. The doctor might not have wanted to consider my opinion, but Dad's unwillingness to listen stung. I'd taken the time to research viable websites, and he didn't care. He just wanted me to be quiet and do what I was told, regardless of how I felt about it.

Regardless of what the medicine did to my body.

A burst of anger surged through me, and I pounded the cup back on the table.

"THERE!" I snapped. "Are you HAPPY NOW?"

Time froze as my father and I stared daggers at one another while Wolfie looked on, speechless. The backs of my legs forced my chair to skid across the floor as I stood. Even Nugget stopped crying for food.

"Where do you think you're going?" Were it not for Dad's gritted teeth, one might mistake his level tone for calm. I threw my wadded napkin into the garbage and grabbed my journal from the island.

"To the tree," I hissed. My heart raced. I'd never spoken to Dad like this. Or any adult, for that matter.

"Sit down," he spat back. "We are eating brunch together."

"I. Am. Not. Hungry." Before I could stop myself, I stormed down the hallway and slid my feet into the weathered hiking boots I kept by the door.

"Twyla, get back here this instant." I opened the door and ran through without looking back. Even as my feet carried me across the lawn, I could hear the front door open. I could hear Dad start to yell for me—only to stop himself. He'd never want to make a scene in front of the neighbors.

I might be in huge trouble when I got back, but I didn't care. Dad had been completely unwilling to listen to me. He'd given me no choice.

When I reached the creek, I splashed to my favorite spot on the bald cypress, ignoring the crayfish that fled in fear. Tears stained my cheeks; I hadn't even realized I'd been crying. I crawled onto the tree, grateful for its sturdiness. Even in the middle of an ever-changing stream, the fallen tree never faltered. Steadfast, strong, and reliable, it nourished and protected the woods, no matter the environment.

Just like my mom had.

My pen clicked to life, shaking in my adrenaline-laced hand.

Dear Mom,
*   YOU would've listened to me. YOU would've known I'm fine. Why is Dad acting like this? WHY???*

I closed my eyes, letting myself find peace in the sound of creek water rushing past. It waited for no one. For nothing. Not for stress, or nausea. Not for Dad. And not for me. I envied its freedom.

Somewhere in the distance, a common loon hooted its wolflike wail, sounding appropriately mournful. Nearby, a thrush warbled, stilling my trembling body. I inhaled the musty smell of my woods, recent rainfall lingering in the air, and my pulse slowed. My stomach growled, angry that I'd stormed off without eating.

Could Dad be right? Was I constipated? I shook the thought away like a tenacious spider web. No. He was wrong. Somehow, in my gut, I just knew he was wrong.

Again, I wrote.

I'm sure I ate something that made me sick. Isn't that what happened? Of course that's what happened.
*   Ugh. I need you, Mom. I need your help. If things*

*really do happen for a reason, I just want to know what
those reasons are. If I could just figure them out, then
I'd know it'll all be okay. And maybe then, Dad wouldn't
make me take that irrelevant, disgusting medicine that
only makes me feel worse. Maybe then, we wouldn't fight.*

I thought about how I'd dumped the Miralax into my napkin. How I'd led him to believe that I'd taken it. That was no different than lying. Guilt filled my chest.

*Please, Mom. I need to know I'm doing the right thing.
I lied to Dad today, and I feel horrible about it. Do you
think maybe you could send me a sign?
Please?*

*Love,
Twyla*

My journal thumped closed and I shut my eyes, praying that something would be different when I opened them again. Maybe the tree would be able to talk, like in *Pocahontas*, or maybe a message would be written in twigs on the bank. But when I opened them again, everything was the same. The babbling creek, the rustling leaves, the cool breeze . . . nothing had changed.

Nothing.

But . . . I still wasn't nauseous. My stomach rumbled. Was *that* the sign? Maybe she wanted me to know that I was better now, because the food poisoning had cleared?

I hugged my knees to my chest. That had to be it.

It just *had* to be.

Chapter 14

DIGGING DEEPER

As it turned out, the beginning of the next school week was the weekend's jerk cousin. Monday's visit to the doctor included some basic labs, but otherwise focused exclusively on my bowel habits and added "anxiety" into the diagnostic mix. It also resulted in a trip to the drugstore for another fateful bottle of liquid nastiness. Then, as punishment for my revolt, Dad had taken away my phone and refused to drive me to or from school. If I was independent enough to choose when I wanted to come and go, he said, then I was independent enough to "get my butt on the bus." Not only that, I was left to my own devices for breakfasts and lunches all week long. Initially, he'd said I would have to make dinners for myself as well. But that had lasted only one night. Thankfully, he preferred to see me eat something other than frozen pizza and granola bars.

Having an architect father who worked from home frequently had its advantages, but I was learning that those did not apply while feuding.

So, in defiant response to my father's punishment, I picked up a habit of which he did not approve—coffee.

"You're only fourteen, Twyla. You should not be drinking coffee."

"I need something to get that disgusting Miralax taste out of my mouth, don't ya think?"

"Don't be sarcastic with me."

"Who says I'm being sarcastic?"

And so it went. For several days, communication between me and Dad was limited to snippy little jibes and short-tempered grunts. Every morning, a tiny, obnoxious cup of Miralax mocked me from the island, and every morning, I dumped it into a napkin when he wasn't looking. At first, I thought I'd be happy exchanging glares and silence with Dad until college. But the bus had proven to be unsustainable. By Thursday, when I arrived at school with gum in my hair and muddy tread marks on my backpack, I was ready to wave a white flag.

When I couldn't find my friends' familiar faces outside the school, I maneuvered my way inside, alone. I made a brief stop in the front office to cut out the sticky lock of hair, then wound my way through the hallways toward the freshman lockers. There, clumped near a group of students studying announcements on the bulletin board, Emilia and Anna chatted with their backs to me. I made a beeline toward them, but something about their hushed tones stopped me only a few feet away.

". . . second time . . . what if . . ."

". . . not sure, Em . . ."

". . . the problem . . . too much stress . . ."

"Twyla!" Anna's blue eyes flashed over Emilia's shoulder, cutting her off mid-sentence. Emilia swung to face me. A mixture of surprise and guilt shaded their features.

"I . . . I looked for you guys outside," I managed. Even though this was the hallway that housed my locker as well, I somehow felt as if I were trespassing. "I didn't mean to interrupt."

Immediately, both girls broke into a flurry of incomplete sentences.

"No, not at . . ."

"Of course, but . . ."

"We were just . . ."

I held up both hands. "Don't worry about it. I've gotta get to class." But as I turned on my heels, I felt the warmth of palms inside my own.

"Wait," Emilia said. She and Anna exchanged a glance, and Emilia sighed. "Listen, we're just really worried about you." Anna nodded in agreement.

"It's true . . . we are. Mom is too, Twy. You were sick so suddenly, and lately, you look sort of frail . . ."

"Says the frail blond," I shot back. Anna bit her lip and let go of my hand. Emilia squared her shoulders, and I could tell she was weighing her words carefully.

"Are you still feeling nauseous?" she asked.

"I feel fine."

"What about that medicine the doctor recommended on Monday? Do you think that helped?"

I'd told my friends about my appointment earlier in the week, but I hadn't admitted to them that I'd been tossing out Miralax behind Dad's back. Not because I was trying to hide it, necessarily . . . it just hadn't come up. And now, with judgment plastered across their faces, I did *not* feel like coming clean. Besides, at this point, I honestly wasn't sure what was or wasn't helping. Obviously, the medicine wasn't, because I wasn't taking it. But my gut told me that constipation was not to blame. Likewise, anxiety might've been affecting me a bit, but I didn't believe it was making me vomit. Especially after the last time at Anna's, where the nausea seemed to strike out of the blue.

For the last four evenings straight, I'd holed myself up in my room to research reasons for nausea and vomiting. I read about countless viruses and bacterial infections, but with no other real symptoms, those felt unlikely at this point (though I still hadn't completely eliminated food poisoning as a possibility). So I realized I had to dig deeper. And as much as I hated to admit it, I *had* been losing weight. I still felt hungry, and I always ate until I was full, but that seemed to happen pretty quickly sometimes. I expanded my research to nausea, vomiting, *and* weight loss . . . but that, too, felt like a dead-end road. I wasn't bulimic, anorexic, or taking laxatives or other medications that might make me sick or cause weight loss (thank goodness). I didn't feel depressed, and my blood work had ruled out thyroid problems and diabetes. In fact, all my labs had been normal. I just seemed to get frequent, random bouts of nausea.

Emilia waved her hand in front of my face.

"Hello? Anyone home?"

"No," I said. "I mean, yes, I'm here, but no, I don't think the medicine helps."

"So you're still nauseous?" Anna asked.

"No!" I shook my head, flustered. "I'm not nauseous. I don't think the medicine makes any difference at all. That's what I'm saying."

I took a swig from my water bottle, shaking the last drops at my friends. "See? I've already finished the whole bottle this morning. And I'm fine. No nausea at all, okay?"

The bell rang, and Anna's hand flew up. "Oh! Guys! I'm taking pics for the yearbook. Hang on a sec." She unsnapped the lens cap from the camera hanging around her neck, and Emilia and I gave each other bunny ears. Then we all waved and headed to our respective classes.

"See you at lunch!" Emilia called.

I waved goodbye and smiled, but my stomach churned at the thought of having lunch with my friends. They were now apparently so concerned about my eating habits that they were talking about me behind my back. Anna was thin too, but no one was secretly gossiping about her diet or pooping habits. I missed the nonchalance of typical, everyday chatter with my friends. And I absolutely detested feeling like I was under a microscope.

I was convinced that the doctors were looking in the wrong places. And I knew my symptoms. I was smart. Maybe, I thought, I could figure out the real reasons for my recent episodes.

I popped open my phone to Google and typed: *Reasons for unexplained weight loss.*

I scanned the result at the top of the page:

Your body weight can regularly fluctuate. But persistent, unintentional loss can be a sign of malnutrition. This is when a person's diet doesn't contain the right amount of nutrients.

I tried to think back to what I'd been eating recently. Had I not been getting the right balance of nutrients? I did like my sugar . . . did I need more veggies? Protein?

Elliott caught my eye near the door. He jutted his chin into the classroom, and I held up one finger to indicate I'd be right there.

Quickly, my fingers tapped: *Good sources of protein.*

Google replied: *Eggs, salmon, almonds, legumes, nuts, chicken breast . . .*

I nodded to myself, vowing to pay better attention to what I was putting in my body. I'd focus on healthier eating and try to build some muscle.

Then, maybe we could all go back to being normal again.

Chapter 15

JELLY BEAN CHROMOSOMES

"Look," Elliott said. I plunked my backpack onto the floor, trying not to let his lopsided grin distract me. He pointed at eight cups of jelly beans on each table. There were four little rows, with two cups in each row, each with a label:

R and *p* on the cups with red and pink jelly beans.

B and *w* on the cups with black and white ones.

G and *b* on the cups with green and blue.

And *O* and *y* on the cups with orange and yellow.

I fingered a ninth cup, filled with toothpicks. A blue jelly bean called to me, so I stabbed it and then slid it off the toothpick with my teeth.

A tiny bit of sugar wouldn't hurt.

"You're not supposed to eat those." Lindy thrust her hip out and blew a bubble in my face. Elliott plucked a green jelly bean from a cup and popped it into his mouth too. Lindy spun on her heels and raised her hand.

"Excuse me, Ms. Givens? Are we allowed to eat the jelly beans?"

"Noooooo." Ms. Givens's voice slid up the scale, and she raised her eyebrows at me and Elliott. "But we're also not supposed to have gum in class." She presented Lindy with a garbage can.

Lindy pouted and spit out her gum. Ms. Givens raised one eyebrow at us, making her warning clear. She strolled back to the front of the classroom, letting her whistle pierce the chatter. "All right, everyone! Take your seats—we've got a lot to cover today. And please . . ."

She looked back at our table again. "Please don't eat today's experiment."

Elliott slouched in his seat and let his bangs fall over his eyes.

"Today we will break up the monotony of cell structure and function by skimming the surface of gene expression. Does anyone remember what alleles are?" Ms. Givens asked. Elliott slid further down in his chair. The new redhead raised her hand.

"Yes, Samantha?"

"Alleles are variants of a gene, on a chromosome. Like the big *T* that's dominant for tongue rolling, or the little *t* that's recessive."

"That's right," Ms. Givens said. "You might have them in pairs, as with tongue rolling, or in larger groups, as with the ABO blood types. They control the type of characteristics you have, and they're genetic. Meaning, they're inherited from your parents." Lindy stuck her hand in the air.

"Yes, Lindy?"

"Is being beautiful dominant or recessive?" she asked. The red-head rolled her eyes. I liked her immediately.

"Well, everybody's definition of beautiful is different, but you will certainly inherit specific traits from your parents," Ms. Givens said. "Genes are encoded in your DNA, and DNA is in every cell of every living thing. It's what makes each of you uniquely *you*."

I glanced around the room. Not a single person had the exact same shade of skin, or the exact same color and thickness of hair. Some people had grown a foot that summer, like Elliott, and others had remained shorter . . . like me. Some had freckles, some had acne, and some had smooth skin. Even the Worthen twins, who somehow both got seated together at table three, looked different enough that I could tell them apart.

How does that work? I wondered.

"DNA is contained in chromosomes, as Samantha wisely pointed out." Ms. Givens winked at Samantha, who blushed.

"Genes," Ms. Givens continued, "are just pieces of DNA that determine the kinds of features you'll have . . . like tongue rolling. Just one chromosome may have over one thousand different genes on it. And that, my dear freshmen, is a lot of coding. Today, I want you and your partner to determine if you're dominant or recessive for four different traits, and we're each going to make a tiny jelly bean chromosome. Let's start with the cups labeled *R* and *p*."

Ms. Givens wrote *R* in red on the smart board, and *p* in pink.

"We already know that tongue rolling is dominant. So if you can roll your tongue, slide a red jelly bean onto a toothpick. If you can't, take a pink. Ask your partner for help if you're unsure."

Elliott and I stuck our rolled tongues out at each other and laughed. Then we stabbed red jelly beans with our toothpicks.

"Next, grab your cups that say *B* and *w*." She wrote a capital *B* in black and a lowercase *w* in white on the board. "I want you to look at your partner's ears and tell them if their earlobes are attached or not." The classroom erupted into amused chatter.

"Aren't everyone's earlobes attached?" Elliott asked. Everyone snickered, and Ms. Givens shook her head.

"I knew you guys would give me a hard time with this one." She turned off the light and the projector flashed two photos onto the board. One showed an earlobe that dangled freely, and the other one showed a lobe that connected to the head all the way to the bottom. Ms. Givens gave us a few seconds to study the photos, then turned the lights back on.

"If your lobes hang, take a black jelly bean. Hanging lobes are dominant. If they're attached, take a white one—those are recessive."

I tilted my head to peek under Elliott's straight, blond hair. My fingers brushed his neck as I moved the strands aside. For a brief second, our eyes met before he looked at the ceiling. I felt my face flush.

"Definitely attached." I handed him a white jelly bean. "How 'bout mine?" I pulled my hair up and presented him with an ear.

"Ummm . . . I think they're dangling?" he said. I smirked.

"You *think*?" I said. "Come on now. Tell me for sure. Attached, or no?" I shoved my ear in his face.

"Okay, okay. Dangling," he laughed. I raised my eyebrows in question.

"For sure," he added. Gently, he tossed me a black jelly bean. I caught it and stabbed it with my toothpick.

"Next, get your *G* and *b* cups," Ms. Givens said. She wrote *G* in green and *b* in blue. "If your eyes are brown or hazel, then you'll need a dominant jelly bean, which is green. If your eyes are blue, then take a recessive, or blue."

Elliott and I both reached for blue jelly beans.

"But your eyes are green," I protested.

"Are they?" He batted his eyelashes like a cartoon vixen and I swatted his shoulder. Then he opened his eyes so wide I half expected him to pull out a chainsaw from under his desk.

"They're blue. See?" he said.

"You look freaky," I countered.

"Blame my mom," he said.

I shrugged. "I'll give you blue-green. There is definitely green in there." *With gold flecks*, I thought.

"Sold," he said. He held his hand out, and I shook it.

"Still a blue jelly bean," he said.

Ms. Givens interrupted our banter. "And finally," she said, "grab your *O* and *y* cups." She turned off the light again, illuminating photos of hairlines that either sailed smoothly over foreheads or dropped to a point in the middle. "These will represent alleles for a widow's peak," she announced. "A widow's peak is dominant, and a straight hairline is recessive." When she turned the light back on, I grabbed an orange jelly bean and groaned.

"You have a thing against orange jelly beans?" Elliott asked. I shrugged with one shoulder.

"It's not the jelly bean. I just . . . I hate my widow's peak. Do you have one?" Elliott pulled his bangs back with a flat hand. My eyes trailed up to his perfectly arched hairline and I gave him a yellow jelly bean.

"Recessive," I said. My chin rested on my hand.

"Why don't you like your widow's peak?" he asked. "I think it's . . ." He glanced over his shoulder, like someone might be hunting him. Reflexively, I looked too. "I kind of like it," he mumbled.

"I don't know. I guess I think it makes me look like a vampire or something. I've never liked it. That's why I've always worn bangs," I said. "My dad doesn't have one," I added. Like that mattered or something.

"So you got yours from . . ." But Elliott stopped short. He dropped his gaze to the floor.

"It's okay," I said, nudging his shoulder. "You're right. I got mine from my mom."

A slow silence grew, pressing heavy against my chest. Suddenly, I could hear the classroom clock tick, tick, ticking. Elliott fished a blue jelly bean out of the cup and handed it to me under the table. My heart fluttered when our hands touched.

"That's my favorite color," I whispered. He grinned.

"I know," he said.

We both jumped when the end-of-class bell sounded.

"Tonight," Ms. Givens yelled, "I want you to write down all the combinations your parents *might have had* to lead to the traits that make up *you*. Have a good day, everyone! Twyla, will you come see me before leaving, please?"

I frowned at Elliott. "Am I in trouble?" I asked. He shook his head.

"That's not her angry voice. See ya later." He waved, and I shoveled everything back into my backpack while my classmates filed out of the room. When the last person had gone, I approached the desk.

"Yes, Ms. Givens?" I said. Her eyes held a gentle smile.

"Sweetie, are you feeling better these days? I've been worried about you." Surprise straightened my spine. For a moment, I felt a strong pull to share everything with her. My worries, my research, the fight with Dad, the inexplicable tension building with friends . . . all of it. But as much as she cared deeply about me as a person, and had for years, she was also my coach. If she knew I'd had two vomiting episodes lately, and if she knew I was losing weight, would she feel a responsibility to make me sit the bench?

She might.

It wasn't a risk I was willing to take.

"I'm feeling better," I lied. Guilt flooded my chest, and I headed toward the door before the truth could crack me open. "I'll be at practice, don't you worry!"

She shook her head. "I'm not worried about practice, Twyla. I'm worried about *you*. I'm here if you need me, okay?"

Without looking back, I waved. "You're the best!" I called.

I rolled the blue jelly bean that Elliott had given me in my hand, thinking about alleles and traits. My parents were both thin. Maybe I was just skinny because they were skinny. Or maybe I . . .

I stopped in my tracks.

Weight loss. Nausea.

Genetics.

What if they were related? What if I inherited some kind of medical problem from my parents?

What if I inherited something from *Mom*?

There's a reason for everything, Twyla.

Suddenly, I knew what I had to do.

Chapter 16

WHY MOM DIED

My white-knuckled fingers gripped the island while I swiveled my butt back and forth in a chair. A pot of water bubbled on the stovetop, while Dad's knife sliced up and down across the peppers with expert speed.

My stomach flip-flopped like an Olympic gymnast. I'd tried to apologize when I got home, but Dad had been deeply focused on a building sketch. When he finally emerged from his office and was ready to start dinner, I followed him around like a puppy.

"You need help with dinner? Want me to set the table?"

Dad eyed me suspiciously. "Sure, that would be great," he said. "You're in a better mood today. Did you do well on a test?"

"Mm-hmm," I said. "Got an A on my math test."

Dad placed an onion on the cutting board. "Well done," he said.

I twisted my hands together, trying to work up the nerve to choke out one little question. Dad's mood seemed neither warm nor cold. As much as I tried, I couldn't get a good read on him. We'd been distant all week, but couldn't he see that I was trying now? I *wanted* to talk to him. I *wanted* his help.

Why was this so difficult?

Chop, chop, chop.

Wolfie scooped chips into his mouth like a squirrel storing acorns for the winter.

"Dude," I said. "It's not good to fill up on chips before dinner."

"Might not be good for my body, but sure is good for my taste

96

buds! Hey . . . did you know that people grow nose hair when they go through puberty?"

I scrunched my face. "First of all, that's a really bizarre transition. But also, isn't that an old man thing, Wolfie? Teens grow armpit hair."

Wolfie laughed. "True, true," he said. "Like, if a man wanted to propose to someone, he could hide the ring *and* the box in his armpit! It's like grown-ups have teddy bears stuffed under their arms!"

I looked to Dad's back for some sort of reaction. A chuckle or something.

Chop, chop, chop.

Nothing.

Just ask, I thought. *What's the worst that can happen?*

"Ummm . . . Dad . . . I have . . . did you . . . can I ask you something?"

He didn't even turn to face me. "Mm-hmm."

"Did . . . Did . . ." *Stop stuttering, Twyla.* I inhaled slowly, then let the words fly.

"Did Mom have any medical problems?"

The chopping slowed for a moment, then stopped. Dad wiped the knife with a towel, and it clicked against the counter. Time froze as Dad braced himself with both hands, leaning into hunched shoulders. I couldn't see his face, but I imagined his eyes were closed.

Nugget meowed at the empty water bowl.

"Awww, buddy, are you thirsty?" Wolfie laughed, oblivious to the momentary tension in the room.

"Wolfie, can you please fill his bowl?" Dad's quiet, even words made my heart pound against my ribs.

"Sure!" Wolfie chirped. He hopped to his feet and started humming the music from Super Mario when the characters move in fast motion.

"Dad? I . . . I'm not . . . I'm sorry if I . . ."

"Your mother was perfectly healthy, Twyla." Dad lifted his

head to look out the window directly in front of him. His sentence seemed to float in the air around him for just a moment, then seep through the cracks in the sill . . . like smoke. Then he picked up his knife and resumed chopping, as if that's where the conversation needed to be cut.

"In science, we're talking about genetics. It just got me thinking—"

"She was healthy, Twyla."

"But if she had any medical problems, don't you think I should—"

"She didn't have any medical problems."

"But what if I inherited—"

Dad spun around to face me, slapping the knife against the counter. "I *said* she was fine! She was healthy! I answered your question! Why are you pushing this right now?"

I balled my hands into fists. No. I would *not* be dismissed again. But if I responded to his anger *with* anger, I also knew I'd wind up taking the bus for another week.

That was not an option.

Dad's eyes, usually soft and warm, jerked back and forth like he couldn't figure out which part of my face he should look at. They looked wild. But then, suddenly, his face drooped, and he choked out one word.

"Why?"

As much as I wanted him to talk to me about Mom's death, as much as I knew direct conversation was the path of least resistance, I realized in that moment that Dad wasn't going to talk to me about it. Ever.

Something was haunting him.

But what?

I chose my words carefully.

"I didn't mean to upset you, Dad. You . . . you know how much I love science."

Dad stared at me, still as stone. For a moment, I thought he might tell me something. Something that would make sense of everything.

"I do," he said. He filled his lungs, softening around the edges. "You got your curiosity from her. You know that?"

A sigh escaped my lips.

"I suppose I did."

Dad mopped his forehead with a kitchen towel, then turned back to his peppers. "You got your beauty from her too."

"But not her complexion," I said. "Wolfie got her complexion."

Wolfie's head snapped up. He'd been crouching on the floor, petting Nugget through the whole conversation. "Who has a complex?" he asked.

"Wolfie, please set the table," Dad said.

And . . . just like that, the topic was closed.

I hopped off my chair. Dad spun back around.

"No walking to the willow, okay? We're having tacos in twenty minutes."

"Okay. Do you need the table set this moment?" I asked.

Dad shrugged one shoulder. "Ten minutes is fine," he said.

My mind raced. I didn't know what exactly I was looking for, so I also didn't know where to look. But instinct told me there was something to be found.

I headed toward Dad's office first. Quietly, I let myself in and moved toward his desk. I slid the mouse a few inches, breathing life into the monitor. When the password prompt popped up, I entered his phone password—0518.

Mom's birthday.

The little rectangle shook, denying me entry.

Darn it.

I tiptoed back out of the office toward the stairs that led to my and my brother's rooms. A manilla folder with my name on it rested on the bottom step. Inside, I found several pages of papers from my last doctor's visit. Name, complaints, medications, blood pressure, weight, that kind of thing.

Nothing but a bunch of medical mumbo-jumbo, I thought. I kept flipping, looking for clues.

And then I gasped.

If Dad kept hard copies of *my* medical records, maybe . . .

The stairs creaked under my feet as I hastily climbed them. I kept looking back over my shoulder, expecting Dad to ask me what I was doing.

You're being crazy, Twyla, I thought. *He's making dinner. He has no reason to follow you.*

But still.

I made a beeline for the rope that dangled from the ceiling in our upstairs hallway. I'd seen Dad go into the attic a billion times, but I'd never had reason to go there before. When I tugged the rope, the attic door creaked open an inch.

I froze.

When no one came, I coughed to disguise the creaking noise and unfolded the ceiling ladder. Then, step by step, I climbed all the way into the attic.

Dust floated, weightless, in rays of evening light, pouring in through a tiny triangular window near the floor. The air felt stuffy and thick, and it smelled a bit like mothballs and wet paper. I paused, allowing my eyes to adjust, and then scanned the small, unfinished room. Fluffy, pink insulation filled the spaces between wooden beams on the walls. The floorboards, however, looked fairly sturdy. If they could hold Dad, surely they could hold me. It only took a few seconds to feel confident that he'd walked across them dozens, if not hundreds, of times. There, against the far wall, stacks and stacks of old boxes teetered as high as the sloped ceiling would allow. I inched toward them, wishing I'd brought a flashlight with me. But then I realized I didn't need it.

Smack dab in the middle of one stack was a box with big, black letters on a strip of masking tape that read:

CELESTE VOGEL

Mom.

One by one, I pulled the other boxes from the top of the stack and set them on the floor, as gently as I could. My heart thudded against my chest as I popped the lid free from Mom's box.

I sucked in my breath.

There were so many photos.

So many photos of her.

As a toddler. At her first communion. On a balance beam. In the dance studio. At Niagara Falls. On stage. With a baby elephant. Holding a python bigger than her. Dozens and dozens of memories I'd never seen before. I closed my eyes, listening for her laugh.

It was there . . . but it was quiet. So quiet.

Acutely aware of the passing time, I blinked back tears and shuffled through more photos until finally, under a large, framed wedding picture of Mom and Dad, a manilla folder appeared. It looked just like the one on the stairs. Hands shaking, I opened it. The very top piece of paper said:

AUTOPSY REPORT

I'd seen enough crime shows with Dad to know that an autopsy report would talk about her cause of death. The question was, what would I find? I hadn't even realized an autopsy was done when Mom died.

"TWYLA?"

My heart stopped. I tiptoed back to the hole in the floor and yelled down.

"Uh . . . yeah?" I forced my voice to stay calm. Casual. Would he be able to tell I wasn't in my room? Would he hear the muffled tone from the insulation? And what if he could? What if he found me up here? Dad wasn't an angry person by any means, but he'd made it crystal clear that this was a closed topic. If he knew, I'd be riding the bus for the rest of my life.

Sweat dripped from the nape of my neck down my back as I waited for him to answer.

Crap. He knew. Crap, crap, crap . . .

"Please come set the table now, okay?"

All my breath escaped in one quick whoosh. He didn't know.

"Okay," I called. "Be right there!"

I ran my finger over lots of long, unfamiliar words, then found a section headed by two words in all caps: PATHOLOGIC DIAGNOSES. At first, all I saw were a bunch of notes about the injuries Mom had sustained in the accident. I skimmed those, not really wanting to know the details. But then, my eyes rested on a word that hit me like a wrecking ball.

Anaphylaxis.

I read it over and over and over again.

Anaphylaxis. Anaphylaxis. Anaphylaxis.

Quickly, I stuffed the papers and photos back into the box, restacked them, and tiptoed down the ladder. With sweaty hands, I shoved the ladder back into its folded position, coughing again to cover the creak as the door folded back into the ceiling.

Mom had been allergic to something. That's what had killed her. That's what had caused the accident. An allergy.

But an allergy to what?

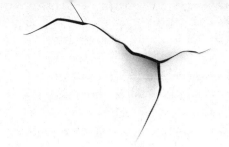

Chapter 17

NUTS

After dinner, my nausea returned . . . and with it, the sinking feeling I was a ticking bomb.

Was it possible that Mom and I could both have the same allergy?

My stomach spun relentlessly at the thought, aided by a gnawing insomnia that began just after my trip to the attic. So, I did the only thing I knew how to do.

Research.

Search: *Anaphylaxis*
Results: *Anaphylaxis is a severe, life-threatening allergic reaction. It can happen seconds or minutes after you've been exposed . . .*

Search: *What happens with anaphylaxis?*
Results: *Anaphylaxis causes the immune system to release a flood of chemicals that cause you to go into shock—blood pressure drops suddenly and the airways narrow, blocking breathing.*

Search: *Can anaphylaxis cause a car accident?*
Results: *Allergies can cause impaired driving.*

Search: *What causes anaphylaxis?*
Results: *The most widely reported triggers of anaphylaxis are:*
  • *Insect stings—particularly wasp and bee stings*

- *Certain medicines—such as antibiotics*
- *Allergies to food*
- *Latex*

My mind raced. Mom had probably been exposed to latex a billion times through surgical gloves alone. It was equally unlikely that she would've taken some brand-new medication right after work or in the car on the way home. It was always possible that an insect could've stung her while she was driving, but given that she was a vet, I likely would've known if she'd had an allergy that was critter-related . . . even if only to insects.

Which left food.

Search: *Foods most likely to cause anaphylaxis*
Results: *The most-common food allergies are milk, eggs, tree nuts, peanuts, shellfish, wheat, soy, and fish.*

There were others too . . . sesame seeds, garlic, celery, and some random fruits like bananas and peaches. So maybe Mom had eaten something that caused an allergic reaction.

Search: *Can you be allergic to a food and not know it?*
Results: *The first time someone is exposed to a food allergen, they usually don't have any symptoms.*

Okay, so that was fine and all, but I found it highly unlikely that Mom would've eaten something in the car that she'd only been exposed to once before. Was it possible . . .

Search: *Can you develop a sudden allergy to food?*
Results: *You can develop an allergy to foods you have eaten for years.*

My pulse quickened on reading this result. The answer didn't feel coincidental. If Mom had autopsy findings reflective of ana-phylaxis, then she most certainly could've been allergic to a food. And if she developed an allergy to food later in life . . .

My fingers shook as I typed.

Search: *Can food allergies be genetic?*

I sucked in my breath, head spinning, as I read.

Results: *Food allergies can be hereditary.*

Now, more than ever, I wished I could ask Dad questions. But since I couldn't, I grabbed my phone and texted Emilia and Anna.

Me: U there?

For ten excruciating seconds, I stared at my phone, wondering if I was going to have to process all of this alone. But then the dots appeared.

EB: I'm here! WYD?

AR: me 2

Me: Found something. Can u come over?

The dots appeared again, the disappeared. Then reappeared. Then disappeared. As I sat, waiting for my friends to respond, my heart sank. Why were they being so cagey?

EB: Can't. Helping Mom clean.

AR: Homework. Sorry!

EB: What did you find?

My thumbs hovered over the keyboard as I considered my response. This wasn't something I wanted to text.

Me: Has to do with my health.

And Mom, I thought.

AR: U ok?

Me: I'd rather talk face-to-face.

AR: U aren't sick again, r u?

Me: No. But I think I know why I was.

EB: Didn't the doc say why already?

Me: Yeah. He's wrong.

EB: I know ur smart. But ur not a doc, T.

What the heck was that supposed to mean? *Ur not a doc, T.* Seriously?

AR: Tell us tomorrow at school?

EB: Yes! Oh, and also—Homecoming! Did you see the posters on Friday?!?

A growl escaped my lips. Was I really this low on their priority list?

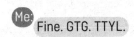
Me: Fine. GTG. TTYL.

My phone hit the pillow with a soft *thunk*. Was I being demanding? Unreasonable? We lived in the same neighborhood, a quick bike ride away. It wasn't raining out. And there was still plenty of time in the day left to clean or do homework. I turned to face my laptop again, grumbling.

Fine. I could figure this out on my own.

Again, I reviewed the list of most-common food allergies.

First on the list was milk. I didn't really like drinking milk, but we ate cheese all the time. If I were allergic to milk, I'd be sick constantly. I could cross that one off.

Eggs were next on the list. I'd had eggs for breakfast that morning, but I'd felt fine after. I didn't feel great now, but I also hadn't eaten eggs with dinner. So that wasn't it, either.

My eyes scanned the next two items on the list. I chewed the inside of my lip, thinking.

Tree nuts. Peanuts.

Hmmm.

I didn't often snack on just plain nuts. In fact, I couldn't remember my parents ever keeping nuts around the house. Did we even eat peanuts before Mom died? Perhaps it was my memory grasping at straws, but it seemed like peanut butter was something I'd just discovered in the last couple of years. And now I loved it—in fact, I'd just eaten chocolate–peanut butter cheesecake for dessert. Screwing my eyes shut, I wracked my brain to remember the other times I'd gotten sick.

Wait a minute.

The peanut butter ball milkshake.

Then, at Anna's house . . . peanut pad thai.

It couldn't be a coincidence . . . could it?

I tapped out one last question on my laptop.

Search: *How long does it take to get food allergies out of your system?*

Results: *Food allergies may take a few hours to a few days to disappear.*

A few days, at most. I breathed a sigh of relief.

I just had to give up eating nuts—easy-peasy. Then, in no time, I'd be feeling better.

Everything would be normal again soon.

Chapter 18

LIES, LIES, AND MORE LIES

"Did you know that you have enough cells in your body to circle the earth *twice*?" Wolfie stuffed a handful of popcorn into his mouth.

"No more, Wolfie. You're gonna ruin your dinner." Dad started the timer and slid a pan into the oven.

I plucked my science homework from my backpack and pulled a chair up to the island. For the most part, school that day had been fine. I'd had no nuts, no nausea, and no conflict. After Emilia's comment that I was smart, but not a doctor, and my friends' apparent disinterest in my attic findings, I'd decided not to say anything about the suspected food allergy—either mine *or* Mom's. I believed I was onto something, and I didn't need anyone bringing me down. They had inquired, of course, but they hadn't pursued the topic. And neither had I. In fact, the conversation had gone like this:

"So, what did you want to tell us about your health, Twy?" Anna had asked.

"Oh—nothing," I'd said, throwing the idea aside with my hand as if it were a passing breeze. "I'm just . . . I'm feeling better! But what about those Homecoming posters?"

And *boom!* Just like that, the topic had changed. I felt a tad bit guilty about lying to my friends, but it really was just a tiny white lie. After all, I *was* feeling better.

Dad waltzed around to read over my shoulder.

"Still your favorite subject?" he asked. I nodded.

"Is Ms. Givens a good teacher?"

I nodded again.

"Guess I'm not surprised," Dad said.

The TV babbled in the background about Taylor Swift and the Grammys they thought she would win for her latest album.

"If I won an award, I'd win Best Armpit Farter," Wolfie said. He tucked his palm into his armpit and pumped it up and down, making farting noises while singing "Trouble."

Now I'm lying on the cold, hard ground
FART
FART
FART
Trouble, trouble, trouble . . .

"How do you even know the words to that song?" I asked.

"YouTube," Wolfie said. "Remember? That video with the screaming goats?"

"Ah," I said. "Of course." A few months back, Wolfie and some friends had laughed until they almost peed their pants while watching videos of goats screaming over Taylor's chorus for at least an hour straight.

It had been slightly annoying.

"When I was in high school," Dad said, "I won an award for Best Eyes."

I raised my brow. "Really?" I asked.

Dad snickered and batted his eyelashes at me. "Is that so hard to believe?"

"What if a cyclops won that award?" Wolfie said. "Would it be called Best Eye?" He laughed so hard, he fell on the ground.

"And what about you, Wolfie? What's your favorite class this year?" Dad asked. He stretched out a hand and pulled Wolfie back to his feet.

"Lu-uuuuunch!" Wolfie sang.

"Besides lunch," Dad said. Wolfie tapped his chin.

"Reeee-cesssss!" he sang again.

Dad drummed his fingers on the counter.

"Oh-kay. Then . . . art! And also, I like sitting on the yoga ball in class. I like that Ms. Whitley lets us sit on them as long as we put our butts on them. She doesn't like us rolling around on them, though. If you roll on the ball, then she'll move your clip down one color on the chart. Soooo . . . I don't want that! I'd be okay with getting greens, but my goal is to get blues and purples and PINKS! Pink is the best color, but you have to be on your best behavior to get a pink. But I'll bet I can get pi-ink, pi-ink, pi-ink . . ."

"Wolfie! Don't jump on the couch!" Dad waved his hand, and Wolfie jumped one more time before bouncing off.

"So what's for dinner? Smells good." As I gathered plates and silverware to set the table, my stomach growled.

"Mahi, baked sweet potatoes, and green beans in mushroom sauce," Dad said. Wolfie hopped back into the kitchen like he was jumping rope.

"I like mushrooms," he said. "They're kind of like wet pretzels."

I wrinkled one side of my face at him.

"Hey! I have a joke!" Dad grinned. "What do you call a fake noodle?"

Wolfie and I exchanged a here-he-goes-again glance and shrugged.

"An impasta. Get it? Im-PASTA?" Dad raised his hot mitts like he made a touchdown, and Wolfie gave him a gut-bursting laugh that could be heard on the moon. Then Dad pulled the pan from the oven and walked past me to the table.

For a second, I stopped breathing.

"Dad? What is *that*?" I pointed to the fish, coated in brownish stuff.

"I already told you. It's mahi."

"But what is *on* the mahi?" My heart quickened.

"Well . . . it's breadcrumbs, parsley, salt, pepper, and crushed nuts," Dad said.

"I can't eat THAT!" The words burst from my mouth with a force that pushed Dad backward.

"And why *not*?" Dad sounded defensive, and I stood still, paralyzed.

"I . . . I . . ."

My mouth scrambled to form the words that my brain couldn't find. A tiny white lie was bad enough. But what was I supposed to say now?

I can't eat that because I found Mom's autopsy report in the attic, after you refused to talk to me . . .

I can't eat that because I'm pretty sure I'm allergic to the same thing that Mom was . . .

I can't eat that because it might kill me too.

No. I couldn't tell him why I wasn't eating nuts without creating major tension or causing another fight. No one wanted that.

I had no choice but to lie.

I steadied my voice, swallowing my defensiveness.

"I can't eat that because I'm really not very hungry, that's all." The excuse sounded lame, and we both knew it. Dad squinted at me, skeptical. I doubled down.

"I ate a huge lunch."

Dad pulled the oven mitt off his hand too calmly. His jaw tensed over clenched teeth.

"Twyla," he said, "did you take your Miralax this morning?"

Suddenly, everything ruptured inside me. The fear, the anxiety, the worry. The frustration that came from not being listened to. The resentment of not being believed. It all boiled to the surface at the mention of that stupid, friggin' medication. The stupid, friggin' medication that made me feel worse, not better. The stupid, friggin' medication that I did not need.

Not now. Not ever.

"*Seriously?*" My rant started off slow but built quickly to the point of explosion. "Oh my gosh, Dad! I'm not hungry, so what—now you think everything happens because I can't take a dump? You think I'm avoiding food because I'm constipated? Is that what you think? YES, okay? Yes, I took the stupid medicine! Is that what you care about? Congrats! You win!" I grabbed my journal off the island and bolted down the hallway.

"Twyla! Don't you DARE do this again, or—"

But before he could finish his sentence, I was gone. I huffed past the tree line and through the woods. I let my feet fly as fast as they could carry me, all the way to the willow.

Only then, when I'd reached the safety of twilight's early quiet, did I begin to wonder.

Would I ever be able to tell him about my allergy?

Would I ever be able to tell *anyone*?

Chapter 19

SOMEONE WHO GETS ME

Dear Mom,
  I know.
  I know I shouldn't have lied to Dad.
  But OMG, he isn't giving me a choice! If you were
here, I know you'd listen. You'd understand.

I dipped one toe in the creek and chewed my pen cap. Then, for a few minutes, I closed my eyes and focused on slowing my breathing, like Mom taught me when I was little. I listened to the sounds of nature around me. The babbling water, the rattle of the breeze through the leaves, the protective chatter of mama birds. When my breaths once again felt even, I opened my eyes, letting the soft chill of fall's dimming light engulf me.

Maybe I couldn't tell anyone about my allergy just yet, but once I started feeling better, I would come clean. About everything.

My stomach rumbled. Nausea wasn't a problem that evening, but hunger was. I knew I'd have to figure out my own nut-free sustenance this week. I had no intention of eating school fruit and squishy peas for lunches all week, so I had to figure out what I'd be packing myself. Thanks to my little explosion, Dad wouldn't be helping me find meals anytime soon. I guessed I'd be taking the bus for a while too.

Sigh.

For tonight, though, I'd raid the pantry when everyone went to bed. Simple enough.

Rumble, rumble.

A goldfinch zoomed past my head to a branch in a nearby sapling. It startled me. They usually nested closer to homes, out in the open. Not in the middle of the woods.

"Hey, little guy. You lost?" I kicked the water.

Two baby birds bobbed their heads out of the nest, beaks open toward their mother. A bright-yellow male swooped in, delivering seeds. When he flew away, the mother continued feeding her babies. I groaned.

Even among lost birds . . . I was still the most lost.

> *Miss you, Mom.*
> *Wish you were here.*
> > *Love,*
> > *Twyla*

I closed my journal again and frowned at the family. All cozy, together in one nest . . . eating food that didn't make them sick. And no one forcing gross, pointless medicine down anyone's throat.

My fingers traced a perfect skipping stone, embedded in the wet bark of my fallen cypress. I unwedged it and brushed off the dirt, then pulled my arm back to the side. With one quick flick, I released the stone and counted.

One, two, three, four, five . . .

Not bad.

I dipped my hand into the creek and felt around for another. The next one was smoother. Softer.

I whipped it even harder down the creek. One, two, three, four, five, six, seven. That was more like it.

Twigs crackled behind me, and I jumped.

"You've got quite an arm."

My head whipped around. A girl I'd never seen, about my age, crouched beside the willow. Her long, black hair whipped in the wind around her angled face. She wore jeans, rolled up at the ankles, a plain black shirt knotted at the side, and a pair of well-loved sneakers that had probably been white when they were new. A scruffy puppy with floppy ears thumped its tail beside her. Its curly, mottled fur made me think it had some poodle in it. The girl examined something in her hands, brushed it clean, then held it up for me to see. A perfectly round stone. She grinned like Wolfie did when he had a secret.

She waded into the cool, shallow water and set it beside me on the cypress.

It was the most flawless skipping stone I'd ever seen in my life. Smoother, rounder, and softer than the one from the creek. And it was the perfect size for my small hands.

"May I?" I asked.

She motioned toward the stone as if to say, "Be my guest."

I picked it up, then wound my arm back and angled the stone so it would hit the water at right around twenty degrees, like my mom had taught me when I was little. Then I let it fly.

One, two, three, four, five, six, seven, eight, NINE, TEN, ELEVEN . . . the stone skipped so quickly, so many times, that I couldn't even count it anymore, before it finally sank back to the bottom of the creek. I jumped off the cypress and splashed in circles.

"Whoa! Did you see that?"

The girl laughed and the puppy bounced up and down. "Pretty amazing!" she said. We both stood still, watching until the surface of the creek was once again still. Then we waded back to the bank. I sat on a stump and the puppy approached, wiggling its butt.

"I'm Twyla," I said. "Can I pet your dog?"

"Sure," she said. "Her name's Sophie. I'm Angela."

"I love her name! Sophie's a character in my favorite book," I said. I ran my fingers through Sophie's long, soft curls. Random patches of black, brown, and white covered most of her body, but her face was split almost straight down the middle. The left half was black, with one brown eye, and the right half was light brown, with one blue eye. The two halves of her face were connected by a thick, white strip of fur that ran straight down her nose, sort of like a skunk. And all her paws, still too big for her body, looked like they'd been dipped in white paint.

"What kind is she?" I asked.

Angela shrugged. "Probably an Aussie mix of some kind?"

"Maybe mixed with poodle," I offered.

"I could see that."

The puppy handed me her paw. "And she's smart too!" I laughed.

"Oh! Wait until you see this!" Angela sat down on the ground with her legs straight out in front of her.

"Sophie? Cover," she commanded.

The puppy stretched across her legs, lying down, and Angela scratched her ears. "Yes, you did cover, didn't you? You're such a good dog. Okay! Stand!" Together they stood, and Angela brushed the debris off her jeans. Sophie sat, patiently waiting, until Angela pulled a treat from her pocket and held it in front of her. They both sat still as stone until Angela said, "Okay." Sophie gently took it between her teeth.

"She's a really good dog," I said. Sophie wagged her tail. Angela nodded, then gazed toward the treetops. She breathed in deeply, eyes closed.

"Is it always this peaceful back here?" she asked.

"It is," I said. "Do you want to check out the creek?"

"Sure."

As we began winding our way down the bank, Sophie charged ahead. Angela and I walked side by side, silent. I kept expecting to feel like I'd need to fill the silence with words, but they felt unnecessary. It was nice.

"You can hear a million different sounds back here," she said. She stopped and closed her eyes again. "There's . . . the creek. And the wind, of course. And listen . . ."

A distinct *purt-ee, purt-ee, purt-ee, purt-ee* followed by a quick chirping sound rang through the trees.

"Do you hear the cardinal?" she asked.

"Yes! You know your bird calls?"

Angela smiled. "I love birds," she said.

"Me too." For a moment, we stood in place, listening for the songs of warblers, sparrows, and chickadees. Every bird I knew, she knew too.

"I don't think I've seen you around here before," I said. Angela picked at a leaf, tossing the bits onto the surface of the creek.

"We just moved here," she said. "From out of town. I don't know anyone yet."

"Oh! Will you be going to Springfield? That's my school." Angela shook her head, and my heart sank.

"No," she said. "We're homeschooled."

"You are? Isn't that weird?" As soon as the words left my mouth, I wanted to suck them back in. My face flushed. "I'm sorry—that came out wrong. I meant . . . don't you miss being around people?"

She laughed. "I'm around people! See? I'm around you!"

"I suppose," I said. My feet shuffled through the leafy debris. "But doesn't it feel weird to be around the same people, day in and day out?"

Angela shook her head. "I don't think it feels any weirder than it would to be around the same friends every day, at a typical school. But I do enjoy getting out occasionally . . . like today. It gives me a chance to be by myself, train Sophie, or meet new people. Like you."

"Who's we, by the way?" I asked. "You said, 'We're home-schooled.'"

"Oh! That would be me and my siblings," Angela answered. "I'm one of nine."

"Nine?" My eyes widened. "That's a lot of kids! Where do you fall in the lineup?"

"I'm the oldest."

"Do you like it? Having that many people around, all the time?"

Angela lifted another leaf from the forest floor, spinning the stem. "I do. Most of the time, anyway. We all need breaks sometimes. That's why I'm out here now!" Angela fished a hand into her coat pocket and pulled out two granola bars.

"You hungry?" she asked.

My stomach growled, but I hesitated. "Does it . . . does it have nuts?"

"Oh no," she said. "I'm allergic."

"Me too!" The spontaneous admission shocked me, but it felt refreshing. Like the first swallow of ice water on a scorching summer day. I unwrapped the bar and sank my teeth in. The mix of chocolate, salt, caramel, and granola satisfied every craving I'd had for the last month. For several minutes, Angela and I walked together in silence behind Sophie, eating.

And then I saw it.

About fifteen feet in front of us, four little legs kicked the air. An upside-down turtle. Sophie sniffed it and yipped.

"I wonder why that happens," I mused. We ambled over toward the turtle and knelt down beside it.

"Well, it can actually happen for any number of reasons. Maybe . . ." Angela glanced at the turtle's long, thick tail. "Maybe he's sick. Or maybe he got into a fight with another male over some female. Or maybe . . ." She looked around and motioned to the hill, right beside the turtle. "Maybe he just took a tumble."

Angela talked to him, just as I had talked to the goldfinch. "Hey, sweet little turtle. How did you turn yourself upside down?"

I reached out and picked him up. The turtle sucked himself back into his shell, so I set him back down, right side up, and stood beside my new friend. The sun was now low on the horizon, a bright orange ball in a sea of blue sky. I wondered how angry Dad was going to be by the time I returned.

"Well . . . I think I'd better get back home. My dad is going to be worried about me. I sort of . . . left quickly," I admitted. Angela studied me, but she didn't ask any questions. I felt grateful for the space.

"Want to meet back here on Friday?" she asked. My heart skipped a beat.

"I'd love to!" I said. "Same time?"

"Same time!"

I waved and ran back toward my house, re-energized. It felt good to have someone I could talk to, openly and without judgment.

For the first time in several days, I felt like I wasn't alone.

Chapter 20

WHY TURTLES FLIP

According to Google, turtles can turn upside down for several reasons.

For example, they might flip if they're sick—like, with a respiratory infection. A turtle's lungs help them stay upright; so if they have a lung infection, their balance could be wonky as a result. Google noted this can be especially dangerous for swimming turtles, who can flip over and find their heads stuck underwater—a potentially fatal situation, seeing as turtles are without gills. I didn't know how long they can hold their breath, exactly (though I bet Wolfie would know). But no matter how long they can stay underwater, they still need air to live. Just like us.

Next, Google said nutritional deficiencies could throw of their balance. It turns out that turtles can get sick when they eat the wrong things, just like people.

I wondered if any of them have nut allergies.

As Angela and I expected, Google also confirmed that turtles can flip in certain environments. They can fall or get wedged in areas where they don't have leverage to flip themselves back over . . . like that steep hill by our willow.

And finally, it turns out that Angela was right—upside-down turtles are sometimes the result of a turtle fight. It *is* possible that one aggressive turtle could flip another one over. But learning this only made me want to go back to the woods to find every upside-down turtle in existence. If I could, I'd flip them all upright again.

Interestingly, Google also stated that healthy turtles should be able to flip themselves back over, but I wasn't sure if I believed that. The turtles I'd found all seemed fairly healthy, but they also seemed fairly stuck. I couldn't begin to imagine how kicking those tiny legs into the air might help them upright themselves.

Personally, I thought they're probably pretty relieved when people come by to help. Maybe I kept finding these upside-down turtles because that was one of my jobs in this world: to flip them all back over again.

Of course, Google also said that sometimes there's no real reason for turtles to flip. Sometimes, it said, it just happens.

And that is why I concluded that Google is stupid.

Nothing "just happens."

Ever.

Chapter 21

LOOKING UP

Smack!

The ball flew low and straight across the field, like a speedboat on smooth water. I raced toward the goal, stick down, ready for the next chance to score. Emilia dodged around our teammates in white pinnies, looking for an open blue. I called to her, and she shot the ball back to me. *Smack! Aaaaand . . . score!*

Shortly after eliminating nuts, my game had returned. Within only a few weeks, sharper reflexes, quicker feet, and a stronger stomach allowed me to lead our team to victory after victory. And even though we still hadn't gotten together outside of school, conversations with Emilia and Anna once again felt relaxed and organic. To be fair, I could also understand why there had been a dearth of get-togethers. Anna, who'd proven to be mad talented in photography, had been spending hours upon hours shooting pictures. The images she'd shown me captured a beautiful vulnerability within people that was inexplicable, given how new she was to the artform. Likewise, no one advocated like Emilia. She was determined to protect human rights—for *all* humans—as a leader in the Amnesty Club. I didn't want to begrudge either one of them the activities they loved. But one of the things I'd always treasured about my besties was that we'd invariably been able to prioritize ourselves while simultaneously prioritizing one another. And lately, it felt like "one another" somehow . . . I don't know. Mattered less. I kept trying to put my finger on a reason for the change, but nothing stuck. And like it often did, my mind spun through possible scenarios like Wolfie through a new box of Pokémon cards. I glanced up at the stands, watching Anna shoot candids of unsuspecting, bubble-blowing children. Then I turned to our team's bench, where Emilia chatted with teammates. I bit my lip.

The last time we'd all gotten together, I'd brought up the funeral. Had *that* pushed them away? Was it too dark? Too depressing? But why would that be? It had been *my* mom who died, after all. And it wasn't like it was a new topic for them.

Emilia seemed pretty boy crazy lately. Could it be that I was simply becoming less important to her? Less interesting? Did she think we didn't have as much in common anymore? But then, if that was the case, why would she still be hanging out with Anna so much? Anna was even more reluctant to talk about boys than I was. And why would Anna be pulling away too?

Both of Anna's parents were doctors. Could Anna be upset that I was in advanced classes and she wasn't? Did she maybe think I was acting elitist about AP Biology? Or was it possible that she was jealous? Was I being insensitive?

Emilia trotted toward me. "Nice shot, girlfriend! Don't ever do that if we're practicing on opposite sides, okay? You'll make me look bad." We high-fived and I shook off my doubts. I was being stupid. Maybe I was imagining tension between us. Other than field hockey, I didn't really have an extra activity like Emilia and Anna did. Maybe I just had too much solo free time on my hands.

"How could I ever make you look bad? You're the queen of assists! And look at those arms . . . Brie Larson ain't got nothin' on you." We did full arm circles, our hands connecting down low as we walked past one another. We both turned and pointed at one another at the same time, laughing.

Coach Givens called us all back to the bench.

"Okay, girls, good practice today. I love what I've been seeing from you recently. Keep stretching, keep running to build your endurance, and I'll see you tomorrow."

I stuffed my stick into my bag and clicked my mouth guard container closed.

"Twyla?" Coach motioned me over. "You looked really good today. Actually, you have for a while now. Are you feeling better?" she asked.

"*So* much better," I said. It felt good to say the words truthfully.

"Glad to hear it. I was worried about you." Coach Givens waved toward the parking lot. "Your dad just pulled in. Say hi to him and Wolfie for me, okay?"

"Will do," I called, jogging to the car.

"Hi, boys!" I opened the door and tossed my bag in. My humongous empty water bottle clanked on the floorboard.

"Did you drink that whole thing?" Dad asked.

I nodded. "Yeah. And I actually refilled it today too!"

Emilia and Anna crossed the parking lot, chatting and laughing. Dad jutted his chin toward them.

"It's been a while since the girls have come over," he said. "Why don't you invite them for a sleepover on Friday?"

I bit my lip. It really had been a minute since we'd spent quality time together. On the one hand, I missed them. I felt like I was losing my mind a bit, trying to justify reasons we'd been distant. On the other hand . . .

I let out a sigh. There was only one hand. These were my best friends, and I was being stupid.

I bolted toward them.

"Emilia! Anna! Hang on a sec!" As I sprinted over, Anna chewed her thumbnail and Emilia stuck out her hip. I almost changed my mind, but then Anna held her arms out for a hug. I took a deep breath, heart in my throat.

"You guys wanna sleep over on Friday?"

Emilia glanced at Anna, then back to me.

Silence.

Anna released the hug. I wanted to flee, but my feet remained cemented firmly in place.

"It's just—it's been a while," I said.

Emilia spoke first. "I . . . I'm sorry, Twy. I promised my mom I'd stay home for a reading."

"Can't you do a reading with her on Saturday? She'll understand." I turned to Anna for backup. "Tell her that her mom can help her find her purpose later."

"Actually . . ." The word lingered in the air until Anna finally finished with, "I can't either." Her thumbnail went back between her teeth, and I looked from one friend to the other. My stomach sank as I considered the possibility that our friendship was dissipating. Curling up, up, up, like smoke into the air, until the edges were so thin that it no longer held its own space.

Just like the memory of Mom's voice.

I was about ready to turn and run, feeling a mix of embarrassed, mortified, and alone, when Anna's eyes brightened. "But hey! Why don't we all get together Friday right after school? That would be fun! I miss you too." She squeezed one arm around my shoulder.

Emilia nodded enthusiastically. "Yes! That's a great idea! We don't have practice, so we can hit balls on the school field and talk about *boys*." Emilia made jazz hands when she said the word *boys*.

If they were truly pulling away, they wouldn't offer to hang out after school, would they? They seemed genuine—excited, even. Maybe they really did miss me?

I shoved all misgivings back down into my gut and embraced the offer.

"No to the boys," I said. "But yes to the field. Though . . . I really do want to do a sleepover again soon, okay? We could stay up late and"—I looked at Anna—"watch a romance?"

Anna scrunched her nose and groaned.

"What?" Emilia teased. "I saw Malik helping you with those books today, like a knight in shining armor . . ." She placed both hands on her chest, letting the words drip dramatically from her lips.

Anna rolled her eyes. "Could you be more insane? I *accidentally* dropped those books in the middle of the hallway, Emilia. Right in front of him! He had two choices: trip over them or help me pick them up."

"Yes," Emilia said. "And he *chose* to help you."

Anna grunted with exasperation. "He's in photography club with me, Em! What's he supposed to do. Ignore me? And Elliott helped too, by the way."

"Ah, yes," Emilia oozed, "but Elliott's heart belongs to another."

Anna snorted.

"Oh, please," I sighed.

"He does look at you a lot," Anna said softly.

"Now *this* is more my speed." Emilia laughed.

"See you guys Friday, then." I saluted, then jogged back to the car.

"Can they come?" Dad asked as I crawled into the passenger seat.

"No, but we'll get together after school on Friday to hit balls at the field."

Dad studied me. "Don't you guys usually hit balls in our yard?"

"Yeah," I said. "But I guess they want to stick around after school instead this time."

I buckled myself in, then twisted around to watch Wolfie's quick fingers defeat Bowser.

"Ha, ha, HA!" Wolfie said. "I'm pretty good with technology. Did you know that? It's kinda like my sixth sense."

I shook my head.

"And did you know that *Yoshi* isn't even Yoshi's full name?

It's T. Yoshisauer Munchakoopas. It's Yoshisauer because he's a dinosaur."

"What's the *T* stand for?" I asked.

Wolfie shrugged. "Maybe Taco? Or . . . no! Tyrannosaurus? I'll bet that's it! Or maybe it stands for Troublemaker, because you know Yoshi can be a troublemaker sometimes . . ."

As my brother babbled on about his game, the world zoomed by. It had been nearly a month since my first episode, with very little nausea. Food almost seemed to taste better, and water went down more easily. Dad had even stopped bugging me about Miralax, so I no longer had to dump it into my napkin behind his back. My stomach growled.

"What's for dinner tonight?" I asked.

"Actually," Dad said, grinning into the rearview mirror, "I was thinking I didn't feel like cooking tonight."

Wolfie sucked in his breath. "WHAAAA??"

"How does pizza sound?" Dad asked.

"PIZZA!" Wolfie shouted.

Dad laughed. "How 'bout you, Twilight? There's a new Italian place near us. Sound good?"

Relieved it was something I could definitely eat, I nodded. "I'm famished!"

Wolfie leaned up to high-five me in the passenger seat.

"Then . . . pizza it is!" Dad exclaimed.

Wolfie went back to his game, and I watched the sun dance across the trees and houses on the horizon. It really had been a pretty good day. I'd gotten an A on tests in Algebra II and AP Biology, we were going out for pizza on a school night, we'd had a good field hockey practice, and even though Emilia and Anna weren't sleeping over on Friday . . .

Wait! Friday! Suddenly, I was grateful they'd said no. Angela and I had been meeting by the willow every Friday. Now, I realized, I'd get the best of both worlds. I could hit balls on the field with Emilia and Anna right after school, then be back at the creek with Angela by twilight. I smiled as the sun appeared, bold and full and unencumbered, illuminating a big stretch of open sky.

I could feel it.

Things were finally looking up.

Chapter 22
A MESSAGE FROM MOM

"*Do you both* want pepperoni?" Dad asked.

"I do!" Wolfie cheered.

"Could we get peppers on half?" I asked. Dad gave me a thumbs-up and turned to our waiter.

"Okay, we'll have a large pepperoni pizza with peppers added on one half, an appetizer of garlic knots, and I'll try your . . ." Dad's eyes scanned the menu one last time. "Your . . . spaghetti and meatballs, please. Oh, and extra sauce on the side for the kids." Dad winked at me as the waiter scurried back to the kitchen. I'd bathe in pizza sauce if I could.

"Wait . . . SPAghetti?" Wolfie's mouth gaped. "So pasketti is really SPAghetti?"

"How old are you?" I said.

Wolfie flopped forward, banging his forehead on the table. "My whole life has been a lie."

I crossed my arms and leaned my back against the side wall, putting my feet up on the booth bench between us. "Did you seriously not know how to pronounce spaghetti until now? You're in the fifth grade, Wolfie."

Wolfie sat up and rubbed the forehead spot he'd just smacked. "No, I seriously did not know, so don't make me feel bad about it, okay?" His skin reddened under his fingers. Sometimes, I wondered how he'd made it this far without getting a concussion.

Garlic and olive oil wafted through the air, making my mouth water. Iron-backed chairs surrounded heavy, wooden tables in the middle of the restaurant, and booths like ours lined the outer walls containing floor-to-ceiling windows. Quick-handed cooks slid wood-fired pizzas in and out of a massive copper oven just behind the bar, and every table received a golden loaf of rosemary focaccia made with grains ground right there in the building. Even our drinks were served with fancy little sprigs of mint. I let out a long, slow whistle.

"This place is niiiiiiice, Dad. Can we come here every night?"

"No, but I was thinking of opening my own restaurant," Dad said. "One that serves only pizza and crab." Wolfie and I gawked at him.

"I'll call it the Crust Station."

For a moment, I stared at Dad in silence, wondering if he was seriously thinking of leaving architecture. And then Wolfie burst out laughing. Dad smirked, and I couldn't help myself. I smiled and shook my head.

The crustacean.

It actually *was* pretty funny.

"So, speaking of work . . . how was your day?" I loved hearing about Dad's new building designs. I always thought of him as more of an artist than anything else.

"Great, actually! The university wants a new waterfront stadium, and they just retained our firm to design it. I'm really excited. But I *will* need to work some evenings in the coming weeks."

"Good thing you have a home office," I said. Dad tilted his water glass toward mine in a toast.

"I think you should design a museum that flies," Wolfie said. "Or . . . oh! I know! An underwater aquarium, where all the visitors get scuba suits and swim through the whole building with the fish."

"Yeah, Wolfie, that'd be great until one of the patrons gets eaten by a shark," I said.

The paper sleeve from Wolfie's straw struck my temple, and I glared at my brother.

"Ac-tu-al-ly"—Wolfie emphasized each syllable with a finger strike in the air—"sharks rarely eat people." He blew bubbles in his water through his straw.

"Really? Tell that to Bethany Hamilton." We'd once watched a documentary on Bethany, who lost an arm to a tiger shark while surfing in Hawaii. But that didn't stop her. She *still* surfed professionally. I thought she was one of the coolest people in the world. Well, her, but also Bindi and Terri Irwin, at Australia's zoo.

They reminded me of me and Mom.

"Well," Wolfie protested, finger in the air again, "there are, like, three hundred species of sharks, but only, like, ten or twelve of them have ever attacked people. So those kinds would have to be in different sections of the aquarium, of course, with, like, thick glass separating them from all the visitors. Easy-peasy."

While Wolfie prattled on, I carefully removed the top part of the paper sleeve from my straw under the table. As soon as he took a breath, I stole my chance. I rolled my tongue to catch his attention, then stuck the straw in the roll and blew the sleeve right at his chin.

BAM! Perfect shot. Wolfie swatted me.

"Hey!" he said. "I can do that too!" Sure enough, he stuck his tongue out and rolled it into a perfect loop. "And I can touch my nose with it like this . . . and I can turn it upside down . . . thith way . . . and thith way . . ."

I began peeling the paper off another straw, preparing to strike again.

Wolfie turned to Dad. "Can you do thith, Dad?" he asked.

Dad shook his head. "Nope," he said. "I can't even roll my tongue."

My hand froze. The straw dropped to the table.

"Wait. What did you say?" My jaw hung slack, waiting for his reply.

"I said, I can't even roll my tongue."

My heart raced, like I'd just discovered the location of a lost Imperial Fabergé egg, and my eyes brimmed with tears. If Dad couldn't roll his tongue but both Wolfie and I could, that meant . . .

"Hey . . . Twyla. You okay?" I jumped when Dad touched my hand.

"Yeah," I said, wiping my tears. I threaded my fingers through his and squeezed, then I smiled at my brother. For just a moment, it had felt like she was right there with us.

And in that moment, I felt whole again.

Chapter 23

THE LOOK

The moment the bell rang, feet pounded through the halls like a stampede of frightened buffalo. I squeezed between bodies to reach locker 216, crouched down, and balanced notebooks on my knees to unlock the door. I hated having a bottom locker. It always felt like I could be trampled at any moment.

It was Friday, and I should've been excited about creek-walking and meeting up with Angela. But I'd been unable to escape my suspicion that my friends didn't want to spend the night tonight for a reason. Hadn't wanted to spend the night for weeks. In fact, they hadn't even tried to get together outside of school once since movie night at Anna's.

I'd been replaying the moment over and over in my head, trying to figure out what caused the sudden tension after practice when I'd asked if they wanted to come over. Especially since the next day at school, it was like everything was perfectly normal again. Well, maybe not normal—but certainly not bad. They still wanted to eat together, and we all showed up early to study or hang out before the bell rang. At school, it was like nothing ever happened. But outside of school . . .

Nothing ever happened.

"Twyla?"

I blew my bangs out of my eyes. "Oh, hey, Elliott." My blue three-ring binder slid perfectly between my AP Biology book and a stack of alphabetized, multicolored folders. I swung the backpack off my shoulder and wedged it onto the top shelf.

"Aren't you gonna miss the bus?" he asked.

I stood and kicked the door shut.

"I'm not taking the bus today," I said. "I'm staying after to hit some balls with Emilia and Anna. Besides, I'm out of bus jail now." In fact, today was the end of my one-month bus sentence, which had started after I exploded at Dad at the dinner table.

"Don't you usually practice at your house?" he asked.

I shrugged. "Apparently not today," I grumped. I began walking toward his mom's room and he fell into stride beside me. "Emilia wanted to hit at the field."

Elliott side-eyed me. "You sound mad," he said.

"You sound observant."

Elliott stopped walking. "I didn't . . . You're not mad at me, right?" he asked.

I twisted to face him, confused. "No! Of course not! I . . ." I sighed. "I'm sorry. I guess I'm just in a mood."

He kicked the toe of his shoe into a wall but said nothing.

Great, I thought. *Now you've pissed off Elliott. Way to go, Twy.*

"I . . ." I paused, trying to find words that would lighten the mood. "I couldn't fit my field hockey bag in my locker, so . . . it's in your mom's room . . ." I thumbed the air in the direction of AP Biology. When he still didn't move, I said, "You're going there anyway . . . right?"

Elliott's head popped up. "Yeah! I am."

"Well, then . . ." I turned to continue walking toward her room, and Elliott ran to catch up with me. But just before we reached the room, he touched my arm. "Twy, I wondered—"

The AP Biology door burst open, followed by Emilia walking backward and waving. "Good to see you too, Coach! I'll— Heeeey!" Emilia froze mid-sentence when she saw us, a sly smile spreading across her face. She was holding my field hockey bag up in the air, as if to prove she had a reason for existing.

"I was just on my way to get that," I said. She raised her left eyebrow at me.

"Whatcha guys talkin' bout, huh?" Emilia's voice dripped with giddiness.

I snagged my bag away from her. Elliott rushed through the door like he was escaping fire, pausing only long enough to mumble, "See ya later, Twyla."

I glowered at her. "Nice, Emilia."

"What?"

Feeling too uncomfortable to say anything to either Elliott or Ms. Givens, I brushed past Emilia toward the exit. "Where's Anna?" I asked, choosing distraction over whatever Emilia was about to say.

"She's at the field, setting up cones. Did he ask you?" Emilia's eyes popped, her hands spinning in circles like she'd just had six cups of coffee.

"Ask me what?"

She pursed her lips. "To Homecoming, dimwit."

"No, he did not ask me to Homecoming."

"So what were you doing together?"

I stopped walking and crossed my arms. "Emilia, he has been my friend—*and neighbor*—since kindergarten. We bumped into each other in the hallway. His mother drives him home, because she is *his mother*. And my field hockey bag was in her office, so we were headed the same direction."

Emilia crossed her arms, mirroring my stance. She drummed her right fingers on her left elbow, obviously expecting me to say more.

"The. End."

Emilia smirked. "Whatever you say, Twy."

We walked the rest of the way to the field in silence. As soon as Anna saw us, her face fell.

"Who died?" she said.

Emilia muttered, "Twyla's sense of reality." I mouthed the word *STOP* to her, and she held up her hands in surrender.

For the next forty-five minutes, Emilia and I ran drills while Anna timed us. It was an unseasonably warm October afternoon, and the heat was beginning to get to me. Pain stabbed behind my eyes, making me feel a little dizzy. I polished off my water while Anna repositioned the cones for my favorite drill. We always ended practice with this particular one.

And I always won.

"Positions, girls!" Anna called.

I shook off my unease and stood at the top of my lane, stick down, waiting for Anna's whistle. Sweat dripped down my forehead, stinging my eyes. Despite the fact that she was almost six inches taller than my five-foot frame, Emilia typically couldn't beat my times, no matter what the thermometer read. But today had been a struggle for me.

"What's the matter, slowpoke?" Emilia teased. "You gonna let me beat you every drill, or what?" I gritted my teeth. On a normal day, losing made me want to scream. But losing to Emilia on this day, on this drill, when she seemed determined to irritate me, would be particularly exasperating. Emilia tapped her stick once to the left of the cone, then to the right, then back to the left again.

"What's the matter with *you*?" I said. "Afraid you can't beat me without your superstitious rituals?" Emilia laughed. It was a dumb dig, but it was all I had.

"You never know, Twy. Maybe there's something to these superstitions," Anna said.

"Not you too, Anna."

"A lot of people believe in them. There's gotta be a reason," she said. She glanced at me briefly before her eyes flickered down. "And you like reasons too."

She had me there.

"Ready?" Emilia asked. I took a deep breath and nodded.

Anna's whistle blew and we both took off flying, dribbling our balls first one way, then another through the cone mazes. As my cleats caught the grass on the last turn, the ball stuck to my stick like cockleburs to socks. I rounded before Emilia and dug in.

But as I began my sprint back to the starting line, a sharp pain stabbed my temples. Convinced I could overcome a little discomfort, I kept my eyes trained on the ball. But when I crossed the finish line and the stopwatch clicked, Anna wasn't pointing to me.

"Emilia wins by a hair!" Anna said. "That was sixteen-point-two seconds, Em. Twy, you were less than a quarter second behind her!"

Emilia whooped. "That's my fastest time yet!" she said. I smacked the ball across the field to no one in particular. Anna grabbed my stick from me and jogged after the ball.

"Nice drill," I grumbled.

Emilia nodded. "Thanks."

"Fore!" Anna positioned herself like she was about to hit a golf ball, then whacked the field hockey ball back toward us. Hard. Emilia raised her eyebrows.

"Remind me again why you don't want to play?" she asked. Anna shrugged.

"Not my thing," Anna said. "I don't mind watching, but playing sports stresses me out."

"I thought boys stressed you out?" Emilia teased.

"Yeah, well . . . them too."

Emilia twirled her stick like a baton, but it kept whacking her hip, so she rested on it like a cane instead. "Soooo . . ."

"I'm going to refill my water bottle," I interrupted.

"Because you don't want to talk about boys," Emilia said.

"Because it's empty," I quipped.

As I turned toward the school, Emilia called after me, "You can't avoid the subject forever!"

"Watch me!" I called back.

Truthfully, I didn't want to talk about boys. But the relentless pain behind my eyes weighed my lids into a squint. So water—and shade—were my priorities.

But when I refilled my bottle, a brightly colored poster framed with streamers and lights caught my attention. Swirly letters curved across the top, announcing, "Homecoming is where the heart is." I couldn't help but think about my conversation with Elliott.

He had said, *I wondered* . . . but what was he going to say after that? *What* did he wonder? Was it possible that he might've been about to ask me to the dance?

The water overflowed, drenching my hand. I swallowed an almost curse word, wiped the wet bottle on my shorts, and then screwed the lid back on.

As I reapproached the field, I slowed. Emilia and Anna huddled together near a tree, whispering. At first, I thought someone else might be near them, but then I realized no one was in sight.

They looked like they were talking about someone. My stomach sank and I froze, wishing I could make myself invisible. Anna nodded, her eyes sad. She chewed on a blond lock of hair, her other arm tucked across her stomach. Emilia appeared more animated, but she, too, looked like she might cry. She was shaking her head, shrugging. Then her eyes sank to the ground, as if she were . . . defeated, maybe?

Suddenly, I felt ridiculous. Here I was, making the situation all about me when it probably had nothing to do with me at all. Something looked wrong—really, really wrong. What had happened? Had one of them gotten a call? Were their parents okay?

My heart stopped. Had someone gotten hurt?

My pulse quickened, redness creeping up my neck and heating my face. I broke into a run, panicked. "Guys?" I called. "Is everything—"

My friends stiffened. They turned toward me, but not before they gave one another a look.

A look I would never forget.

Chapter 24

SEAMS OF HOPE

My feet shuffled through the leaves on the wooded path, replaying every detail. The slack-jawed, wide-eyed looks they'd exchanged. The stuttering, ridiculous protests that they hadn't been talking about me. The laughable claim that they'd been discussing an assignment in English.

It stunk of lies. All of it.

Were they angry with me? Had I done or said something to offend them? Had I somehow let them down? Was Emilia angry I'd made a crack about her superstitions when we were running field hockey drills? Anna had commented that there could be something to Emilia's superstitions . . . were they both believers now? And if that was the case, did they think that I was the one being stupid for not believing?

I closed my eyes, pressing my fingers into the bridge of my nose like Dad did when he was stressed. The more I thought about it, the crazier I felt. Of *course* Emilia's mom couldn't read my mind. And I honestly didn't believe she could predict the future.

But did Emilia? And if Emilia believed it . . . could she convince Anna of it too?

No. That couldn't be it. And besides, they didn't really look *mad*. They looked *sad*. Though if they were sad, why wouldn't they talk to me about it? I'd talked to *them* when *I* was sad about my mom. I'd trusted *them* with *my* feelings.

But I knew it to my core. They were hiding something. But *what*? And why?

None of it made any sense.

As I meandered along the path, lost in thought, a deep, drumming noise caught my attention. I stopped walking and tilted my head, slowly turning to pinpoint the source. A loud, clear series of piping bird calls took my breath away. My eyes darted from tree to tree, finally landing on a dead snag only about six feet away. And there, about halfway up the trunk, was the most glorious bird I'd ever seen.

A pileated woodpecker. And he was staring straight at me.

He was bigger than a bowling pin, with white stripes on his face and neck, and a flaming-red crest and matching mustache. I tried not to breathe, for fear I'd ruin the moment. *Our* moment. Me, a short, freckled firecracker and this magnificent symbol of . . . of what again? My mother had loved these birds, and even Emilia's mom regularly talked about their spiritual symbolism. I scoured my memory bank until it hit me: loyalty. They stood for loyalty. Strength.

Determination.

The woodpecker released the tree and swooped overhead, revealing a shock of white underwings. He flew upward in an undulating pattern, until finally disappearing into the woods. Only then did I realize I'd stopped breathing. I stood there, motionless, grateful that he'd revealed himself to me.

"Isn't he beautiful?" Angela's voice should have surprised me, but it didn't. She knelt by the snagged tree, slowly spinning a large maple leaf in her hands. I smiled.

"Did you see him fly right over my head?" I asked. "I can't believe how close he got!"

Angela didn't answer, but instead hunched over the bright-red leaf. Her fingers thoughtfully trailed its delicate gold veins. I approached quietly, so as not to disturb her. Overhead, a stunning autumn blanket of oranges, reds, yellows, and greens covered our heads like a patchwork umbrella. The creek, soon to be quieted by the winter cold, rushed by in a constant, steady *shhhhhh*. A few songbirds chirped in the distance. My shoulders relaxed and my breathing slowed, as I witnessed Angela's moment of peace.

"Have you ever heard of kintsugi?" Angela whispered.

"No," I said. She closed her eyes, running her fingers over the leaf's veins.

"It's the Japanese artform of repairing broken pottery with gold seams. It respects the breaks as part of that object's history, rather than viewing them as a flaw that should be hidden. To me, this leaf . . ." Angela opened her eyes. "It looks like a piece of kintsugi pottery. It also reminds me of that Ernest Hemingway quote: 'The world breaks everyone, and afterward, some are strong at the broken places.'" She smiled and set it on a stump. I began to pick it up, then paused.

"May I?" I asked.

"Of course!" she said.

My heart fluttered. The bright, cherry red made the leaf appear freshly painted, and the vivid gold veins looked almost fake . . . but purposeful. I envisioned it as having once been nothing but broken pieces, with no identity, now made whole again by Mother Nature's hand. Fractures, repaired by something not quite as strong, yet still just as beautiful.

I touched a scar on my arm, where I'd cut myself on a shard of glass when I was four. The thick skin shone brightly, like a pearl. I'd always hated that ragged scar. I'd thought of it as ugly. A flaw. But maybe . . . maybe it was just a golden seam, created to make me whole again. A reminder that nothing, and no one, can go from birth to death without cracking a little.

"Thank you," I said to Angela. The sun shone on her hair, like a golden crown atop polished onyx.

I smiled, then furrowed my brow. "Hey," I said. "Where's Sophie?"

At the mention of her name, Sophie came bounding through the creek, with a stick bigger than her body clamped in her teeth. Angela laughed.

"She likes to explore too," she said.

Sophie dropped the stick at my feet and nuzzled my hand, ears perked and tail wagging. I scratched her head.

"My kind of girl," I said.

I sat up and tossed the stick back into the creek. Sophie splashed after it.

Angela rose to her feet, and I carefully tucked the leaf between the pages of my journal. I'd meant to write in it before meeting with Angela, but my thoughts and the woodpecker had distracted me. Angela and I ambled toward the willow, then sat in silence for what felt like hours, listening to the world around us. The birds, the creek, Sophie's curiosity, the leaves rustling in the wind, and a nearby chorus of bullfrogs. Sounds that painted a beautiful picture when woven together in the woods.

Golden seams in a kintsugi forest.

I inhaled the smells of fall and stood.

"Well, I guess I'd better get back," I said. "Dad's gonna serve dinner soon." Angela smiled, and a thought struck.

"Hey," I said. "A week from Saturday, my field hockey team plays at nine in the morning at school. It's our Homecoming game, so it's sort of a big one. You should come!"

Angela smiled. "That sounds really fun," she said. "I'll see if I can make it!"

"Okay, well . . ." I tapped my journal and grinned. "Thanks again for the leaf."

Angela smiled. "Anytime. See you next Friday? Same place?"

I started to nod, but Friday suddenly felt too far away. "Friday works," I said, "but I'll probably be back out here again tomorrow. And maybe Sunday too."

Angela studied me as if she could see straight through to my soul. Her forehead creased and her eyes teared ever so slightly, like she could feel my pain too. She offered a small, gentle smile.

"Sophie *does* love her late-afternoon walks," she said. Sophie barked, and we both laughed.

"Me too," I agreed.

It felt good to have a friend who knew what I needed, without me even having to say a word. We both waved, and slowly, I turned back toward home.

Even though I'd been feeling less nauseous lately, something inside me still felt off. Broken. Maybe that's why kintsugi resonated with me. It made me feel understood.

And it gave me hope.

Hope that if I kept piecing myself back together, maybe I, too, could be stronger at the seams.

Chapter 25

SOAP OR SALSA

All day Monday, the hallways buzzed with excitement. Gold and white streamers zigzagged from one side of the hallway to the other, then back again, all over the school. Some signs boasted hackneyed slogans like, "There's No Place like Homecoming," while others promised "all your favorite songs," or special treats, like chocolate fountains with strawberries and marshmallows. Life-sized posters beckoned seniors to vote for their favorite Homecoming Court nominees, and hopeful candidates smiled from glossy photos on the walls. The king and queen were to be announced at Friday's varsity football game during halftime by a skydiver, who would land on the field and present the winners with flowers. Even the most chill seniors were bouncing off the walls with excitement.

Then, on Saturday morning, our JV field hockey team would play right before the varsity team. Both teams had been playing well, and everyone anticipated wins before the big Homecoming Dance that night . . . my first high school formal.

I just hoped my friends and I were getting along by then.

I clicked my locker shut and rubbed my temples. Emilia and Anna had both repeatedly texted and called over the weekend to check on me, but I hadn't wanted to chat. In fact, I hadn't even looked at the flurry of messages on my phone until Sunday night.

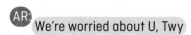

AR: We're worried about U, Twy

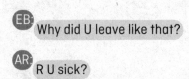

EB: Why did U leave like that?

AR: R U sick?

EB: Will U B in school Monday?

AR: ♥U

EB: R U OK?

On Saturday afternoon, I'd told Angela about the recent weirdness with my friends. How they whispered when I approached, then appeared uncomfortable when I made my presence known. How they'd been avoiding sleepovers, but still ate lunch with me at school. She'd agreed their reactions sounded fishy . . . but she'd also encouraged me to keep lines of communication open.

"Why don't you just ask them what they were talking about?" she'd said.

"*I* shouldn't have to ask! *They* were the ones excluding *me*!"

"I know you *shouldn't*. But maybe you'd feel better if you *did*."

"Well, truth is, I *did* ask. And they told me they were talking about an English assignment. Which they *weren't*, Angela. They were talking about *me*."

She had sighed at that. And I realized there was no possible way to make me feel better. No one—even Angela—could convince me that my friends weren't talking about me without coming across as gaslighting. And agreeing out loud that they *were* talking about me did nothing but worsen my paranoia.

It was a lose-lose situation.

I'd asked Angela if she wanted to sleep over sometime, but she said her parents didn't allow that. Evenings, they said, were for family. So instead, we'd spent the rest of our time in silence on the cypress, skipping rocks and tossing sticks for Sophie.

The weekend's undercurrent of friend-related tension had given me a splitting headache, so, with some moderate pleading, Dad had agreed to let me sleep in and drive me to school late on Monday. But as the bell rang just before choir, I knew there was no more avoiding Emilia and Anna. Immediately after choir was lunch. I either had to skip class and try to sneak lunch into the library, or face the music.

Literally.

Head down, I walked toward my chair in the front row of the soprano section. Emilia's voice carried from the middle alto row.

"TWYLA!"

My head snapped up just in time to see Emilia dragging a crimson-faced Anna by the arm.

"Where have *you* been all weekend?" Emilia demanded of me. "And why weren't you at school this morning?"

"Were you sick?" Anna asked.

Emilia turned toward Anna, finger wagging. "*You* don't get to talk yet. I cannot even believe you didn't call us with your news."

As much as I wanted to be angry, my curiosity was piqued. And I didn't feel like talking about the weekend.

"What news?" I asked.

Anna looked at her feet. "It's no big deal," she mumbled.

"Oh, it's a very big deal," Emilia said.

Anna rolled her eyes. ""Well . . . I got a call over the week-end . . . about next weekend . . . and . . ."

"Malik asked her to Homecoming," Emilia announced. Anna smacked her arm.

My jaw dropped. "Malik? From photography club?"

Anna shrugged, and my eyebrows shot up to my hairline.

"I thought boys were gross?" I said.

"We're just friends," Anna insisted. She locked eyes with me. "But seriously, Twy. What happened to you this weekend?"

For a beat, I let my gaze linger on Anna before switching my focus to Emilia. Both of them now stared at me, unflinching.

On the one hand, I ached to tell them how they'd made me feel on Friday. How much it hurt to feel isolated, especially by my best friends. I wanted to tell them I didn't buy that they were talking about a stupid English assignment. I wanted to ask them why they had lied to me.

But then, doubt filled my chest. Why would they immediately run my way, the moment they saw me, if they were truly hiding anything? Wouldn't they still be avoiding me if they felt guilty? And wouldn't they feel guilty if they had lied to me? I hadn't been sleeping well lately. Was my exhaustion getting the better of me?

Was I making something out of nothing?

I sighed.

"You know what?" I opened my arms to welcome them into a hug. They both obliged. "I spent a lot of my weekend outside, guys. I'm sorry I didn't text back."

It was true enough. I *had* spent a lot of time outside. Emilia pulled away from the hug just far enough to glare at Anna.

"And what about you? Are *you* sorry you didn't call?"

Anna shoved Emilia's face away with a gentle hand. "I'm going back to my seat now," she said.

"Fine," Emilia said, waving her off and squeezing my shoulder. "Be that way! I guess it's just you and me now, Twy," she sighed.

As the bell rang, indicating class was about to begin, Emilia and I caught sight of Elliott's best friend, Tanner, rushing past the choir room.

"Unless . . ." She wiggled her fingers at me, poking her head out the door and letting her eyes trail after him down the hallway.

Anna shook her head. "She's shameless," she said.

Emilia feigned indignation.

And I felt like I was home again.

• • •

When I walked into AP Bio the next morning, my headache was immediately amplified by Lindy's nasal drawl.

"It will be the *absolute cutest* dress that *anyone* has ever worn!" Lindy flipped through pictures on her phone in front of Samantha, who looked like she was trying to slide off her chair and under the table.

I decided to take the long way around the room. There was not enough ibuprofen in the world to numb me from that.

When I reached our table, Elliott wielded two jelly bean–covered toothpicks. "Remember these?" he said.

I tilted my head. "Yeah . . ."

Ms. Givens whistled. "Okay, everybody. Take your seats! POP QUIZ!"

Everyone groaned in unison. I tucked my backpack under my chair and plopped down next to Elliott, who drummed his pencil rhythmically on the table's edge.

"Whatcha playin'?" I whispered.

"'Sucker,'" he whispered back.

"Jonas Brothers?"

He nodded.

"Huh. I didn't know you liked them."

"There's a lot you don't know about me," he said.

His eyes twinkled playfully, and my stomach danced.

"Yeah? Like what?" I asked.

Was he blushing?

"Like—"

"Ms. Vogel, are you and Mr. Givens going to join us for class today?" Ms. Givens leaned between us from behind.

"Sorry," I squeaked. Lindy snorted.

"Sorry, Mom," Elliott murmured. She patted the table between us and strolled back to the front of the room.

"You will see that you all have your jelly bean chromosomes from the beginning of school on your tables. Today, I want to know who remembers what it means to have dominant versus recessive genes. So, using your jelly beans and your lab partner's jelly beans as 'parent' chromosomes, I want you to list *all* the kinds of traits, or phenotypes, a baby *could* have."

I chewed the end of my pencil and shifted in my chair. Elliott shook his head so his bangs covered his eyes.

"Excuse me, Ms. Givens?"

Ugh. Lindy.

"I can't take this quiz. I would *never* have a baby with *her*." She jerked her thumb toward Samantha, who looked like she wished she were invisible.

"If your preference is to settle for a failing grade, Ms. Michaels, then you are welcome to do that. But otherwise, you can take this quiz figuratively, as it is meant to be taken, and list the potential phenotypes that would be created by a combination of your chromosome with Ms. McNally's. Understood?" Ms. Givens turned her eyes to the class. "Flip your paper over when you're done. Now . . . you have ten minutes. GO!"

Everyone consulted their jelly beans, then scribbled phenotypes onto their papers. Once ten minutes had passed, Ms. Givens whistled again.

"Time's up! Pencils down." As she walked around the room collecting quizzes, Ms. Givens deposited a cup with leafy green stuff in front of each student. I smelled it and wrinkled my nose. It looked like parsley, but it didn't smell like parsley.

Once everyone had a cup, Ms. Givens said, "Without saying anything to anyone else, I want you to taste what's in your cup. You all have the same thing." Miko, a quiet soccer player, peered in his cup suspiciously.

"I promise, it's edible," Ms. Givens added.

I pinched a leaf off the little stalk and touched it to my tongue. The taste was familiar, but I couldn't quite place it . . . so I began chewing.

And then I spit it out.

I swigged from my water bottle, swishing it around in my mouth as long as I could. Ms. Givens laughed.

"Twyla, why don't you tell the class what it tastes like to you."

The taste stuck to my tongue like superglue to skin. "Ugh, it tastes like soap," I said.

Lindy burst out laughing. "It does *not* taste like soap," she said. "It's cilantro. It's in salsa, and *everyone loves* salsa."

Elliott wrinkled his nose. "It tastes like soap to me too," he said.

Ms. Givens looked questioningly at Elliott. "Lindy's right," she said. "It's cilantro."

Lindy smirked and leaned back in her chair.

"But," Ms. Givens continued, "everyone definitely does not love it." Lindy crossed her arms and stuck out her bottom lip.

"Sometimes," Ms. Givens continued, "it's not all about dominant or recessive genes, like it is with eye color or tongue rolling. Sometimes it's more complicated than that. Cilantro is one of those examples. Whether someone likes it or not depends on variations in their olfactory, or smelling, receptors. To some people, it's a tasty addition to salsa. To others, it tastes like soap."

While Ms. Givens chatted on about genetic variations, Elliott absentmindedly picked a leaf from his stalk. He was about to put it into his mouth when I grabbed his arm.

"What are you doing?" I whispered. "Don't you hate that?"

Elliott shrugged. "Nah," he said. "I love it." He popped it into his mouth and grinned. "I just wanted Lindy to shut up."

And in that moment, I couldn't help but wonder:

What else didn't I know about him?

Chapter 26

THE GAME

On Friday afternoon, I tried on three different outfits before the football game. Nothing looked right. Nothing felt right. And my flipping head *still* hurt. When I'd finally settled on my favorite pair of jeans, a fitted lavender top with a lacey off-white cardigan, and suede ankle boots in the perfect shade of caramel, I hopped in the car.

"Are you meeting your friends at the game?" Dad asked.

"Yes," I answered, half-truthfully. "Just drop me by the front gate."

Although I anticipated finding Emilia and Anna, we hadn't exactly settled on a place—or a time, for that matter. We'd talked about the game off and on all week, so I knew they'd be attending. But no one had talked about anything beyond that. To be honest, I hadn't thought about it until I returned from my walk with Angela, when I finally texted to ask them about plans. I checked my phone again for responses.

Nothing.

As we drove to the game, I rested my head against the passenger window, the world blurring by. The cool, crisp nip of fall crept through the glass. My forehead rolled against the surface, reveling in its chill, until Wolfie began kicking the back of the passenger seat.

"Stop it, Wolfie," I said.

He kicked again.

"Stop," I said, more forcefully this time.

Seconds later, a steady pressure pushed into the center of my spine.

"WOLFIE! I SAID STOP IT!"

"I'm not kicking," he said, defensively.

"But you're PUSHING!" I snapped.

"But I'm not KICKING," he snapped back.

"Stop! Both of you!" Dad warned.

"I don't understand why I can't go to the game too," Wolfie whined. "I never get to do anything with Twyla anymore."

"Really? We eat together, like, every night, Wolfie," I said.

"I meant something *fun*," he said.

Dad stretched his arm into the backseat. "Your sister needs time with her friends too, Wolfie. We can do something fun tonight, just you and me."

I heard Wolfie's head fall against his seat, and the bulge against my back disappeared. "It's not the same," he mumbled.

Normally, I tried to have a little sympathy for my brother, but lately he'd just been omnipresent. He wanted my help on his homework. Wanted me to read to him. Wanted me to tuck him in at night. I couldn't even pee anymore without him knocking on the bathroom door, asking me what I was doing. It was beyond irritating.

My eyes scanned the parking lot as we turned toward the football field. Horns and drums blared fight songs from the field, riling up the crowd. Students, teachers, and parents donned Springfield High spirit wear and milled about, slowing traffic. A lone cheerleader jogged from the school, dodging cars and fixing her ponytail. Dad stopped to let her pass.

"I'll just get out here," I said. "I'll text you when the game is over, okay?"

Dad nodded. I hopped out and slammed the door behind me, a little harder than I'd intended.

Weaving through the mass of people, I kept my eyes peeled for my friends. I finally spotted them near the snack shack.

"Hey!" I called. Emilia was placing an order, but Anna turned and waved.

"Twyla! Over here!"

By the time I reached them, Emilia held three bags of buttered popcorn. She handed one to each of us, and we wandered toward the stands.

"So." I started speaking before I really knew what I wanted to say, but Emilia was staring at me now. Anna shoved a handful of popcorn into her mouth. "So," I repeated. "Did you guys get my text earlier this afternoon?"

Mouth full, Anna shook her head.

"Oh, I meant to respond! Sorry about that," Emilia said. After a quick scan of the crowd, her eyes lit up. "Follow me," she sang.

I followed Emilia and Anna into the stands, wondering if she was actually going to answer my question. They almost always responded quickly to my texts, but Emilia's nonchalance was playing tug-of-war with my paranoia. I fought to keep my stomach from sinking.

Within seconds, I knew where we were headed. Tanner and Elliott chatted near an aisle, toward the top of the stands. The wind tousled Tanner's shaggy brown mop, but Elliott's straight hair was flattened by a backward ball cap. My stomach fluttered and I took a deep breath. This was my *friend*. Surely, when he looked at *me*, that's all he saw—his childhood friend. His neighbor. It felt creepy to suddenly notice these little details about him.

These . . . adorable little details.

As we approached the boys, Elliott gave me his signature crooked smile. My pulse quickened, despite myself.

"Hiiiiiii, Tannnnnnner." Emilia dragged out the words, her voice unnaturally high and singsongy. She pushed past Elliott and plopped to the right of Tanner, who looked a bit like he wished the ground might open and swallow him whole. Anna followed, sitting to Emilia's right. I shrugged apologetically, squeezing past them all to sit beside Anna.

The sky melted from hues of blue to black as the sun set behind us. Bright stadium lights attracted a flurry of bugs that looked like tornados of stardust overhead. Energy permeated the crowd as our Dragons went up during the first half of the game, fourteen to seven. When Ozzy Osbourne's "Crazy Train" finally called the cheerleaders to the field at halftime, Tanner stood and stretched.

"Well, I guess I'm gonna go get another popcorn . . ." His eyes darted to Emilia, then back to the stairs.

"I'll go with you," Emilia said, surprising no one.

Elliott handed ten dollars to Tanner. "Grab another bag for me, will you? And a water?" He turned to me and Anna. "Do you guys want anything?"

We shook our heads, and Anna gave Emilia a thumbs-up as she followed Tanner back down to the snack shack. The three of us sat together for ten awkward seconds before Anna popped up and said, "I'm going to the bathroom. Back soon," and bolted down the stairs.

"I haven't seen her move that quickly since Mama Rose told her she had sixty seconds to pick as many books as she could hold for her birthday," I said. Elliott laughed. "I think she grabbed every mystery in that store. I couldn't even see her face above the stack."

"Which section would you have emptied? Contemporary fiction?" he asked.

My eyes widened. "How did you know that?"

He snorted. "Are you kidding? You used to spend hours reading on your porch! Then you'd leave your books on that table outside when you went walking in the woods."

I shook my head. "I didn't know you noticed that!"

Elliott looked at his feet. "I notice more than you think I do," he said.

I wasn't sure if it was the words he'd spoken, or just the way he'd said them . . . but a flush of embarrassment crept up my neck to the tops of my ears. Elliott fixed his gaze and fiddled with his hands. Although we were outside with hundreds of people, all I could hear was silence. My head spun. Did he regret saying that? Is that why he was so quiet now? Or did he think I'd assume it meant something different? Something . . . that it didn't mean? Or was I supposed to say something now? Was he expecting *me* to fill the void?

Why was I being so stupid?

When the song "Mickey" played and cheerleaders started dancing, I was grateful for the distraction. I barely noticed when Emilia and Anna pranced back up the stands with Tanner in tow. Giddiness oozed from Emilia's pores.

"Okay," I said when she sat down. "What happened?"

"He asked me to Homecoming," she whisper-shrieked.

"Or, you asked him," Anna teased.

"Whatevs. We're going together."

My lips smiled, but my stomach sank as I realized they both had dates to the dance and I did not. As Anna and Emilia prattled on about hairstyles and nails, I wished I could read Elliott's mind. Did he already have a date? No . . . I would know. Wouldn't I? Maybe *I* wouldn't, but surely Emilia would. She had her thumb on the pulse of everyone's crushes in school. But why should I care if he did? We were just friends.

Weren't we?

I leaned down and pretended to fix my shoe, then stole a glance past Anna, Emilia, and Tanner. At Elliott.

Watching *me*.

My stomach fluttered, and I sat back up feeling much better than I had ten seconds prior.

Maybe he really *did* notice more than I thought.

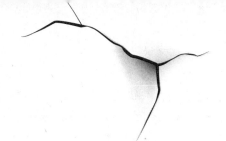

Chapter 27

THE MOST IMPORTANT GOAL

"Do you have everything?" Dad locked the car door while Wolfie banged a stick against a tree. Field hockey players milled about.

I ran through my mental checklist, nodding with the thought of each item.

"I've got everything," I said.

Excitement pounded through my veins. Yesterday's visit to the tree, followed by our football team's win, felt like good omens. Angela and I had found two box turtles (both right side up) and one adorable little ringneck snake, and we'd enjoyed a magnificent welcome from the pileated woodpecker, whom I'd named Zeeno (because it meant "loyal and courageous"). It was hard not to feel left out, being the only one flying solo at Homecoming. But Emilia and Anna both promised me that they wouldn't be with the boys all night. And, as far as I knew, Elliott still didn't have a date.

So there was always that.

As soon as my family started hiking toward the field, Wolfie threw his body in front of me and Dad, pointing about four feet ahead into the grass.

"That looks like fresh poop, straight outta the butt! Come on down, a dollar ninety-nine. Kitty litter sold separately!"

I laughed at my brother. "You could've just told us there was poop in the grass, you know," I said. "And I feel fairly certain it's not cat poop. But hang on . . . can I have the car keys for a sec?"

Dad fished the keys from his pocket and tossed them to me. I dropped my field hockey bag, ran back to the car, pulled out an empty plastic bag from under a seat, and jogged back to pick up the poop.

"Dad, why don't we have a dog?" I asked.

"We did, when you were little," he said.

"I know. But why didn't we ever get another one?"

Dad sighed. "Well, we moved shortly after Bernie died, and then we got Nugget, and then without Mom . . ." Dad's voice trailed off, and we walked in silence for a bit. "I don't know, Twyla. I guess we've all just enjoyed being part of nature's family while outside. And with just the three of us plus a cat, it's too much to bring a dog into the picture."

Dad nodded absentmindedly, and I knew. The subject was closed.

"Did you know that a dog's sense of smell is at least ten thousand times better than ours?" Wolfie said. "And Mr. A Game has a cat named Bella. She's soooooooo cute. But he doesn't have her anymore because she had to go back to live with Nonna. She's not dead or anything."

"Who's Mr. A Game?" Dad asked.

"That's Wolfie's favorite YouTuber. He plays video games," I said.

Dad shook his head. "I will never understand that."

"Hey, Twyla!" Emilia and Anna motioned to me from the sidelines. But my eyes trailed just above their heads, to the stands. My heart swelled. There, in the very top row, was Angela. I grinned and waved.

Emilia followed my gaze, shielding her eyes from the sun with one hand. "Who are you waving at?" she asked.

Suddenly, I realized I'd never mentioned Angela to the girls. I'd considered it a few times, but it never felt like the right moment. There'd been so much tension with them lately . . . and, in all honesty, Angela had been *my* safe space. I sort of felt like I didn't want to share her.

"Just someone from my neighborhood," I said.

Emilia frowned.

"Twyla! Can I see you for a second?" Coach Givens called me to the middle of the field. When I reached her, she gave me a serious look. "I know you've been doing better lately, but I just wanted to be sure you're still feeling strong enough to start today."

I nodded. "For sure."

She gave me a thumbs-up, then whistled to the rest of the team. "Time to warm up, girls. Two laps around the field. GO!"

Instead of waiting for Emilia, I began my run alone. And instead of pacing myself, I sprinted the entire way. My legs felt strong, my heart pounded, and my chest burned. When I returned to the bench, I draped a cooling towel around my neck and drained my water bottle. Lindy sidled up beside me as I refilled it from the team cooler.

"Hold tight to that water bottle, or you might just blow away in the wind," she said.

Emilia's voice caught me off guard. "You should know about wind, Lindy. You *are* full of it, you know."

Lindy's eyes rolled, and Emilia winked at me. Then she pulled a necklace out from beneath her jersey and kissed it.

"New ritual?" I asked.

She nodded, showing me the necklace. It looked sort of like an eagle with its wings spread wide.

"What is it?" I asked.

"A thunderbird," she said. "Mom gave it to me. It's a symbol of strength and protection."

"I like it," I said.

She tucked it back into her jersey and patted it. "Me too. Did you rub your snow globe?" she asked.

"Of course I did." A pang of guilt cut through me about the summer game—when all my problems started—and the words came out a little sharper than I'd intended. If Emilia noticed, she didn't let on.

"Awesome! Then let's go win this game!".

"Okay, girls. Huddle up." Coach Givens called us together, then listed the usual starters. When we hit the field, I glanced back up to the stands. Angela grinned.

The whistle blew, and my stick was ready. I passed to Lindy, whose mother shrieked predictably from the stands. When Lindy met a wall of defenders, Erin rescued her and passed it to Emilia, who shot it through a defender's legs back to me.

Our team maintained control of the ball for most of the next two minutes. Finally, an opening finally presented itself. Emilia saw it too. I posted to the goal. She spun past a player and whacked the ball to me . . . but a defender cut in front of me, blocking my shot. Lindy sprinted to the other side of the goal, so I hit the ball back to her. She pulled back her stick and whacked it straight into the net.

Score!

Lindy looked to her mom, who pursed her lips and nodded once. Lindy ceremoniously lifted her stick, and we all ran back to the bench for water. My eyes scanned the bleachers to be sure Angela was still watching.

She was.

My adrenaline flowed. An assist was great, but I felt a strong urge—a *need*—for Angela to see me score. Maybe it was because I hoped she'd fall in love with the game when she saw how much I loved it. And if she saw how much I loved it, maybe she'd want to come to school and play too. Or maybe it was just ego.

Whatever it was, it felt important.

For the rest of the first half, the ball volleyed between teams, up and down the field. Players came in and out, resting, rehydrating, refueling. And every time Coach glanced my way, I nodded to indicate I felt fine.

I would not leave the game until I'd scored.

About ten minutes into the second half, Emilia scored—this time, assisted by Lindy. Lindy's mother paced the field, red-faced and scowling. I thought she was going to pop a vein.

"WHY DIDN'T YOU TAKE THAT SHOT, LINDY? YOU HAD THAT!"

Emilia approached Lindy to click sticks as acknowledgment of the shared goal, but Lindy brushed right past her.

Emilia rolled her eyes.

With two minutes left in the game, I looked to the stands again. Angela did not wave. She did not give me a thumbs-up. She simply nodded, like she knew it was my time.

I nodded back.

And then, I ran. Every time defenders tried to double-team me, I passed. Every time they ran toward me, I ran faster. And when they fought for the ball, I fought harder.

My energy, contagious and feverish, spread through the team. Emilia met my speed, step for step. And when the next opportunity presented itself, I did not allow anyone else to get between me and the net. I dug in. I shot.

I scored.

Angela's cheer echoed from the stands, and a smile split my face. This girl, who shared my love of nature, who understood my need to sit in occasional silence, had now also witnessed my love for the best sport in the world.

"Twy-LA! Emil-IA! Goooooo, DRAGONS!" My eyes trailed to the bottom row, where Dad and Wolfie danced and cheered. Behind them, Anna and Mama Rose screamed on their feet. My chest swelled.

We won the game, three to zero.

As players laughed and patted one another on the back, Lindy filled her water bottle by the bench. Alone. Empathy got the better of me, so I inhaled deeply and walked over.

"Nice game," I said. She flipped her ponytail and glared at me. Her mom stood on the sidelines, arms crossed, foot tapping the turf. Lindy glanced nervously in her direction while she gathered her stuff.

"One goal and one assist," I said. "I'm sure your mom's proud of you . . ."

"How would *you* know what my mom feels?" Lindy spat. "You have no idea what *anyone's* mom feels, Twyla. You don't even *have* a mom."

It felt like she'd knocked the wind from my lungs. My body froze, paralyzed, unable to do anything but watch her walk away.

As Lindy neared the stands, her mother hissed, "Way to let other people do all the work for you, Lindy. And that defense! Pathetic . . ."

Hmmph, I thought. *They deserve each other.*

"Hey! Twyla!" Elliott's voice startled me as I slung my bag over one shoulder. He jogged toward me, and a grin tugged at my lips.

"Hey! I didn't know you were here!" I said.

He flipped his bangs out of his eyes. "Good game," he said.

"Thanks!"

"So . . . I have a question." Elliott looked at his feet and kicked the grass. The air thickened around us, and my mouth went dry.

"Will you . . . are you . . . will you go with me?"

For a moment, I thought I'd heard him incorrectly. Or maybe I hadn't understood him. Go with him? Right now? Or . . . did he mean . . .

"To Homecoming?" I asked. I felt like a doofus, but I needed the clarification. With my luck of late, I'd assume he meant Homecoming when really, he was inviting me to the grocery store.

"Yeah," he said. My stomach twisted in all the best ways, and I nodded.

"I'd love to go with you."

He nodded too, and we both stood there, nodding in awkward silence. Finally, after what felt like a year, he spoke.

"Good."

"Good?" I asked.

"Good," he said again.

Elliott ran his hand through his hair. "So . . . I'll come by to get you?"

"Sounds good," I said, feeling stupid for saying the word *good* again. "What time?"

Panic flashed through his eyes, and I felt the need to rescue him. "It's okay," I said. "You can text me later."

Relief washed over him. "Good," he said. I laughed.

"Good," I repeated.

Elliott gave me his crooked grin, turned, and walked back to the stands.

A cool wind blew across my face and I smiled at the sky. I had a date. An actual date. To my first high school dance.

With *Elliott*!

The field came back into focus, like I was emerging from a dream. I scanned the upper row, but this time, Angela was gone.

"Nice game, kiddo." Dad approached and tugged my ponytail. "You ready for the dance tonight?"

My eyes trailed to Elliott, and I smiled.

"Yeah," I said. "I think I am."

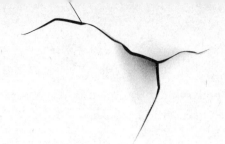

Chapter 28

BROKEN

Imagine Dragons thumped in our ears as Emilia, Tanner, Anna, Malik, Elliott, and I maneuvered our way through the auditorium, now transformed by dark lights and disco balls. Fairy lights twinkled inside mason jars on every table, and black plates, cups, and napkins with gold and silver confetti patterns sat next to a chocolate fountain. A mountain of props teetered on a table next to a photo booth. We took pictures with "Royal Court" signs, "We Won" speech bubbles, massive glasses, funny hats, tiaras, and an errant "I'm with Stupid" arrow that had somehow found its way into the mix.

Emilia looked exquisite in a sleeveless royal blue dress. The entire bodice was covered in beadwork that shimmered in the disco lights and cascaded below the waistline into a short, flowy chiffon skirt. Her long, dark locks were tied back in a fancy half-up, half-down do with loose waves that flowed down her back, almost all the way to her waistline. A few spiral tendrils framed her angular face, and a shimmer blush accented her naturally high cheekbones.

In keeping with trending styles, Anna and I also wore short dresses. Anna's, a baby pink chiffon frock, had adorable capped sleeves and a thin rhinestone belt that accentuated her delicate features. Anna, too, had chosen to wear her hair half up, half down, but unlike Emilia's, hers was straight and sleek. Her side locks were clipped back in a barrette adorned with a porcelain pink flower and waterfall pearls that dripped two inches below the clip.

164

The moment Elliott entered the door to my house, I'd been happy with my own choice. The sage green complemented my red highlights, and the full skirt made perfect waves when I twirled. The bodice was covered in sequins that twinkled in the lights, and the bare back with thin, crisscross straps made me feel both mature and beautiful. I'd gone minimalist on makeup, accentuating my eyes with black mascara, my lips with a nude gloss, and my cheekbones with a light rose blush. My hair fell free in gentle waves that tickled my collarbones.

"Wow," was all he'd managed to say. It had been the perfect greeting.

Despite the fact the boys had asked us (or, in Emilia's case, she had asked) to Homecoming so late, we'd somehow managed to find a florist who created matching corsages and boutonnieres. Anna's was delicate, with pink sweetheart roses, baby's breath, miniature white carnations, and white ribbons, while Emilia's was more robust with blue delphinium, white roses, greenery, and sparkly gold-and-royal blue ribbon. They fit their personalities perfectly. Mine, too, seemed as if it had been made just for me. White calla lilies and bicolor white-and-pink alstroemeria complemented my sage dress beautifully. I wasn't sure how Ms. Givens had managed, but even Elliott's shirt matched my dress perfectly.

"Who's ready to dance?" Emilia asked. Without waiting for an answer, she grabbed Tanner's hand and steered him toward the dance floor. I tugged on Elliott's shirt, thrusting my chin in Tanner's direction.

"Is he okay with this situation?" I asked.

Elliott chuckled. "I think so," he said.

"Hey, guys, Malik and I are gonna grab our cameras," Anna said.

"We want to get some pics for the yearbook," Malik added.

As if on cue, the auditorium doors flew open, letting in a burst of light from the hallway. Like a Broadway star entering the stage,

Lindy glided in wearing the most massive bubblegum-pink dress I'd ever seen. The bottom fluffed out way wider than her arms, which were clad in long, white gloves. A bedazzled tiara sat atop her head.

Anna groaned. "She looks like Princess Peach," she said, heading back to her locker with Malik.

She wasn't wrong.

For the next thirty minutes, Elliott and I hit the dance floor while Anna and Malik circled the crowd, shooting pictures. When "Sucker" by the Jonas Brothers started playing, we sang along, tapping invisible desks with invisible pencils.

When the song ended, "Thinking Out Loud" by Ed Sheeran began to play.

"Oh, I love this song," I said. All around us, the space between couples disappeared. I looked at the floor. "But I'm okay if you're tired of dancing," I said.

I felt Elliott's fingers entwine with mine, and I looked up.

"I'm not tired of dancing," he said. "Unless you are."

Speechless, I shook my head. He pulled me close and wrapped one arm around my waist, holding my hand with his other. My head rested against his chest, feeling the *thump, thump, thump* of his heart.

When Elliott began singing along, I almost pulled away in shock. I'd never heard him sing before. His voice was soft. Sweet.

Gently, I began singing along with him as we swayed to the music. When the song got to the part about kissing under the stars, Elliott's hold on me loosened. I tilted by head up in question.

We stopped moving.

For a moment, and for an eternity, we stood still. Couples rocked from side to side all around us as we stared at one another, barely breathing. Elliott leaned his face closer to mine.

A wave of nausea washed over me. It hit hard and fast.

"I . . . I think I've gotta go."

I released Elliott's hands and made a beeline for the door, but suddenly felt like I had tunnel vision. I could see nothing but the light from the hallway, shining through the tiny windows of the auditorium doors. I prayed I would make it to the bathroom.

I had to.

When the door was almost within grasp, my left hip smacked something hard. As if in slow motion, the folding table with the punch bowl collapsed on one side, sending the massive bowl of bright-red liquid flying into the air. But I couldn't stop.

Behind me, I heard a familiar, nasal shriek.

Lindy.

I bolted into the hallway and pushed my way into the closest bathroom I could find. I barely made it to the toilet before the vomiting started. And once it started, it did not stop.

Wave after wave after wave of relentless, violent vomiting took over. Two, three, four, five minutes. By the time Emilia came, it felt like forever had passed.

"I . . . couldn't . . . find . . . you," she panted. Her sentences came out in breathless, staccato bursts. "I . . . I looked . . . everywhere." I felt her hand on my back as Emilia caught her breath.

"You're in the teacher's bathroom," she said. "Elliott sent me. Anna's calling your dad. What's going on? Are you sick?"

But I couldn't answer. It felt like my insides all wanted to come out.

Why? I thought. *Why now? Why tonight?* This was the exact same kind of nausea I'd felt during our last sleepover, and again at movie night. Why had it come back? Had I missed something on a label somewhere? No . . . I felt sure I hadn't! I'd even been avoiding everything marked "Made in a factory with." EVERYTHING! So why was I sick again? WHY?

The bathroom door squeaked open behind me.

"Elliott called Mr. Vogel. I couldn't find my phone." Anna's voice echoed off the bathroom walls. She spoke again, but this time in almost a whisper. To Emilia.

"Did I leave it at your place last night?"

My heart dropped, shocked, into my spinning stomach. Last night? Anna was at Emilia's last night?

Without me?

Emilia's hand shifted on my back, indicating that she was shaking her head. I began to cry.

Elliott's voice carried from the hallway.

"Is she any better?"

As my tears fell, another wave of vomiting began.

No. I was no better. In fact, I was *worse* than no better.

I was broken.

Completely, irreparably broken.

Chapter 29

RUNNING OUT OF TIME

Wolfie lay stomach-down on the doctor's stool, propelling himself by pushing his hands against the floor until he spun so fast, his fingers couldn't keep up. With his arms and knees tucked in, he flew around in a blur, the stool squeaking under his weight. Then he stuck his arms and legs straight out like Superman, slowing himself instantly. When the chair stopped completely, he tucked his knees and reached for the floor again.

And again.

And again.

Dad sat in a non-spinning chair, legs straight out, ankles crossed, head against the wall. I couldn't tell if he was staring at the ceiling or asleep. Dark circles cupped his eyes. His mouth hung slightly open, his button-down shirt was untucked on one side, and his long stubble made it look like he was trying to grow a beard. Ever since the dance the week before, he'd walked around hunched over, staring blankly ahead.

Stuck.

Just like the turtles by the creek.

I'd wanted to flip him back over, so I tried to tell him I was fine. That I must've eaten something that made me sick, and I knew I could figure it out. I wasn't ready to admit what I knew about Mom yet, but I'd explained that I'd been monitoring my diet, and in the process had learned certain foods didn't sit well with me.

I'd obviously missed something, which had made me feel poorly at Homecoming. Maybe I'd even eaten something that had been contaminated. It certainly was possible, with all the hands flinging snacks around that night.

But Dad had insisted that Miralax would make me feel better. I'd tried to protest, only to realize that I couldn't tell him he was wrong without admitting I'd lied about taking it.

In the end, he'd poured a dose of the milky white medicine, handed it to me with sad, tired eyes, and simply said, "Please, Twilight?"

So I took it. For four straight days, I took it. And when the cramping became intolerable, I began tossing it in secret again.

All the while, I tracked every last thing I put into my mouth. Headaches started plaguing me along with the nausea, and even though it didn't seem possible with my already-protruding ribs and chicken legs, I'd dropped two pounds in just one week. My belt was now on its last notch.

Google said protein intake was imperative for weight gain, so I'd been requesting a lot of chicken, fish, and beans, and Dad even made avocado toast with dried fruit a few mornings. But he always seemed to want to add peanut butter to smoothies, so those, too, needed to be dumped.

I'd hoped that my quest for nutritional knowledge would pack on the pounds, eliminate nausea, and prevent a visit to the doctor.

But here we were.

Wolfie finally tired of spinning and hopped up next to me on the exam table.

"What's a pe-di-a-tric gas-tro-ent-er-o-lo-gist?" He read the diploma on the wall one syllable at a time.

"That's the specialist Twyla's seeing for her stomach problems," Dad said.

Wolfie pulled the otoscope off the wall and a light automatically came on. He peered through the lens.

"Seems like an awfully fancy name for someone who talks about pooping and throwing up all day."

"Don't play with that, Wolfie."

"Hey! Did you know you have three bones in each ear? And they're so teeny-tiny, itty-bitty small that they can all fit together on one penny!" He started leaning toward my ear and I pushed him away.

"Not right now, Wolfie."

"Wolfie! I said don't touch that! It's not a toy," Dad snapped.

Wolfie stuck out his lower lip and replaced the otoscope.

The door swung open and in walked a tall, slender man with long, white hair and a matching beard. He reminded me of Dumbledore and, for just a minute, I wondered if he might pull out a wand and fix me with a spell and a flick of his wrist. He peered at me from over his half-glasses, then looked back down at the chart in his hands. The nurse in Mickey Mouse scrubs, who'd initially taken my temperature and weighed me, pushed a computer on a rolling table and followed the doctor in.

For a few seconds, no one said anything. I almost wished Wolfie would spin on the squeaky stool again. Finally, Dr. Dumbledore broke the silence.

"I'm Dr. Hawley," he said. "You must be Twyla."

I nodded. More silence. More peering.

"I looked over your labs and your films, and it does look like you are a little constipated. Can you lie down so I can—"

"I'm not constipated," I spat. "I mean . . . I'm pooping fine." I forced calm into my voice and bit my tongue to keep from saying anything I might regret. Dr. Dumbledore raised his eyebrows and looked back at my chart.

"I . . . see you're prescribed Miralax." He peered at me over his glasses again. "Have you been taking that?"

I glanced at Dad, whose eyes warned: *Do not argue about this.*

I nodded. Clearly able to read my mind without his wand, Dr. Dumbledore frowned. I silently begged him to drop the subject.

He did.

"Well, I was going to say that I do think there may be some constipation, but I also agree that there might be some other problem," he said. He tilted his head, studying me. He inhaled slowly, hands in his pockets, and rolled from his heels to his toes, then back again.

"But I'd like to examine you first." His voice was gentle. Respectful. "Can I do that?"

I nodded, relief washing over me. This did not strike me as the kind of doctor who wanted to force a quick opinion on me.

"Go ahead and lie down then, when you're ready. Here, young man." Dr. Dumbledore patted his chair. "Why don't you take this for a spin?"

Wolfie jumped off the table and jumped back on the chair.

After a bit of pushing and prodding, Dr. Dumbledore sighed.

"Constipation really shouldn't be causing this kind of upset," he said. He turned to my dad.

"I'd like to schedule Twyla for a gastric emptying study." Then he turned back to me.

"I wonder if your stomach isn't emptying into your intestines the way it's supposed to after meals. Is the nausea worse in the evening?"

"Yeah," I said.

"And you often feel bloated and gassy?"

"Mm–hmm."

"Do you feel full quickly? Maybe even after eating small amounts?"

I twisted my face in thought. "I guess, maybe? Some?"

The doctor scribbled something on a piece of paper, ripped it off of the pad, and handed it to the nurse, who'd been frantically typing since he'd entered the room. "How soon does Nuclear Medicine have an opening?" he asked.

The nurse tucked her frayed bangs behind her ears and typed

for a few more seconds. "They had a cancelation tomorrow at seven," she squeaked.

The doctor directed his attention back to my father. "Do you think you can make it that soon?"

Dad nodded weakly. "How long does this test take?" he asked.

"About four and a half hours."

Dad sighed. "I'll tell work I'll be in late."

Once more, Dr. Dumbledore peered at me over his spectacles. "Twyla," he said, "although I think there may be something else wrong, I'd like you to *stay* on the Miralax. Okay?" The way he said *stay* made me want to leap off the table and run out of the room.

"'Kay," I mumbled.

While the nurse explained the study in more detail to Dad, my mind raced. Maybe there was some constipation, but that couldn't be my primary problem. I'd been feeling better for too long, and Miralax had never helped me feel better—not once. I wanted to share this with the doctor, but I couldn't. Not without making Dad mad. Besides, I *had* to have a nut allergy. I hadn't had an emergency like the one at the dance since I started avoiding them. And it was in my genetic code . . . wasn't it? I'd thought it was as much a part of me as it had been a part of Mom.

My head throbbed, the bright ceiling lights piercing through me.

But even though I'd been so careful about my diet . . . it was seeming less and less likely that it was the only thing causing my symptoms. I could've eaten something contaminated at the dance, but that wouldn't explain why I was still feeling nauseous for the past week. Maybe there *was* something else wrong with me.

And maybe, just maybe, this study would tell us what it was.

It *had* to.

Because deep in my gut, I was starting to feel like we were running out of time.

Chapter 30

LOSING CONTROL

I folded my tater tots inside a pancake and stuck a fork through the top, so it would hold its shape. Then I leaned back to study my creation.

"Looks a little like the Leaning Tower of Pisa," Anna said.

Emilia frowned. "Twy, what's wrong? You love breakfast-for-lunch day. Did the test go okay?"

Anna leaned toward me on her elbows, sipping her orange juice from a straw.

I shrugged. I'd had no interest in discussing the test with them, or anything else for that matter. Ever since the revelation that Anna and Emilia had gotten together without me, I'd spent my free time researching, journaling, and walking in the woods with Angela. Emilia and Anna had continued texting me like nothing was wrong, but we could all feel the tension in the air.

Even if no one wanted to admit it was there.

Besides, the truth was, the test had sucked. I hadn't been allowed to eat or drink anything all morning, which was the only time of day I seemed to be able to eat without feeling sick anymore. When I'd arrived at the hospital (way too early), a surly nurse took my temperature, almost squeezed my arm off with a blood pressure cuff, scoffed at my weight, then led me to a room with a machine that looked like a human panini press. She'd then delivered toast and jelly on a plastic plate, a small glass of water, and two lukewarm scrambled eggs that apparently had been mixed with some kind of radioactive dye.

I'd wondered if they'd make me glow in the dark.

"Don't care if ya eat the toast," she barked, "but ya've got ten minutes to finish the eggs, and ya have to eat 'em all. Understand?" She didn't wait for me to answer. She just waddled away like a pissy, elderly penguin.

The eggs tasted like crap and my stomach felt like it might revolt, but I'd managed to force them down. When she came back, she put me in the panini press, took some X-rays, then led me to a dingy, yellow waiting room with Dad.

I thought about the small boy I'd seen there, his diaper poking out of the top of his jeans. He'd been sitting at a table with a toy that looked like a roller coaster gone wrong. Lots of colorful metal wires attached to a wooden base, spinning up, down, and every which way around one another. The boy made happy *zoom, zoom* noises while he pushed bright wooden balls along the wired maze. There was no point to the toy that I could see, really. No clear beginning or ending. Just a bunch of craziness with a mess of balls. Yet the boy seemed perfectly content to keep pushing the balls back and forth, up and down. Over and over again.

Part of me thought it was the most ridiculous toy ever. But part of me couldn't look away. It had no clear purpose. No reason for being.

And yet.

Nurse Pissy-Penguin had come back to get me for more X-rays after an hour of radiated-egg digestion, then again after another hour, and then again after two more hours. I'd wanted to ask if I could see the pictures, but I didn't. I just ate my eggs, sat still for my pictures, and watched the world fly by on the way home.

I realized Emilia and Anna were still staring at me, waiting for an answer. But right then, sitting at that lunch table with my Leaning Tower of Pancakes and the two girls who were supposed to be my best friends, I didn't feel like sharing anything.

"It was fine," I lied.

Anna slurped the last bit of OJ from her glass.

"Fine?" Emilia asked. "What does that mean?"

I shrugged. "It was no big deal. They did this X-ray thing because the doctor thinks I'm constipated, even though I told them I thought it was something I ate. But they still want to make sure I'm digesting food normally. That was it. Then Dad brought me here. No big deal."

"Oh," Anna said. "Okay. Well . . . that's good then, right?"

"Right," I said. I pushed the fork into my pancake tower until it fell over and clanked against the plate.

"Well then, let's talk about Halloween! Are we trick-or-treating this year?" Emilia asked.

"I think we're probably too old for that," Anna said. "Should we give out candy from my house—"

Anna's body jerked like she had been kicked under the table, and she never finished the sentence. I didn't have the energy to worry about why.

Someone walked by with a fresh tray, and the smell of pancakes and syrup hit me like a toxic landfill. I swung my leg off the bench and grabbed my tray.

"I'll do whatever. I've gotta go, guys. See ya later."

Notably, Emilia and Anna didn't stop me.

I dumped my food and tossed the dishes into the soapy bin, wondering how the kitchen staff could stand the smell of left-overs and dirty plates all day. I was about to find a bathroom when Elliott's voice drifted over my shoulder.

"Hey," he said.

I turned to face him. Concern filled his eyes, his brows stitched together in worry. I ignored the urge to hug him.

"Hey," I answered.

"Mom said you had a test that took all morning. That sucks."

It wasn't a question. It was a statement of empathy. My shoulders softened with gratitude.

"Yeah," I said. "It did." I fiddled with the hem of my shirt. "I'm sorry I bolted like that at the dance."

Elliott's forehead relaxed, his eyes smiling at the corners. "So you've said."

My gaze dropped to the floor. Was I annoying him by apologizing too often? In the week since Homecoming, I'd probably said I was sorry about a dozen times. He'd been really gracious about it, but I couldn't help but feel like I'd ruined something that night.

Leave it to me to break something that isn't even a thing yet.

Cafeteria chatter floated down the hallway, filling the space between us. Elliott cleared his throat.

"So . . . Kentucky Kingdom is doing Halloscream with mazes and food and stuff. I was thinking maybe we could do that on Halloween. You know, with all of us?"

With all of us? My stomach lurched at the phrasing, which made it sound like I'd been friend-zoned. I plastered a smile on my face.

"Sounds good," I said. "Text me details, okay?"

Without waiting for a reply, I waved and darted down the hall, turning a corner to dash into the nearest bathroom. I prayed no one would find me there. The last thing I wanted was another scene. No one needed an audience as they vomited radioactive eggs.

Nobody understands, I thought. *Nobody understands what it's like to feel sick all the time, and to have to read food labels, and worry about dying from anaphylaxis.* All everyone cared about was dances and Halloween. I just wanted to stop feeling like every bite I took was going to come back up or kill me. I just wanted to figure this out and feel normal again.

Normal. Ha. Whatever that was.

I leaned over the toilet, prayed I wouldn't lose the few calories I'd eaten, and made a decision. I wouldn't just avoid nuts. Now, I'd log everything. Every bite, every ounce of protein, every gram of fat, every medication, every sip, every little thing that went into my mouth. I'd track it all on paper. Then, when I figured out exactly what was making me sick, I would explain to everyone what I'd been going through. I'd share it all. No doubt, my friends would feel bad that they hadn't been more supportive. Dad would feel guilty for forcing me to take Miralax. And in the end, everyone would be proud of me for figuring it out, and they'd be grateful that I hadn't worried them for no reason.

Maybe *this* was why Mom died.

To make me aware. To make me question everything.

To save me.

Hope washed over me. Soon, everything would be better. I could fix this.

The wave of nausea passed, so I left the stall to clean my hands in the sink. The cold water felt good, so I splashed some on my face and rubbed the color back into my cheeks.

I watched the water drip down my face's reflection, finding comfort in gravity's predictable nature. Then, I dabbed the droplets away.

Everything was under control.

Chapter 31

JUST LIKE MOM

"Hey, Twyla . . . if a fly didn't have wings, would it be called a walk?" Wolfie pressed his nose against the car window, then pulled his face back to make smiley faces in the steam. His steady stream of happy babble irritated me today.

"I learned about friction in school and now I'm not in school and I'm getting ready for the weekend. Today is a much better day," he chattered.

More breathing. More smiley faces.

"Hey, Twyla . . ."

"Wolfie, please," I grumbled. "Not right now."

Wolfie pulled a sucker from his backpack. He threw the wrapper onto the floor and popped it into his mouth. "Mmm . . . mmmm! Mystery flavor! This is a yum factory right here."

I wondered how long Wolfie could carry on a whole conversation by himself.

Dad parked the car in the driveway. When I opened the door, his voice startled me. He hadn't said a word the whole way home from school.

"Don't go running off yet, Twyla. Let's go inside and talk," he said.

I scowled. "Why?" I asked. "What's wrong?"

If possible, Dad appeared even more haggard than he had the day we met Dr. Dumbledore. His wrinkled clothes looked three days old.

"The doctor called," he sighed. "Let's go talk."

My stomach dropped. I didn't know what to ask, so I just followed Dad out of the car in silence. Once inside, Wolfie spun like a tornado and disappeared up the stairs. Dad flopped down and patted the spot on the couch beside him.

My heart raced. I sat, feeling a little like I was about to be grounded.

"You know that day in the hospital, they were testing how fast you can digest food, right?"

I nodded, but he kept talking like he hadn't seen me. Like his words were rehearsed.

"In other words, they were looking to see how quickly food moves from your stomach through your intestines. You understand that?"

"Yes, Dad. I understand. Would you please just tell me what's wrong?" Dad's elbows pressed into his knees. He started to reach one hand toward me, but at the last minute he pulled it back. His head hung low.

"Twyla, you have something called gastroparesis. It means you digest food slowly. They think it started with a virus, and they called today to schedule you for a scope."

My mind whirred. Nothing he was saying made any sense. A virus? I hadn't even been sick lately. A scope? What did that even mean?

"They'll use medicine to put you to sleep, and then they're going to put a camera through a tube down your throat to look around . . ."

"Wait . . . what? A camera? Down my *throat*? Are you kidding me? *WHY*?"

Dad's face sagged. Exhaustion pulled him against the back of the couch, and pain creased his forehead, drawing his eyebrows together.

"You'll be under anesthesia, so you won't remember any of it,

Twyla. They need to take tissue samples, and they'll look at them under a microscope. The procedure is going to be on October thirty-first, and—"

"Tissue samples? On HALLOWEEN? I can't have a procedure on *Halloween*!"

Dad's expression hardened, ever so slightly. "You can, Twyla. And you will."

"Will I be better by that night?" I asked.

Dad shook his head. "It takes time to recover from anesthesia."

I tried to slow my breaths, but the unfairness of it all overwhelmed me. I felt panicky . . . unable to stop the flow of words.

"So you're just going to let them march forward and do a bunch of stupid, USELESS tests on me? It's *my* body, and no one wants to listen to anything I have to say about what *I* think is wrong! Maybe I have some ideas that are worth listening to! Did you ever think of *that*? Homecoming was a total bust, and now I can't do anything with my friends on Halloween either? Could this get any worse? This isn't fair!"

"LIFE'S. NOT. FAIR. TWYLA!" Dad slapped the couch cushion beside him, and a loud *POP* echoed through the living room. For a moment, my jaw hung slack, stunned. We glared at each other, both sapped yet unyielding.

A sudden movement caught my attention from the corner of my eye. Wolfie stood halfway down the stairs in the shadows, paralyzed. His eyes glowed, full and round. Something about the sight of him crushed me. I swallowed tears, stood, and turned back to Dad.

"No." The word was fire, breathed through gritted teeth. "They do NOT need to take tissue samples. They do NOT need to put a camera down my throat. They were wrong about the constipation, and now they are wrong about this. And you know why? You know why they don't have the right answer? Because . . ."

The words bubbled up into my throat. I knew that once they

were out, I couldn't take them back. But the doctors were wrong. They were all wrong. I should've just listened to my gut from the start. I was done with being ignored.

Done.

"Because I have an allergy," I hissed. "I'm allergic to nuts." I spit the next words at him, knowing they would sting. Knowing they would hurt.

I *wanted* them to hurt.

"Just. Like. Mom."

Chapter 32

THE KINGSNAKE

Dad hadn't even tried to stop me. This time, I think he wanted me gone too.

Dead sticks cracked under the weight of my feet pounding the dirt as I ran. I didn't stop to listen to the creek. I didn't stop to look for my new woodpecker friend, Zeeno. I didn't stop for anything until I reached the comfort of my willow. Only then, when I could finally hide beneath her branches, did I sink to the ground and sob.

Memories flooded my brain. The siren. The officer who told us Mom had been in an accident. Dad, leaving for the hospital, and then coming home . . . crying, crying, crying. He'd knelt down and patted his knee for me to come to him, but I hadn't. Instead, I'd run outside, barefooted, into the darkness. Into the storm. Dad had followed me, splashing through puddles. I remembered the cold, wet ground beneath my feet. How my clothes stuck to my body. How I'd tripped and fallen in the grass, tears and raindrops streaking my face. How Dad had scooped me up, rocking me, our bodies shaking with sorrow.

How he hadn't said a word, but I'd known anyway.

Mom was gone.

Minutes passed, the tears demanding to fall. Memories demanding to be replayed. Finally, when the nausea outweighed the heartache, I pulled my knees to my chest, wrapped my arms around my legs, and tucked my face into the darkness. I pressed my pounding temples into the palms of my hands, willing the pain to stop.

Why hadn't I grabbed my journal? If ever I needed to write, it was now.

Crack.

A twig nearby broke. And footsteps.

Someone was there. In my space. But it was Tuesday.

Angela never came out on Tuesdays. She was always helping her siblings with schoolwork then.

Crack.

They were closer now.

"Twyla? Is that you? Are you okay?" The breeze carried Angela's soft voice down from the top of the hill. My breath caught and I broke my tiny bubble, peering through the branches to search for my friend. There she was, sliding down the hill, face etched with concern. Her long, dark hair tangled with fallen leaves as she rushed toward me, Sophie on her heels.

"Angela!" I sprang to my feet. Sobs racked my entire body as I threw my arms around her neck and sank into the safety of her hug. She rubbed my hair until I could breathe again, then took my hand. Together, we sat by the willow.

"Cover," Angela told Sophie.

I was surprised when Sophie lay down across *my* legs. The weight of her body brought a sense of peace. I stroked her head.

"Tell me what happened," Angela said.

So I did. I told her about Homecoming, genetics class, and my mom's autopsy report. I told her about the scope, the camera, and Halloween. I told her about Dad trying to force Miralax on me, even though I was certain I didn't need it. I told her how much I missed music in the house, and how sad Dad looked recently. I told her about Wolfie's nonstop babbling, my bizarre nausea, and my distant friends. I even told her about Elliott. Everything came gushing out in a messy tidal wave of tears, sadness, and confusion. Through it all, Angela just sat and listened.

When my thoughts finally exhausted themselves, I rested my

head on her shoulder. For a long while, we watched the creek swim by.

"I'm sorry things have been so hard," Angela said. "But hey—I wanted to tell you . . . you did a great job at the field hockey game."

I half smiled. "I was sort of hoping you'd love the game as much as I do, so maybe you'd come to school with me."

"I don't know." She laughed. "That one girl, who kept glaring at you . . . she looked a little mean. Like a bulldog chewing a wasp."

I pulled back, shocked.

"What?" she asked.

"It's just . . ." I shook my head. "That expression. I haven't heard it in a long time." I sniffled, and Angela put her arm around my shoulder.

"Well, it's a good expression. Can't you just picture it? A cute little bulldog? Chewing a *wasp*?" She tugged me into both arms, hugging tight. I hugged her back. "I know I risk frustrating you by saying this . . ." Angela's voice trailed off and I pulled away. "But I bet your dad just wants you to take the Miralax because he cares about you."

I sighed. "I know," I said. "But I wish he would listen to me. It's my body."

Angela nodded. "It is," she agreed, "and he's probably worried about it right now."

I dug my toes into a pile of leaves and sighed.

Angela released me and rested her hand on my knee. "You're going to be okay, you know."

I let my eyes drift across the clear blue sky. Crows cawed in the distance.

"Did you know a group of crows is called a murder?" I asked. "Isn't that creepy?"

Angela laughed. "Sort of perfect for Halloween," she said. "Did you learn that from your brother, who talks too much?"

I nodded and sighed.

"Can I ask you a question?" I said.

Angela tilted her head. "Anything."

I pushed myself to stand and brushed my pants. "You said I'm going to be okay."

She nodded.

"How do you know? How do you know I'm going to be okay?"

Angela stood beside me, brushed her own pants, and followed my gaze to the sky.

"I don't suppose I do," she admitted. "But you're stronger than you think you are. And you aren't alone." She took my hand.

"I'm glad you came today," I said. "The scope is on Friday, so I won't even get to see you again before . . ."

Angela squeezed as I fought tears.

"Do you still have your kintsugi leaf?" she asked.

"Yeah."

She hugged my shoulders with one arm. "Then bring it with you, and I'll be right there, the whole time."

Together, we stood there, listening to the murder of crows until the last caw faded away.

Sophie yipped.

"You hungry, girl?" Angela scratched her ear, and Sophie's wagging tail brushed clean a pile of leaves. Angela turned to face me.

"I'm glad I came today too," she said. "See you after the scope, okay?"

I nodded, waving to my friend as she followed her dog down the bank of the creek.

As I began slowly hiking home, I scanned the surroundings for Zeeno, upside-down turtles, or other critters that might bring a little joy. My shoes scattered rocks, sending centipedes scurrying and one green frog to find shelter. But close to our house, under a large fallen branch, one magnificent finding took my breath away.

A stunning, black kingsnake.

A stunning, black, *injured* kingsnake.

Her black-and-white-checkered belly seemed unharmed, but the smooth, shiny scales on her black back had two deep, red ridges. Gently, I picked her up, scanned the length of her body, striped with thin, white bands—but I could see no other injuries. She looked as if she'd been hit by a lawn mower. She didn't try to slither away, bite me, or release musk like other snakes I'd caught. But her body still moved. It still held life.

I'd never found a kingsnake before, but Dad had. He'd shown me and Wolfie pictures and talked about finding them in Tennessee. Non-venomous, beautiful, and gentle, they were one of his favorites.

He would know what to do.

Gently, I lifted her up and cradled her coiled body. Then I bolted across our backyard and burst into the house through the garage door.

"DAD!" I yelled.

Silence.

"Dad?" I skidded into the living room. Wolfie stood in the middle, absorbed in some virtual reality video game, so I ran through the hallway toward Dad's room. But when I turned the corner, I stopped in my tracks. There he was, sprawled across the top of his comforter on his bed.

Out cold.

I furrowed my brow at the slow-moving snake in my hands. She needed help. But Dad . . . we hadn't exactly parted on the best terms. And he'd been so tired lately. So, so tired.

My mind whirred. Heart racing, I grabbed a bucket from the garage, filled it with dirt and grass, and put the snake inside. Then I carried the bucket to our computer, plopped down in the chair, and typed into Google: *Reptile vets near me.*

I could fix this on my own.

And if I could fix *her* . . .

Maybe then, he'd see.

Maybe then, he'd listen.

And maybe then . . . everything would be okay.

HOPE

"But she's really hurt!"

"What am I supposed to do? Just let her die?"

"She's a *kingsnake*! Do you know how rare these are around here?"

After pleading every which way with six different vets, I'd gotten nowhere. Well, I'd learned the term *pro bono*, which apparently means someone will offer their services for free . . . but not a single vet would exchange their knowledge, or their time, for her life.

I only had one more number to call. Hope filled my lungs, and I dialed.

"Hi, my name is Twyla Vogel, and I'm calling to leave a message for Dr. Ellis about a kingsnake I found. She is not my pet, and I don't expect to have her returned to me. I only want someone to help her and release her back into the wild."

My heart hammered against my chest. No one had let me get that far before interrupting me yet.

"Did you say a kingsnake?" The man's voice was gentle. Old.

"Yes, sir," I said. "She's beautiful, and she looks like she got hit by a lawn mower. My mom was a vet, and she would've saved her if she . . ." Sadness tugged at my throat, and I couldn't finish my sentence.

"What'dya say your name is again, little lady?"

"Twyla Vogel," I whispered.

"Well, you hold tight, Twyla Vogel. Let me go see if Dr. Ellis is free."

A recording started to play about Dr. Ellis, her vet practice, and her love of all things living. The woman in the recording told me their address, their hours, and who to call in case of an emergency. She told me what kinds of animals she saw (all of them, though she preferred to send horses to a local equine specialist), and she welcomed calls about . . .

Injured wildlife.

Chills blanketed my body. This was my vet. It had to be.

A woman's voice came through the receiver. "Twyla?"

"Yes! This is Twyla," I said.

"This is Dr. Ellis. Cedric says you have an injured kingsnake on your hands. Do you think you could bring her to me tonight? Before we close?"

Excitement pulsed through my veins. "I . . . I do! I have to ask my dad to drive me, but . . . I'm sure he will!"

"Oh, that's wonderful. We'll stay open and wait for you. I won't be able to give her back to you when she's better, though. You know that, right?"

"I don't want her! I mean . . . I'm not looking to keep her as a pet or anything. I just want her to live."

Dr. Ellis laughed. "Well, I do too. Do you have my address?"

I confirmed that I did, thanked her, and hung up the phone. The snake curled under a clump of grass and dirt in the bucket.

"You're gonna live, sweet girl," I said. As I crouched down to pick up the bucket, a thought drew me back to the computer.

I had one more thing to do. I typed: *What does the name Ellis mean?*

My stomach fluttered. *Ellis* meant kind, or benevolent. I googled Dr. Ellis's address to get a sense of how far away her office was, then peeked into the bucket once more.

"Well, Ellis, let's go wake my dad."

If the name was good enough for the vet, then it was good enough for the snake.

The floorboards creaked as I carried Ellis down the hallway to my father's room. I checked my watch. Almost six o'clock. Dinnertime.

"Dad?" I tapped his leg. "Dad?"

"Wha . . . Twyla? Oh my gosh, what time is it?" Dad bolted upright and rubbed his eyes. "I must've fallen asleep," he said. As his eyes focused on me, his body slumped a little. Gently, I offered him the bucket.

"What's this . . ." Dad's soft gasp warmed my heart. But his smile faded as quickly as it had appeared. He fished Ellis out of the bucket and turned her over in his hands.

"Oh, Twyla. She's hurt."

"I know," I said, "but I called seven vets and I found one, a lady named Dr. Ellis, who's—"

"Wait. You called . . . seven vets?" Dad's eyes widened in surprise.

"Yes!" I said. "And she's willing to fix her and release her into the wild. Pro bono! They're supposed to be closing at six, but she's willing to wait there for us. I googled her address. She's only twenty minutes away! But we need to leave right now, okay? Can we? Can we go?"

"Do you know what kind of snake this is, Twyla?"

I scoffed. "Of course, Dad. She's a kingsnake. And her name is Ellis, and I don't want her to die, so can we please go? Now?"

A grin tugged at Dad's mouth. "How do you know she's a female?"

"I . . ." I frowned. "I don't know," I admitted. "I guess I just thought she looked like a *she*."

Ellis slithered slowly through Dad's relaxed fingers.

"Lampropeltis getula," he whispered. "That's her Latin name."

Ellis curled into the warmth of Dad's cupped hands, her tail still encircling his forearm. Dad's mouth hung open ever so slightly and his eyes welled up, as if caught between a memory and words.

Together, they sat there, motionless, and I wanted to ask Dad what he was thinking. But then Ellis's tail released its grip, and Dad blinked back the tears. Ellis's forked tongue licked the air.

The moment was gone.

"Well, you're right. She's a she." Dad's tired eyes crinkled in the corners. He pointed to her swollen lower half. "Do you see those bumps? She's gravid—meaning, she's pregnant. And they're only gravid for about a month, so she should lay her clutch soon."

Dad put Ellis back in the bucket and straightened his shirt. "So we'd better get going, don't you think?"

"But . . ." I held up my hand, stopping him. "Is she going to live?"

Dad's eyes reddened and welled, but then he cleared his throat and rubbed them both with the finger and thumb of each hand.

"Yeah," he said. "Yeah. If we get her to the vet, she should live."

I wanted to hug him, but it was like an invisible force pushed us apart. The tension from our earlier fight still hung in the air.

So, with Ellis's bucket in my hands, I followed him out of the room.

In silence.

Chapter 34

PUZZLED

When Mama Rose learned that I'd be having a scope on Halloween, she apparently deemed my recent distance "unacceptable" and took it upon herself to invite me over after school. I'd been torn as to whether or not I should accept the invitation, but Mama Rose had been insistent. For their parts, Emilia and Anna seemed agreeable enough, nodding and smiling when Mama Rose asked in the parking lot at school . . . though I noticed Emilia's hand never left her thunderbird. It was like she thought she needed protection from the black cloud hanging over my head.

"Emilia, this is impossible without looking at the box!" Anna pawed through puzzle pieces, trying to find just the right pink so she could finish her flamingo. "If I knew what was next to the flamingo, then this wouldn't take so long!"

"But if you looked at the picture while doing the puzzle, then *I* would have to save you from all the bad luck you'd suffer over the next year. And that, my dear Anna, would be entirely unacceptable. I wish only good luck for you. So." Emilia smirked. "Get over it. No picture."

Anna growled but continued her search. Mama Rose put a plate of sugar cookies on the table and Anna stuffed one into her mouth.

"Hey. Earth to Twyla!" Emilia waved her hand in front of my face. "Are you still working on that same corner?"

I nodded, squinting at the pieces in front of me. It felt like someone was stabbing me above my left eye; it was a minor miracle

I hadn't crashed my bike on the way over. So far, my best efforts at helping with the puzzle involved feeling for edge shapes that might fit together. I felt slow and awkward, like Buddy the Elf trying to make a toy in a room full of real elves.

"But whoever heard of getting bad luck from looking at a picture on a puzzle box?" Anna complained. "I mean, come on, Em. Don't you think that's slightly . . ."

"No. Box." Emilia raised one eyebrow at Anna. "And quit spraying cookie spit on the puzzle."

As Anna and Emilia argued about whether or not a peek at the puzzle picture would turn Anna into a lonely, old, crazy cat woman, I reran the conversation with Dad in my head. The doctor said I have gastroparesis. Okay. Fine. That, supposedly, was the cause of my nausea and vomiting. Okay again. Maybe that was true. But what, then, was the cause of the gastroparesis?

When I'd googled "causes of gastroparesis," I'd learned the main suspects were:

1. Injury to the vagus nerve during surgery (I hadn't had surgery, so . . . nope).
2. Hypothyroidism (they'd ruled this out with a blood test).
3. Certain autoimmune disorders (I didn't fit the picture of anything in this category).
4. Certain nervous system disorders (again, my symptoms didn't match anything like this).
5. And finally, the most common cause of gastroparesis in kids like me . . . a viral infection (but I hadn't been sick. Nope, nope, nope).

When my dad explained this to the doctor, the doctor said that sometimes they just didn't know the reason. Sometimes, gastroparesis just happened.

Uh, no. That would be a big, fat, no freaking way. Nothing "just happened."

They were missing something. We were all missing something. But what?

"Twyla, honey, are you okay?" Mama Rose touched my shoulder, and I jumped. Only then did I realize that I'd been rubbing my temples with my eyes squeezed shut. Emilia and Anna stared, like wide-eyed statues.

I shifted from one foot to the other, feeling the weight of everyone's stares like a vise grip on my lungs.

"I . . . I . . . I'm fine, really," I stammered, blinking a few times to refocus. "A little tired, that's all. And this puzzle! It's so tough." I forced a laugh and winked at Anna. "Without the picture, I mean. It's impossible, don't you think?"

"So now you're taking *her* side? Come ON!" Emilia's stance relaxed and Anna laughed, but Mama Rose's face held firm. I felt naked under her stare, so I leaned my elbows on the table and poured all my focus into the puzzle.

"Do you guys have any other edge pieces over there? I swear, some are missing." The pieces blurred in front of me as I strained to ignore Mama Rose.

"Ah! Look! There's one." Anna handed me an edge piece and I patted it in with a flourish, completing one side of the puzzle. A whoosh of relief escaped my lungs as Mama Rose climbed the stairs.

"So," Emilia said. "Indoor field hockey is coming up right after Halloween! Do you guys think Coach is going to start Lindy? She's been so unpredictable lately, not wanting to pass and all. You know Twyla's a shoo-in, but I wonder what the rest of the lineup will look like. I feel like she played me for less time in the last few games. Do you think she's losing faith in me?"

"Of course she's not losing faith in you," I said.

"How could she?" Anna added. "You and Twyla are amazeballs."

Emilia said, "Oh, stop," while motioning toward herself repeatedly, like we should keep talking.

As I watched her hand circle around, the puzzle pieces in front of me seemed to disappear into a black hole. A sharp pain over my left eye forced me off balance, and Anna caught my arm.

"Twyla . . . ?"

"Oh! Sorry . . ." I held my hand up in apology. "I must've tripped on your foot."

"But you didn't touch my foot . . ."

"Well . . . I must've . . . I need a glass of water."

I felt their eyes bore holes in my back as I climbed the steps, dizzy. Sleep had been elusive lately, and I wondered if I should just go home and try to nap. Or maybe I needed more protein? From what I'd been reading, a lack of balance in my diet could definitely cause headaches, fatigue, and a general sense of malaise. As hard as I tried, tracking the nutritional content of everything I ate had proven to be difficult. I'd found an app on my phone that made it a little easier to look up certain items, like pre-packaged foods, but homemade dishes required a lot more work. I couldn't measure things like salad dressing, sauces, or butter without raising eyebrows at home, so nothing was perfectly accurate . . . and it all just took so much time to log. Carbs, saturated fats, unsaturated fats, grams of protein, sugar, salt—there was so much to balance.

I'd just paused in front of the kitchen cabinet to press on the pain over my eye when Mama Rose placed a glass of water beside me, then wrapped her arms around me in a massive bear hug.

"I'm worried about you, sweetheart," she said. She pulled away and looked me in the eyes. I softened.

"Drink some water," she said. I did.

Outside of Kristin Givens, there were few adult women in my life who cared for me the way Mama Rose did. She and Mom had been good friends, frequently talking science, reading side by side, or going on walks together. She was basically family to me.

"Talk to me," she whispered.

"I'm . . ." I sighed. "I don't know, Mama Rose. I think I know what's wrong with me. But . . ."

Mama Rose studied me, her eyes quizzical. "But . . . ?"

She released me from the hug, and I leaned back against the hall wall. "I don't mean this to sound wrong . . ." I paused, waiting for Mama Rose to interrupt me. She did not. I considered my words carefully.

"I think the doctors are missing something. I don't think this is all constipation, or even gastroparesis."

"What does your dad think?" she asked.

I sighed. "I don't think he's willing to consider the possibility that it's anything else."

"Why not?"

I shrugged. "I wish I knew," I said.

Mama Rose pursed her lips. "Would you like me to talk to him for you?" she asked.

I shook my head. "No." Just the thought was enough to shut me down. I had no desire to fight with Dad over this again.

"No," I repeated, more gently this time. "I'm okay, Mama Rose. Really. I'll figure it out."

She twisted up one side of her mouth and sighed. "Okay, Twyla. I won't bug you about it anymore today. But I hope you know I'm here for you."

I hugged her again before heading down the hall to the bathroom, leaving Mama Rose in the kitchen. I wanted to splash water on my face before heading back downstairs. But before I reached the bathroom, a stack of photos sitting on a console table caught my attention.

Homecoming photos.

I flipped through the first few, feeling a combination of wistful and sentimental. The six of us laughing in the photo booth, holding goofy signs and pointing at one another. Me and Emilia dipping strawberries in chocolate. Malik looking through his camera at Anna, who was shooting the picture, and a similar photo of Anna doing the same. Emilia and Tanner dancing, their faces full of joy and laughter. Me and Elliott, slow dancing.

Then, chaos.

Shocked faces. Cups flying. Fruit punch everywhere. And Elliott . . . cleaning Lindy's dress.

Holding her hand.

Whispering in her ear.

And she was smiling.

My heart stopped. The searing pain returned just above my left eye, and suddenly, all I wanted was to get out. To go home. To sit by my tree, with my creek and my wildlife. To breathe.

I threw the pictures back on the console and rushed down the hall, calling over my shoulder to Mama Rose as I reached the front door. "Tell the girls I realized I had to turn in some homework before my test tomorrow, okay?"

"Twyla, wait . . ."

As I flipped the kickstand up on my bike, Mama Rose came out.

"Twyla?" she called. "Can I drive you home?"

I waved her off. "No, really . . . I'm fine . . ."

Emilia and Anna edged through the open door behind Mama Rose, looking confused. With one hand I snapped on my helmet, waved over my shoulder, and pedaled into the road.

Tears and humiliation burned my throat. How could I have been so stupid as to think he'd like me? Sure, Lindy had the personality of a scorpion, but I could never compete with her glamour. Her perfect hair and clothes. No boy was going to choose a girl with dirty fingernails over someone who looked like . . . her.

Stupid, stupid, stupid.

My feet couldn't pedal fast enough. I wanted my legs to burn. I wanted the wind to whip my face.

I wanted to fly away, as fast and as far as I could.

Chapter 35

MORE THAN A WASHCLOTH

I turned the snow globe over and over and over in my hands, trying to lose myself in bits of light reflecting off swirling stars. "Godspeed" plinked along steadily, a metronome to pace my breaths. When I stopped moving, tiny whirlpools of stars spun around the moon for several seconds. I gazed out the window at the sky.

Twilight.

I closed my eyes, searching for Mom's voice in my head as the music slowed. Finally, after what felt like an hour, I could hear her again. I hated how long it took to retrieve certain memories now. Time was sort of cruel that way. Mercifully, it eased the crushing pain I felt when she first died . . . but it came at such a precious cost.

As the stars settled at the bottom of the globe, I let my mind wander to other worries. No matter how hard I tried, I couldn't get Anna's photographs out of my mind. They haunted me: Elliott, cleaning Lindy's ballgown. Elliott, holding Lindy's hand. Elliott, whispering sweet nothings into Lindy's ear.

We'd been neighbors and friends for so long, how could I possibly believe that he'd developed feelings for *me*? Short, freckled *me*? And how could I be so stupid as to fall for his crap . . . saying he didn't like Lindy, when all this time, he did. He'd probably been telling me that just so I'd help him in AP Biology. And he'd probably only asked me to Homecoming because his best friend went with my best friend. Ugh. Maybe he'd just asked me to try and make Lindy jealous.

My heart shattered thinking about the possibilities.

Nugget kneaded the comforter by my feet, turned in two circles, and finally curled into a ball. Wolfie bounded up the steps, then back and forth through the hall outside my door.

"HAS ANYONE SEEN NUGGET?" His shout pierced the walls.

"WOLFIE! Don't YELL!" Dad yelled.

Oh, the irony.

I scratched between Nugget's ears. "Don't worry," I whispered. "I won't tell."

"NUHHHHH-GET? Where AAARRRRE YOOOUUU?" My door flew open and a massive smile split Wolfie's face. "Nugget!"

"Wolfie, please don't move him," I begged. "He's happy."

Wolfie flopped on his belly across the bottom of my bed with his face about an inch from Nugget's.

"Aren't you the cutest thing ever? Aren't you just the sweetest little thing?" He cooed like a mother to her newborn baby. Nugget's ears pointed back.

"He's not happy, Wolfie." My brother crawled up next to me.

"Can I hold your snow globe?"

"Not right now, no," I said.

"You wanna watch something with me? Mr. A Game just released a new Mail Time. Or have you seen the video where Mr. Beast buries himself? Wanna watch that with me?"

A massive breath escaped my lungs, and I dug the heel of my hand into the spot above my left eye. "My head really hurts, Wolfie. I don't want to watch anything."

"We don't have to watch that. We could watch something else! Let's watch funny cat videos. Or funny test answers! Or we could—"

"Wolfie, STOP! Will you just SHUT UP already? I don't feel well!"

The sudden admission took me by surprise. Tears welled in my eyes, and I squeezed my head. Wolfie scrunched his face.

"I'm sorry," I said. "I didn't mean to snap."

Wolfie patted my hand, kissed Nugget on the top of the head, and ran out the door.

Great. Things were completely weird with my friends, I was lab partners with someone who liked my mortal enemy, my father and I had an invisible wall between us, and now I'd trampled my brother's feelings.

Nugget leapt off the bed.

"Figures," I muttered.

I wrapped the snow globe in Mom's old *Wicked* shirt, slid the box back under my bed, and sat down at my desk with my journal. For a moment, I thought about going to see if Angela was around . . . but it was Thursday, and we hadn't agreed to meet that night. Besides, my head ached. A trip *anywhere* sounded painful. I flipped open the journal and stared at the empty page.

I hadn't written to Mom in ages.

I poised my pen over the paper and thought.

Hi Mom,

Feeling pretty alone these days. I mean, I'm surrounded by people . . . but no one understands what I'm going through. Except maybe Angela. She's this girl I met by the willow. But I can't see her tonight. I feel horrible.

I massaged my temples.

I have to miss Halloween, and everything seems to be falling apart. Emilia and Anna don't ever want to be with me. I thought Elliott liked me, but he doesn't. Dad and Wolfie and I fight all the time.

My head is killing me, Mom. I'm hungry, but food never sounds good. The doctor is going to look at my stomach more closely tomorrow. He's going to give me medicine to make me sleep and do a scope, with a camera down my throat.

I don't want a camera down my throat. Even if it is tiny.

I don't know how to explain it, but I know this isn't the right problem. I know the doctors are wrong. They're missing something with me, just like they missed something with you. Can you please watch over me? And can you please help me figure out what's really causing all these problems?

Please, Mom . . . help me find my reasons.

Love,

Twyla

As I set my pen down, my phone dinged, alerting me to a new text. I glanced at the screen.

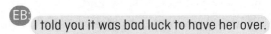

Confusion etched itself across my face. Emilia was texting on a thread with me and Anna. But . . . was she talking about me?

Ding.

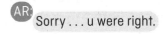

My mouth went dry as I stared at the phone.

Pop! Pop!

The texts suddenly disappeared, followed by two quick automated messages.

Emilia Bernard unsent a message

My stomach sank. They were. They were talking about me.

As quickly as the sadness struck, anger took over. So . . . this nausea. The headaches. All my symptoms—my best friends thought they were my fault? That I was bringing them on . . . *myself*? And if they thought I was bad luck, then what? Did they think I was going to rub off on them? Start causing problems for them too?

Was *this* their idea of friendship?

For one hot, angry moment, I thought about writing something to let them know that I'd seen their messages. To let them know that there was no unsending something that had already done damage.

But why? Did it really matter? By now, it was glaringly obvious that they'd moved on. Emilia. Anna. Even Elliott.

My shoulders slumped. Could I really blame them? If I was in their shoes, would I want to be around someone like me? Someone who was nothing more than a burden to shoulder? I weighed down sleepovers and Homecoming dances. Movie nights . . . even puzzles.

No wonder Emilia was wearing a charm to protect herself. It wouldn't shock me if Anna showed up with one too.

Maybe they were both right. Maybe I *was* cursed.

I closed the journal and rested my head on my folded hands, fighting tears. The bedroom door creaked. I turned to see Wolfie tiptoeing toward me with a cold washcloth and a glass of water.

"Here," he said.

I tilted my head, took the glass, and sipped. Then I frowned at the cold cloth.

"Why did you . . . ?"

Wolfie walked back to my door. "You said your head hurts, right?"

"Yeah," I said.

He shrugged. "Well, then . . . there's a cold washcloth. That's what Mom would've done, right?" Then he disappeared into the hall.

I stared at the doorway, where my brother had stood just a moment before. He'd been too young to remember that she would've brought a cold washcloth to ease a hurting head. How had he . . .

Wiping tears on my sleeve, I crawled into bed and let the cool cloth fall across my forehead.

I still didn't know my reasons.

But at least I knew she'd heard me.

Chapter 36
MISSING EVERYTHING

"Do you have any other questions before we take her back?"

The doctor towered over me while the walls breathed in and out like they were filled with liquid. I stared at the bandage on my arm, hiding the tube that entered my vein. I looked like a mummy.

Maybe I *was* a mummy.

"How long will the procedure take?" Dad asked.

"No longer than an hour, but you can follow along with our progress if you downloaded the app on your phone. And if you didn't, you'll still see screens in the waiting room. Did they give you a card with a number on it at registration?"

I touched my face while they talked. It felt like it belonged to someone else. I giggled.

Dad frantically fished through his pockets, finally plucking out a wrinkled card. He squinted at it, then held it up so the doctor could see it.

"Is this it?" Dad asked.

"Yes," she said. "See that number right there? You can track her progress next to that number on the LED screens in the waiting room. When she's done, they'll notify you. Did you or your wife give a phone number to the nurse?"

Your wife? Did she say *your wife*?

Mom. They meant my mom.

The lights on the ceiling blurred, like stars in the night sky. Suddenly, I was crying, and the lights twinkled.

204

Twinkling, leaky stars.

"My wife passed away years ago," I heard Dad say.

So much sadness. Sadness in my throat, in my belly, in my head. Inescapable, deep fingers of sadness, roping me in.

Sobs.

"Can you give her something else to calm her, please?" Now Dad's sadness, seeping into my ears.

Shuffling. People dressed in scrubs, in and out.

Dad's eyes. Teary eyes.

Beeeeeep.

Stars. Lots of stars.

Darkness.

Quiet.

• • •

My head lolled from side to side, a seat belt digging uncomfortably into my neck. I forced my eyes open and tried to make sense of the world whirring by. The leaves were so pretty, but this spinning felt so wrong. Like I was in the teacup ride at an amusement park, spinning round and round among the maples and oaks, yet somehow also on a roller coaster racing straight ahead.

A teacup roller coaster.

I frowned.

A tissue flew from the driver's seat to the passenger seat. A crumpled, used tissue. I wiped drool from my chin with the back of my hand.

And there, there was another one. By my feet. It was wet.

A low, quiet sob squeezed my heart. But . . . but it wasn't my sob.

It was Dad's.

I focused on the side of his face, trying to make sense of the noises . . . like tired moans of a storm, seeping through cracks of a windowsill. My eyes trailed up to the top half of Dad's face. Wrinkled and wet, like the tissue.

"Daaahhhd?" My voice sounded small.

Dad jumped and wiped his eyes with his sleeve. He kept his gaze forward, but reached his hand over, trying to find my knee, or hand, or some physical proof that I was there. I slid my fingers through his. And that's when I remembered.

The scope. The camera.

I pulled my fingers away and wiggled them in front of my face.

"Hey, Twilight," Dad sniffed. "They gave you an injection through the scope, into the muscle between your stomach and your intestines. It should help that stay open for a while, to help you digest food. They said you should feel better soon. Isn't that great?"

"Yah. Gweat," I slurred.

"And we should get the biopsy results soon, but they didn't see anything really wrong. He said you should be feeling better in no time. Did you hear that part, Twy? Isn't that great?"

"Yah. Gweat," I repeated.

The car kept bumping along the road until finally, we pulled into a road that looked familiar.

My road.

Ms. Givens came out of my house. Why was Ms. Givens in my house?

"Can I help, Dustin?"

"Yeah . . . she's pretty out of it. Can you help her to bed?"

"Mario time . . . oh yeah!" Wolfie burst from the garage. But he didn't look like Wolfie. He wore blue overalls and a red shirt. The red cap on his head had a big *M* on it.

"Wolfie, can you please go back inside? Your sister needs help right now."

"Looks like Mario's gonna have to find a job!" Wolfie bounced around like a kangaroo.

"You want a job, Wolfie? Please carry this bag inside."

"Woo-hoo! I'm-a ready for anything!"

As Wolfie grabbed the bag and bounced up the stairs, I remembered more than just the scope and the camera.

I remembered Halloween.

I was missing Halloscream.

I was missing mazes. And haunted houses. And candy. While my friends were out doing all the things I wanted to be doing . . . while they were out having all the fun . . . I was missing everything.

But was I? Did they even want me there? Was I really missing anything at all?

Were any of them really even my friends?

And as my dad carried me up the stairs to my room, I couldn't help but wonder:

Would anything ever feel "normal" again?

DEFECTIVE

"Fruit flies? Who cares about *fruit flies?"* Lindy snorted, then spun Samantha's paper off the table as I walked by.

I halted. Samantha shifted her weight in her chair and leaned down to pick up the paper, now on the floor by Lindy's feet. I touched Samantha's shoulder, stopping her.

"Lindy, I think you accidentally dropped Samantha's paper on the floor," I said. My voice held the unnatural calm of a hurricane's eye.

Lindy's jaw set and our eyes locked. I imagined Hamilton and Burr, and all the emotions they must've felt in those moments before their duel. The bitterness. The resentment. I didn't even know why she felt that way about me, but that's what flashed in her eyes.

And it sure as heck was in my eyes too.

"Lindy, just pick up the paper." Elliott appeared out of nowhere, stepping between us. Into the line of fire.

She snagged the paper with two fingers, wrinkling it just enough to make a statement, and pushed it toward Samantha.

I faced Elliott, my hands still clenched.

"Thanks, but I don't need saving," I hissed.

"All right, everybody, settle down." Ms. Givens whistled extra loud, cutting the tension in the room. Elliott sped up so he could walk beside me.

"Hey, are you okay?" Elliott whispered. "I'm glad you're back." We slid into our seats.

"I'm fine," I said.

"How did the test go? I was worried . . ."

"Elliott Givens. Do you mind socializing on your own time, please?" Ms. Givens scowled at her son. Lindy flipped her hair over her shoulder, then smirked at me.

Ugh.

Elliott slumped in his chair and shook his bangs over his eyes.

"You will see papers on the table in front of you about fruit flies," Ms. Givens said. "Today, I want you to work with your partner on an extra credit pop quiz."

Double ugh.

She continued. "Discuss the five written questions, debate between yourselves, and decide on your answers together. You have ten minutes. Go!" Even though we were in the classroom, Ms. Givens always sort of sounded like she was coaching our team.

I squinted at my paper, but every time I tried to focus on one fly, another would blur. I'd hoped I'd feel better after the scope, but so far, no luck. Everything just felt . . . off. It was almost like the anesthesia was still in my system, but I wasn't giggly anymore.

"So . . . ummm . . . which set of fruit flies are the lucky parents to this offspring?" Elliott grinned his lopsided grin. I leaned back in my chair.

"Should we give him a name? Like Zeus?" he asked. I kicked the table's leg.

"Twy . . . I know you're good at this stuff, but I'm really bad at it." Elliott's voice began to sound slightly panicked. "Help? Please? We're a team."

As much as I didn't want to help him, I also didn't want to fail. I lifted the paper to my face, squinting. "Well," I said, "the offspring has . . . white eyes, so that would rule out . . . I mean . . ."

But the harder I focused, the more the paper blurred. The more it blurred, the more my head hurt. And the more my head hurt, the worse my nausea became.

"I think the answer is . . . Parents C," I mumbled. "Just put Parents C."

Slowly, Elliott circled *C*. "Should we . . . talk about why you think C is the right answer?" he asked.

I rubbed my eyes. "I really don't feel like talking," I said. I shifted uncomfortably under Elliott's stare. Silently, I pleaded with him not to ask me anything else while I picked at my eraser.

"Okay. Parents C," he said.

The next four questions went exactly the same way. My stomach churned and my head pounded. More than anything, I just wanted to be done with the whole thing. We finished the quiz with three awkward minutes to spare.

I put my head down on the desk.

"So . . . what are you guys doing for Thanksgiving?" Elliott asked.

I sighed. Truth was, I didn't even want to celebrate Thanksgiving this year. The idea of turkey, mashed potatoes, or even pumpkin pie made me want to puke. And in the past, Emilia, Anna, and I would get together for a Saturday-after-Thanksgiving sleepover, where we'd spend the whole day in pajamas, eating leftovers, watching holiday specials, and giving one another mani-pedis. But none of that was going to happen this year. The girls had been waiting for me by my locker that morning, but the air had been thick with tension. Surely, they were looking for me to give them some sign as to whether or not I'd read their texts. But I'd given them nothing.

I was just . . . done.

"Twy? Umm . . . Thanksgiving?" Suddenly, I realized Elliott was still staring at me.

"Oh. Nothing," I said. "We're doing nothing."

"Yeah," he mumbled. "Same."

"Okay, students. You're on the honor system now for grading, okay? The answers to your quiz are B, C, C, A, D." The bell rang and Ms. Givens raised her volume.

"Write your names on the top and put it on my desk. Oh, and our first indoor field hockey game is tomorrow! Come on out and support your Dragons!"

Two right. We'd gotten two out of five right.

Serves him right, I thought. *Using me just for a grade.*

I grabbed my belongings and stuffed everything in my backpack. In my haste, I didn't even zip it closed. Which sucked.

Because on my way out of the room, I crashed into Lindy, scattering books everywhere.

"You defective klutz!" Lindy shrieked. "Can't you watch where you're going? What is the matter with you? Didn't your mother ever teach you to walk?" She thrust her face toward mine.

"Oh, that's right," she hissed. "You don't have a mother, do you?"

I bolted for the door, leaving my books behind. Ms. Givens reprimanded Lindy and Elliott called after me, but I didn't look back. The tears had already begun to flow.

I *had* lost my mother. Things were horrible with my best friends and with Elliott. Dad refused to listen to me. And now, my grades were starting to suffer.

Maybe Lindy was right.

Maybe I was defective.

Chapter 38

FLIPPING TURTLES

"Did you know that I can make myself yawn whenever I want to? Look!" Wolfie's mouth gaped at me for several seconds, until a yawn finally escaped. "Isn't that kind of a talent? Can you do that?"

Wolfie sank his teeth into what was left of his lunch, sending crumbs and bits of peanut butter flying all over the car. I was grateful Dad was able to pick us up from school today, but I wasn't so sure Wolfie's food-spit shower was a price worth paying.

"Look at what I've done—I've done some damage! I'm gonna kill this guy and it doesn't even care, because it's just a sandwich. Mmmmmmm . . ."

The whole world could blow up, and Wolfie would still be talking to himself.

"Wolfie, what are you eating?" Dad's voice had no inflection, like one of those bad actors in car commercials.

"My LU-UNCH!" Wolfie sang.

"Well, it's almost dinner, so just . . . don't. Okay?" Dad sounded as irritated as I felt.

"Hey, you know there's a myth that girls don't fart? Twyla could *kill* that myth." Wolfie laughed at me open-mouthed, sandwich pieces still wedged between his teeth.

"Wolfie, what's with you and all the killing?" I snapped. "And don't talk with food in your mouth. It's disgusting."

"Oh, you know what's disgusting? A bunch of species of horned lizards can squirt blood from their *eyeballs!* They can even

212

aim it at predators! Can you imagine? *Shrroom! Shrroom! Shrroom!*"
Wolfie's fingers burst from his eyes toward everything in the car.
I tuned him out and leaned against the headrest, eyes closed, until
we finally stopped moving.

"Gonna go walking. Bye." I jumped out of the car and expected
Dad to protest, but he didn't. So I crossed the backyard in search
of stillness.

Sometimes, when a canopy of colorful November leaves still
shrouded the Kentucky sky, warm air would hug you as if to say,
"I'm autumn, and I'm still here. Appreciate me. Love me."

But sometimes, on days like today, an ocean of limp, lifeless
leaves squished under your feet. Thousands of naked branches
clicked together overhead, tangled fingers against the fall sky, while
blasts of cold breathed, "I'm winter, and I'm coming for you."

Although my eyes scanned a canopy of colorful leaves and the
air wasn't crisp, my heart still felt a warning. I shivered.

The wind carried a whisper to my ears as I neared the willow.

"You can do it, little guy. Come on. You can do it."

I picked up my pace until Angela's crouched outline appeared
at the bottom of the willow's hill. Sophie sat motionless beside her,
transfixed by four frantic turtle legs kicking the air. I jogged to her
side and reached out to flip the turtle back over. Angela held out
her hand.

"No," she said. "Wait."

I pulled back and sat quietly next to her, so as not to scare the
turtle. Together, we watched him stretch his neck one way, then
the other, squirming for freedom like a worm on a fishhook. I
wondered if Angela might be crazy for letting the poor guy suffer. For five, ten, fifteen minutes, we sat in silence. I thought he'd
exhausted every rock, every stick, every pebble that might help
him, until, finally, determination flipped him back over. As if he
hadn't a care in the world, he ambled off. Soon, the creek—and the
tumble—were left far behind. I shook my head.

"I had no idea they could really do that!" I said. "I mean, I'd read that it was possible . . . but I'd never seen it happen before. That's incredible!"

Angela picked at the edges of an old, dry leaf and flicked fragments into the water. Sophie chased after them. The creek carried some of the pieces away, but others stuck to rocks, protruding just above the surface.

"It's amazing, really, what turtles can do when they stretch their necks out," she said. "We might think they're stuck forever, but if you give them enough time . . . boom. They flip themselves over and keep on going."

We watched the creek pass as I processed Angela's perspective. I wouldn't have believed it if I hadn't seen it for myself.

A dead branch popped like a firecracker, somewhere just beyond the top of the hill. It sounded too big for a squirrel or a raccoon.

"Be right back," I said. I hopped to my feet and ran up the hill.

Hands in his pockets, Elliott kicked at the dirt near Zeeno's snagged tree. He turned rocks over with his feet. "Hey, Twyla," he said. "I thought you might be out here."

I sighed. Only a few days ago, I would've welcomed the opportunity to introduce Elliott to Angela. But I hadn't had a chance to tell her that I'd been wrong about him yet. What was I supposed to say? *Angela, meet Elliott, the guy I went to Homecoming with, who actually likes that girl who you said looks like a bulldog chewing a wasp.*

Yeah. No.

"Can I . . . join you?" Elliott asked. There was no way around it without being a total jerk.

"I guess," I managed. "We were just hanging out."

Elliott searched the woods over my shoulder.

"We?" he asked. "You and . . . the dog?"

I turned back toward the creek, but all I could see was Sophie's wagging tail bounding off in the distance.

Great. Now Angela had left me too. I blew at my bangs in frustration.

"Listen, Twyla," Elliott said. "I just wanted to say I'm sorry I wasn't any help on the quiz today. I actually asked my mom if she'd help me study. I don't blame you for not wanting to give me the answers, and I won't put you in that position again."

He drew circles in the debris with a stick.

"That, and I put your books on your back porch. The ones you dropped. In class."

I picked up a flat rock and released it at an angle across the water. It skipped only three times before it sank.

Crap.

"Did I . . . *do* something?" he asked.

I spun on him, seething, searching his face to understand how he could even ask that question.

"I don't know, Elliott. Did you?"

He fell back, stunned. Silent.

"I mean, it's not like you *owed* me anything, right? We're in high school now." I prattled on, picking up another flat stone. "You're a big boy. You're free to like who you want. If you want to like Lindy, that's *your* business . . ."

Elliott grabbed my wrist just as I was about to release another rock over the water. "Whoa—wait a minute. What the heck are you talking about?"

I yanked my wrist from his grip and whipped the rock at a tree. "I'm talking about the picture I saw at Anna's house. The one of you cleaning Lindy's dress, and the one of you holding her hand, whispering into her ear, while I was in the bathroom sick as a dog. That's what I'm talking about."

Elliott searched my face with soft, confused eyes.

Soft, confused, *blue-green* eyes.

"Twyla—" He rested his hand on my shoulder. "Do you really think I like *Lindy*?"

I shrugged his hand off and bent down to grab another rock. For some reason, his question made me feel stupid.

"You're allowed to like whoever you want," I said, sounding more like a toddler than I wanted to.

Elliott took the rock from my hand and tossed it toward the creek. "Yeah," he said. "I am."

The honesty in tone startled me. We locked eyes.

"But I *don't* like Lindy," he whispered.

A bird chattered in the distance, and an unseasonably warm wind whipped my ponytail. Elliott grinned his lopsided grin, leaning forward to pick a leaf out of my hair.

"Are you, umm, staying here? Or maybe . . . do you wanna . . ." He jerked his head back in the direction of our houses. "Walk back with me?"

I scanned the area once more. Angela and Sophie were gone. Sheepishly, I bit my lip.

"Okay," I said.

But Elliott didn't move. He just stood, feet planted, searching my face.

"Are we?" he asked. "Okay?"

I nodded, wondering when I'd become so stupid.

Side by side, we headed home. The oranges, golds, and reds overhead reflected beams of sunlight that shone between the trees like spotlights from heaven. As we hiked between two large oaks, our hands brushed together, making my skin tingle.

And I wondered . . . what else might I be getting wrong?

Chapter 39

GONE

"Wolfie! Where are your shoes? Did you seriously get in the car without *shoes*? I can't even . . . Twyla, I'm going to have to drop you at the door." Dad smacked the Unlock button and banged the back of his head against the headrest.

"Did you want to do our handshake . . . ?"

"Do you want to be late for the game?" Dad swung around to face me. I knew he *wasn't* mad at me. But he *looked* mad at me.

I shook my head and glared at my brother who, for once, seemed to know better than to open his mouth.

"Then GO! I need to go *all the way* back home for a pair of *shoes*, for God's sake. We'll see you when we see you." He waved me off.

As soon as Dad sped away, I stormed into the facility. Moving at the speed of *GRRRR*, I rounded a corner . . . and collided with Mama Rose. My bag clanked as I tumbled to the ground.

How many people was I going to walk into this week?

"Twyla! Oh, sweetie! Are you okay?" Mama Rose stretched a hand toward me and pulled me to my feet, bracing one elbow as I stood. I pressed the heel of my palm against my left eye.

"I'm fine," I said. "How are you?"

But Mama Rose wasn't having it with my deflection.

"Your head still hurts, doesn't it?" she asked. Concern etched itself across her face.

I sighed. "I think I'm just tired, Mama Rose. I didn't sleep

217

very well last night. I'm sure I'll feel better when I get a good night's rest."

"Why didn't you sleep well?" she pressed.

"Oh. The headache, I guess."

"The headache woke you?" she asked.

I nodded. "Do you mind calling my dad for me? Wolfie forgot his shoes at home. Maybe Dad can grab some Tylenol while he's there."

"Sure. I'll call him now. Anna is . . ." Mama Rose glanced around, finally pointing to the visitor's bench beside the field. "Over there. With Emilia." She picked up my bag and handed it to me. "How's the nausea?" she asked.

I shrugged. "I'm sure it'll get better soon. They did say it can take a few weeks after the scope." I waved to her over my shoulder. "Thanks for calling my dad, Mama Rose."

Emilia saw me coming first. She kissed her thunderbird before she tucked it back into her shirt.

I walked past her to the bench.

"Hi, Twyla?" Anna's greeting sounded more like a question. I nodded at her.

"Did your dad bring you? I don't see him," she said. I knew she was trying to make small talk, but I wasn't feeling it.

"Wolfie forgot his shoes, so he had to go back home." I glanced across the field and spotted Mama Rose on the phone.

Good. She'd reached him.

I lifted my foot to the bench to retie a loose shoe.

"Wait." Emilia held her hand out. "You *did* do the handshake with him before this game, didn't you?"

I had to fight not to roll my eyes at her. "No," I said. "Actually, I didn't."

An invisible vise gripped my head.

Emilia gaped at me. "Well, did you at least rub your snow globe?"

"*Stop*, Emilia, will you just STOP with the superstitious crap?!"

Coach Givens blew her whistle, and Emilia and I stood cemented to the ground in a staring standoff. Finally, Anna reached out to hold both our hands.

"Guys. It's gonna be okay. You're gonna do great today, I know it . . ."

I jerked my arm away and joined the rest of the team, now huddled around Coach Givens. Eventually, Emilia joined the opposite side of the huddle.

Coach Givens listed her usual starters, including Lindy, Emilia, and me. Then she clapped and bent down with her hands on her knees as if she were about to tell us a secret.

"We've had a couple weeks off since the outdoor season ended. Is everyone rested and ready?" she whispered.

"Yes we are!" we murmured back. Coach stood taller.

"We've had a couple weeks off," she repeated, more firmly this time. "Is everyone rested and ready?"

"Yes, we are!" This time, the team's chorus rang louder.

"WE have HAD a COUPLE WEEKS OFF!" Now, Coach was bouncing on the balls of her feet. A smile lit up her face, and her goal became clear: inspiration. "Is EVERYONE RESTED and READY?" she shouted.

"YES, WE ARE!" Cheers echoed from our huddle bubble, and everyone scattered to take their positions. I avoided Emilia's eyes, squinting at the stands instead.

Mama Rose stood, hands on her hips, watching me like a hawk.

Surely, Dad would be back before halftime.

Surely, I could wait until then.

"Hey, Twyla . . ." Lindy's drawl raised the hairs on my arms. Her perfectly manicured fingernails tapped her perfectly tape-wrapped stick. "How do you know when an Irishman has a stomachache?"

I glared at her.

"He's Dublin over." She forced a big, fake laugh and I smacked the turf with my stick. I couldn't focus on Lindy or my stomach problems right now. I couldn't focus on Emilia or Anna. And I couldn't focus on the searing pain above my eye.

I needed to focus on playing well.

The whistle blew and we fell into familiar formations, dribbling, passing, and defending like a well-oiled machine. Unfortunately, so did the other team. For twenty heart-racing, head-pounding minutes, the ball traveled back and forth, with no team clearly on top. Then, with five minutes left in the half, a defender stole from Emilia and passed it to a girl posted right by our goal.

She shot.

Our goalie got the stop. I started to breathe a sigh of relief, but the ball bounced straight back out, in front of Erin, who passed it all the way down the field to me. I swung to pass ... but felt nothing but air. Suddenly, Lindy swooped by, taking off toward our opponent's goal. Her mother went nuts from the stands.

"THAT'S HOW YOU DO IT!" she screamed. "You TAKE THAT BALL! Take it down and SCORE!"

I didn't have time to think about what had happened. I tore down the field, ignoring the pain in my head. I posted by the goal and tried to out-yell Lindy's mother.

"I'M OPEN!"

Lindy, now double-teamed, glanced briefly at her mother, then at Coach Givens.

"Pass it!" Coach shouted.

"SHOOT IT!" her mother screamed.

With no other viable option, Lindy passed between a defender's legs . . . straight toward me.

I swung.

And missed.

Again.

I peeked at the sidelines as Lindy's mother growled and threw her hands into the air.

A defender began to run back toward our goal and Emilia fouled her. When the whistle blew, Lindy stormed toward me.

"You see?" she hissed. "THAT is why I don't pass to you."

Anger pulsed through my veins, stabbing my temples. Frustration shortened my breaths, and disgust flared my nose.

Enough. I had had enough.

"Why do you need to be the center of attention all the time, Lindy?" My voice started soft, controlled. But it didn't stay that way. "And why are you always so fricking mean? Does it make you feel powerful? Does it make you feel good to put everyone else down?"

Emilia sprinted toward us, arm outstretched to push me away from Lindy. But I couldn't stop myself.

"Do you really think being a horrible person somehow makes you BETTER than us? You know, if you weren't such a spoiled brat, MAYBE YOU'D ACTUALLY HAVE FRIENDS!"

Emilia threw her arm around my shoulder, forcing me to turn away. But not before I saw Lindy's lower lip quiver.

"Twyla, stop." Emilia said. I threw her arm off my shoulder and turned on her.

"Why? It's all true! You've said it too! You all . . . everyone . . ."

The air suddenly felt like it was three hundred degrees. Fuming, I stomped to the bench and threw my stick on the ground. Without stopping, I raced toward the restrooms. Lindy's mom's voice trumpeted in my ears like an angry elephant.

"Why HER, Lindy? Why did you pass to HER?"

The incandescent bathroom lighting struck like a punch to the gut. And . . . that smell. Was something burning? Was there a fire somewhere? I glanced under the stalls, then splashed cold water on my face.

"Twyla? Are you okay?"

Spinning. The room was spinning. I backed against a wall and slid to the floor.

"Twyla!"

My vision blurred. But that voice . . . I knew that voice . . .

"Angela?" I whispered.

Angela ran toward me and touched my forehead. "You're cold and clammy, Twyla. And your face . . . you're white as a ghost. Here. Lie down. I'll go get help."

She took off her coat and folded it into a square under my head. I closed my eyes as the pain, the nausea, and the burning all peaked at once.

Just breathe, I thought.

Breathe.

I squinted. There . . . there was Dad, running, running, running toward me, with Mama Rose. And then . . .

Spinning. So much spinning.

Darkness.

Gone.

Chapter 40
VERY, VERY WRONG

For a while, nothing made sense. So many faces peering down. Strangers in navy shirts with patches on their sleeves carrying boards and straps. Ceiling lights flying by.

Sirens.

The strangers counted to three and a sheet carried me to a bed, like a magic carpet. Someone held my hand, never letting go. Then Dad, beside me, in a van.

"Twyla, honey, can you hear me? We're going to the hospital in an ambulance." He wiped his runny nose with his sleeve.

"Angela?" I said.

"No, honey, *ambulance.* The *ambulance* is taking you to the hospital."

"No . . ." I struggled to make sense of the world around me. "Where's *Angela*?"

Dad's eyes drew together. "The girl who found you?" he asked. I nodded. Dad shook his head. "I'm not sure, Twy." Tears filled his eyes.

"What . . . what happened?" I asked.

"You had a seizure," he said, blinking away his fear. "Thank God Dr. Rose was there. She knew immediately what was happening."

The ambulance doors closed behind us, and a siren filled the air.

I'd heard his words. I understood them, even. But they made no sense. I closed my eyes and focused on the *bump, bump, bump* of the road below. I breathed deeply, inhaling the cool oxygen

223

mist from the mask over my mouth and nose. And then something clicked.

Seizure.

Did Mom have a seizure too?

I strained to remember what I'd eaten before the game, but the energy it took to focus stretched me too far . . . so I stopped trying. Dad's forehead now rested on my bed, his hand on my wrist. I flipped it over and let him lace his fingers through mine. When he lifted his head, my heart broke. His face looked exactly like it did at Mom's funeral, when he tried to speak . . . but couldn't. Stained with tears, splotched red with sadness. I squeezed his hand weakly. He looked so . . . helpless.

Like the upside-down turtles.

"It's okay, Daddy," I said. "I'm okay."

Dad's breath caught, and he smiled through his tears. "I know you are, baby," he said.

But I could tell he didn't know at all.

Truth was, I didn't know anymore, either.

The MRI machine looked like a really long donut, with a skinny table in the middle. The whole contraption was housed in a cold, bright room with a window facing another room, so the people running the test could see me. My hand throbbed where they'd stuck a tube in my vein. They said they'd be taking some pictures of my brain, then they'd inject dye into the tube, and then they'd take more pictures. They strapped me onto the table, then put big, squishy headphones over my ears and fastened my head inside some helmetlike thing. I'd been allowed to choose a movie to watch, so I picked *Pitch Perfect*—but I wasn't sure how I was going to see it while I was inside the big donut. A woman put a squeezy ball in my hand.

"If you squeeze this, it calls me, like a nine one one button. So if you get scared or need anything, this is your way of letting me know. I'll be able to hear you, but we'll have to stop the MRI if that happens. That means we'd have to redo that entire section of pictures. Do you understand?"

I couldn't nod with the strap tight across my forehead, so I gave her a thumbs-up.

"Are you cold?" she asked.

"A little," I said.

She motioned to a helper, who immediately left the room.

"There's a mirror on the ceiling in the machine," she said. She pointed and I lifted my eyes enough to see it. "Once you're inside, you'll see it better. You'll be able to watch the movie on the wall behind you, and your dad's in the chair right next to the screen, so you'll be able to see him too. The machine will make lots of clunking noises, but the movie in your headphones should help drown those out. Remember to stay very, very still, okay? If you move, we have to start that part over again. The whole thing should take about forty minutes."

The helper came back and fluffed a thin, warm blanket over my body. It felt like it had just come out of the dryer. I relaxed a little.

Forty minutes. I could do anything for forty minutes.

"The pictures will be taken in sections that are only a few minutes long each. Remember to squeeze that ball if you need me. I'll be back in to give you the dye a little more than halfway through. You ready?"

Another thumbs-up.

She pushed a button on the machine, and the table suddenly began sliding me into the donut. My heart raced as darkness closed in around me. I considered squeezing the ball almost immediately, but when the mirror came into view, I could see Dad in a chair, next to the projection screen on the wall. His smile calmed me. His face was no longer stained by tears. Our eyes locked, he winked, and peace filled my chest. Suddenly, the movie began, and the Treblemakers swept me away with "Please Don't Stop the Music."

For the first half of the movie, my breathing evened. Every time I glanced away from the screen and at Dad, his constant gaze reassured me. Never once was he looking away or doing something else. I couldn't hear him, or speak to him, but I felt him there with me. It was like we were in the machine together.

And then, just as the riff-off was about to begin with the Barden Bellas, Dad's head jerked up. I scanned his face for answers, but he blew me a kiss, mouthed the words, "See you soon," and left.

Again, I considered pushing the button. But if I did, I'd be prolonging the inevitable.

It's okay, I told myself. *You're okay. It's almost over.*

I closed my eyes and listened to the groups compete in the "Ladies of the 80s" category. As the Bellas sang, "Hit Me with Your Best Shot," I forced my shoulders to try and relax.

It didn't work.

The riff-off ended. Ten, twenty minutes passed. Despite the fact the blanket had lost its heat, my body now burned. My mind raced.

Where was he? Why had he left?

When was he coming back?

Finally, forever later, the MRI stopped knocking. I heard footsteps, and my table slid slowly, evenly, back out of the donut hole.

"You're all done," the woman said.

Something about her face seemed different. I let the ball drop to the side of the table. As she unbuckled the straps, I sat up and stepped to the floor.

"Where's my dad?" I asked.

"I'm gonna take you to him now." She smiled at me, but it looked like the kind of smile a teacher might give when telling you she was sure all those girls didn't mean to exclude you, they just forgot.

"Can you walk on your own?" she asked.

I nodded.

I followed her down a long hallway. We passed lots of dark rooms, and I wondered if this part of the hospital was always empty. Then we turned a corner toward a single bright room. Relief washed over me.

And then I saw them.

Dad. And Mama Rose. Both of them, crying. My stomach sank.

Something was wrong.

Very, very wrong.

Chapter 41

SHATTERED

My feet carried me backward . . . away from the room. Away from Dad. Away from Mama Rose.

Away. Away. Away.

"Twyla, please. Come here, honey. We need to talk." Dad's arms opened, like he was welcoming me home from a long trip.

Like he did when he came home after Mom's accident.

Panic drove my heart and tears burned my throat.

No. This wasn't happening.

"Why? Why do we need to talk, Dad?" The shrillness of my voice echoed through the empty halls, and Dad cupped his face. Tears spilled down his face.

"Mama Rose?" I begged. "What's wrong?"

But no one spoke. Just offered tears.

"WHAT IS WRONG WITH ME?" I yelled. "Just TELL ME! TELL ME NOW!" My breaths were quick, my eyes wild, like I was being chased by a murderous clown.

"Dustin?" Mama Rose's voice pushed my father gently, painfully, like she was encouraging him to jump off a cliff.

"I can't," Dad sobbed. "I . . . I can't."

Mama Rose stepped forward and bent down so we were eye to eye. "There is no way to make this easy, Twyla. You have a tumor. In your brain. Please come in the room, so we can talk."

A tumor? In my *brain*?

I shook my head.

"No," I whispered. "No, I don't. You're both wrong. I have an allergy . . . like Mom!"

Time suddenly felt meaningless. Like it was simultaneously rushing by and completely still. I could feel that something major was happening in that moment. Something huge, and life-changing. But it also felt like it wasn't happening to *me*.

It wasn't supposed to be happening to *me*.

I wanted to turn and run.

Far away from the hospital.

Back to my house.

Back

    to

        my

            willow.

Mama Rose walked into the room and swiveled a computer so I could see the screen.

"This is a cross section of your brain, Twyla. You see these two round things, at the top? Those are your eyes." She scrolled through the pictures, one by one, as images jumped by like animated brain slices. Once she'd scrolled past the eyeballs, a bright white circle appeared in the middle of a gray maze. I walked slowly . . . tentatively . . . toward the screen. At some point, I felt my father's presence behind me. He placed a hand on my shoulder.

I shrugged it off.

"Twyla, I know this is hard to hear," Dad whispered. Mama Rose nodded to him. His words caught in his throat. "It's . . . it's *so* hard for me to hear too. But you have a tumor in your hypothalamus . . ."

"No." My voice was soft, but firm. "No."

I was in a horror movie.

    This wasn't true.

        It couldn't be true.

Dad tried to wrap his arms around me, but I wrestled them off.

No, no, no, no, no.

Mama Rose knelt in front of me, but she didn't touch me. "Your hypothalamus affects so many things. Hormone production, appetite, thirst, mood, sleep, body temperature, nausea . . ."

My eyebrows drew together as my breaths grew shallow. Nausea . . . vomiting . . . the feeling that the room was so hot . . .

"The seizure." My voice shook. "Could a tumor cause a seizure?"

Mama Rose nodded. Her eyes were sad.

So sad.

"And gastroparesis?"

Nod.

I thought about all the times the ball had disappeared right in front of me. All the people I'd bumped into.

"What about vision? Could it affect vision?"

"The tumor is sitting on your optic nerve, right here." Mama Rose pointed to a spot on the screen. "So, yes . . . I'm afraid it could."

Suddenly, the word struck me like lightning, over and over and over again.

Tumor.

Tumor.

Tumor.

Tumor.

Tumor.

It was like I was watching the world blow up through a window of a room, locked from the inside. I couldn't run, and I couldn't take cover. My stomach churned as reality sank in.

I faced my father.

"Dad . . . do I have cancer?"

Tears rolled down my father's cheeks as his mouth opened, but no sound came out. I looked to Mama Rose and raised my voice.

"Do. I. Have. CANCER?"

Mama Rose bit her lip, just like Anna always did. "We don't know yet, honey. We'll immediately need to admit you to run some tests, and then you'll need a biopsy first thing Monday . . ."

"A . . . biopsy?" I glanced back at my father. "Dad? Will they have to go into *my brain*?"

Dad nodded, pain contorting his face. Again, he opened his arms. Again, I backed away.

Breaths came fast and hard.

"Can I scream?" I asked.

Dad didn't look to Mama Rose this time. "Yes," he said.

A strange, high-pitched sound escaped from my chest. Like an injured animal, or a lost child. Like the tires that squealed when Felix was hit.

"Can I throw my shoe?"

Tear streaks stained my father's face. He nodded.

I grasped my shoe in my fist and wound back. I tried to scream again, this time reaching down my throat to dig deep into my gut, grabbing all the pain, all the hurt, all the fear, all the questions, all the unknowns that had been beating me down, unanswerable, for so many months. I tried to pull them all up and throw them away with my shoe, as hard and as far as I could throw them. I wanted my shoe to shatter the glass wall into a billion tiny pieces. I wanted it to break for me.

I wanted it to break *like* me.

But my shoe just thunked against the glass and fell to the floor.

Still.

Alone.

My hand wiped a single tear from my cheek.

"We need to admit her now, Dustin," Mama Rose said.

As we left the room behind, the room where my life upended, nothing felt real.

Not the walk back down the hallway.

Not the elevator ride to the ER.

Not the sad-eyed nurse who gave me a teddy bear wearing a cancer ribbon.

Not the quiet receptionist who gave my father her charger for his almost-dead phone.

Nothing.

In the ER, a man about Dad's age with Harry Potter glasses and a bow tie introduced himself as a neurosurgeon. He talked with Mama Rose and Dad, but all the words sludged together like old, dead leaves on the forest floor. Strangers chattered as they passed our room, not knowing that for me, at that moment, everything was changing.

Everything was crumbling.

A cold winter, arriving too soon.

Eventually, I was taken to a private room on the fifth floor, in a wing marked Hematology and Oncology. Dad settled into a corner chair to fill out paperwork. I couldn't tell if a day or an hour had passed. Outside, rain pelted my window as a storm brewed. I thought about the people in the passing cars. Where they might be going. If there were family members fighting or telling jokes. If they'd seen a movie recently. What they'd eaten for dinner.

Maybe somebody had just won the lottery.

Maybe somebody had just had a baby.

Maybe somebody had just lost their mother.

I buried my face in the teddy bear's soft fur and rocked, rocked, rocked.

"Twyla?"

Wolfie. My head popped up. Coach Givens stood at the door, and my father pushed himself out of his chair. "Be right back," he said.

"Okay."

Wolfie cradled a bag in his hands like he was holding a billion dollars in diamonds. He inched into the room, still standing close to the wall.

A world away from me.

"Did you know that Jimmy Carter was the first president to ever be born in a hospital?" he asked. His voice was soft. His eyes, scared.

I turned away, looking back out the window.

"Okay," he breathed. He sounded like he might cry, but this time, I couldn't be strong for him.

"I'm sorry," he said. "Sometimes I try, but I do the wrong thing. But . . . but I brought you something to cheer you up!" I turned back toward Wolfie, who reached into his bag and pulled out a bundle. He smiled and suddenly bolted toward me, offering the treasure in his outstretched hands. As if in slow motion, his toe caught on a cord, lurching his body forward. The bundle in his arms unrolled in mid-air, revealing a word.

A word on a shirt.

Wicked.

"WOLFIE! WAAAAAIT!"

My precious snow globe flew through the air and tumbled toward the floor, where it crashed into bits.

Shattered.

Silver stars lay motionless, scattered across the floor of my hospital room. A silver plate skidded to a stop in front of me. I picked it up and ran my fingers over the engraving.

Godspeed, Little Twyla

No.

No.

NO.

I could save it. I could save it all. I *needed* to save it all. The plate, the stars, the box, the glass, the moon . . . every last piece. Frantic, I began sweeping broken pieces into my hands while Wolfie looked on in horror, pleading with me to stop.

"Twyla, don't! You'll cut yourself . . ."

But even as he spoke, my hands began to bleed, and I realized.

It was hopeless.

I could not save it.

I could not fix it.

Any of it.

"Out," I hissed through gritted teeth. "Get OUT OF MY ROOM!"

As my door closed behind Wolfie, the sounds of his sadness carried through. But I didn't have room for his pain. Not now.

Maybe, not ever.

Everything did *not* happen for a reason. There was no reason for my snow globe to break. For this tumor. For Mom to die. For Felix losing his leg. For my friends to abandon me.

For any of it.

As I lay on my bed and soaked my pillow with tears, my heart broke. All this time, I'd believed her.

My heart shattered like the snow globe as reality sank in.

Mom was wrong.

She'd always been wrong.

Sometimes, there was no reason at all.

Chapter 42

UPSIDE DOWN

I must've fallen asleep, because when I opened my eyes again, the floor was spotless. At first, I'd been confused as to where I was. But when I saw Dad sleeping on the couch by the window, everything came flooding back. The seizure. The MRI. The tumor.

The snow globe.

I slipped out of bed and tiptoed to the garbage can. First, I looked in the can by the sink, but it was empty. When I spied another through the bathroom door, my heart filled with hope . . . but that one was empty too. No glass. No moon. No stars.

Nothing.

Of course it was gone. It wasn't like a hospital would leave broken glass all over the floor. They'd swept away all my memories without a second thought.

I caught my reflection in the bathroom mirror. Heavy, swollen eyes reflected my mood. When I came out, Dad was sitting up, scanning the room. He jumped when he saw me.

"There you are, Twilight. You scared me for a minute." He patted the couch cushion, so I joined him. He sighed and rubbed the spot on his nose between his eyes.

"Twy . . . why did you think Mom had an allergy?" Dad's voice wasn't accusatory or harsh. It was more like a gentle massage on a sore muscle.

For a flash, I considered lying to him. But his gaze said, *It's okay. I won't be mad.*

Level with me.

So I did. I told him about the genetics class, and my trip to the attic. The box with the photos, and the medical records. My realization that nausea always seemed to strike after I'd had nuts, and that I'd been keeping a food log as a result. And finally, the link I'd made between my symptoms and that word on the autopsy report.

Anaphylaxis.

Dad folded my hands into his. "Twyla, honey, that autopsy report didn't confirm that she died from anaphylaxis. It just talked about some of the inflammatory changes they saw. It listed possible reasons why those *might've* been there.

"The truth is, Twyla, your mother also had asthma. It had always been mild, but who knows? Maybe . . ."

Dad's breaths caught. He smiled weakly before continuing.

"The night of the accident, your mother called me before she left the office. She said she wasn't feeling great, but we both thought she was just tired from working an extra-long day, or maybe she was starting to get sick. Now, of course, I can't help but wonder about everything. If her asthma had been acting up, maybe she had an attack on the way home. If maybe . . . maybe, if I'd done something different, insisted she wait until I pick her up . . ."

Tears now streaked my father's face, contorted in pain. I released his hands and crawled into his lap, wrapping my arms around his neck like I used to do when I was little.

"It's not your fault," I whispered.

For several minutes, we sat together, crying, sharing our sadness, until finally Dad leaned his tired forehead against mine.

"Sometimes, I think it's natural for us to want to blame ourselves. To try to make sense of things we don't understand."

"I thought *I* understood," I said.

Dad turned his hand up, palm to the ceiling. He wiggled his fingers.

"Can I hold your hand?" he asked. I laced my fingers through his, and Dad rubbed the back of my hand with his thumb. He drew a deep breath.

"Mama Rose did some allergy testing when they drew your blood."

I searched Dad's face for answers. Were they wrong about the tumor?

Had I been right the whole time?

"You're not allergic to nuts, Twilight. Some mild allergies to dust mites, grass, a few trees . . . but no nuts. No foods at all, really."

My heart stopped. No nut allergies.

So this was all the tumor.

Was it something *anyone* could fix?

"Can they take it out, Dad?"

Dad's eyes again filled with tears.

"A piece of it, maybe? Dr. Rose said it looks like a slow-growing, low-grade mass, called a glioma. But they won't know for sure until the biopsy results come back. You'll need—"

Dad's voice broke and he inhaled deeply, slowly, before he could continue.

"You'll need chemo to keep it from growing more. The goal is to take out as much as we can now, stop the rest, and get you through treatment so you can live a long, happy life."

"Chemo?" My spine straightened. Dad squeezed his arms around me.

"I know. It scares me too," he said.

"For how long? Will it make me sick? Am I . . ." Suddenly, all I could see in my mind's eye were the tiny, bald children in the St. Jude's ads on television. I wanted to vomit.

"Am I going to lose my hair?"

Dad nodded, visibly heartbroken.

"Probably. Your treatment will take about eighteen months

total. And we have no idea how it'll make you feel. They say all kids respond differently." Dad didn't bother to wipe away his tears anymore. "I wish I had *all* the answers for you."

Uncertainty clouded my mind. In twenty-four hours, everything I thought I'd known was proving to be false. How could I have been so wrong about so much?

For a long while, we embraced the silence around us. I leaned my head against Dad's shoulder, breathing in the smell of his shampoo, wishing we could just stay that way forever. Eventually, he spoke.

"I've been distant, Twyla. I don't think I recognized it . . . or at least I didn't really understand why, until now. When you started feeling sick, it just triggered so many worries. I didn't want anything else in our life to spiral out of control. When we lost Mom . . ."

Dad sniffed. I hugged him.

"I don't think I've fully recovered from that. I'm not sure I ever will. But I don't think I was ready to deal with another tragedy, and that was selfish of me. I'm so sorry, Twilight." Dad pulled away just enough to look directly into my eyes. "I will always be here for you. I will never, ever abandon you. I want you to be able to come talk to me when you're scared. I want you to trust me . . . which means I have to be trustworthy. So I promise to try harder. I promise not to shut down or close myself off when things get scary. No matter what. We will get through this together, okay?"

A lump burned my throat. I nodded.

"Oh . . ." Dad leaned back against the couch and smiled. "Your friends have been calling to check on you. They'd all like to visit before surgery. Is that okay?"

My stomach dropped as I thought about my last interaction with Emilia and Anna. I knew I shouldn't have been so short with them.

I also knew silence wouldn't help anything.

"Which friends?" I asked.

"Emilia, Anna, and Elliot," Dad said. He tried to look casual when he said Elliott's name, but I could see the smile in his eyes. "Oh, and the girl who found you in the bathroom," he added.

My heart skipped, and I nodded. "I'd like to see them all."

A woman popped her head into the room. "Mr. Vogel? Hi . . . I'm Bridget. Your social worker. I have some materials I'd like to review with you. Would you rather come out here, or should I come in?"

Dad raised his eyebrows at me in a question. "I'm kind of tired," I said. "Do you mind going into the hall?"

Dad kissed my forehead. "I'll be just outside your door, if you need me. I love you, Twilight."

"Love you too, Dad."

As the door closed, I stood to walk back to my bed. But I tripped on a cord, bending my toe backward. I braced myself on the sink, preventing a fall . . . but not before I caught another glimpse of myself in the mirror.

Mats clumped my hair, and the hospital gown hung limp on my frail frame. Circles lined my eyes, which looked sunken in the middle of my pale face.

My hair was out of control. My clothes were out of control. My *life* was out of control.

Maybe Dad wasn't the upside-down turtle after all, I thought.

Maybe *I* was.

Chapter 43

CONFESSIONS

The ophthalmologist packed up her supplies at my bedside.

"We're going to need to do another exam in my office, where I have all my equipment that's too big to move. But it can wait until after surgery. And I'll be seeing you every three months through treatment, at least. Do you have any questions for me, Twyla?"

I shook my head. Questions would probably come to me in time, but countless doctors, nurses, pharmacists, therapists, and other people had already been in my room since I'd been admitted. I could no longer keep track of anything.

"Okay, then. I'll see you soon." She smiled warmly. As she wheeled her bag to the door, two familiar faces poked their way in.

Emilia and Anna.

I grinned. "Hey," I said.

"Your dad said it was okay for us to come by. Is now good?" Emilia asked.

"Sure, come on in."

"They're only letting two people in the room at a time," Anna said, "so Mom's in the cafeteria with your dad and Wolfie."

Anna set a big basket filled with games, slime, crafts, and tons of snacks on my table. Emilia handed me a stuffed dog holding a bouquet of balloons and a big manila envelope.

"The team made you cards," she said. She looked at her feet. "Everyone's worried about you."

For a minute, I thought she'd looked down because of

the tension between us . . . but then I saw the tears. She wiped them away.

"I'm sorry," Emilia whispered. "I promised myself I wouldn't cry."

Anna's lip trembled too. She put her arm around Emilia.

Looking at them, I felt like we were back in kindergarten. I remembered how we bonded over princesses and fluffernutter sandwiches. I remembered how Emilia joined me and Anna that first day at lunch because we were laughing, and she wanted to be part of the fun. I thought of the handshakes and pinky swears we'd made over the years.

I crawled toward them on my bed, wrapped my arms around their necks, and for a long time, we hugged and cried. I didn't pull away until I absolutely had to blow my nose. I balled the tissue in my hand and threw it toward the garbage. It missed. Anna picked it up and threw it away.

These were the kind of friends who would grab my snot-drenched tissue without flinching.

These *were* my people.

"Guys . . . I have a confession," I said.

Emilia tilted her head at me. Anna chewed her thumbnail.

"All these weeks, pretty much since summer, I thought I had a nut allergy. I found Mom's autopsy report, and . . . well, I read it wrong. I thought Mom died from a nut allergy. I should've told you. Things were so weird . . ."

I swallowed the rest of my sentence. I didn't have to finish. They understood.

Emilia pulled a tissue from the box and handed it to me.

"I have a confession too," Emilia said. My heart sank. Was this where she was going to tell me they thought I was cursed?

Emilia inhaled deeply.

"We were always around, Twyla. Every time. I . . . I can't believe I'm saying this. But I thought you were sick *because of* us. I thought we were jinxing you or something. I made Anna promise we'd give you space, to be sure we weren't the reason you . . . to be sure you were sick because . . . ugh. That's why I got the thunderbird. I thought it might protect you from us. And all this time . . ."

Big, fat tears rolled down her cheeks. "I'm so, so sorry," she said.

My chest tightened. *That* was why they'd been avoiding me? To try and *protect* me?

Anna nodded, then her face fell. "While we're making confessions . . ." She chewed the inside of her lip. "I owe you an apology too, Twyla."

My eyes widened.

"You know that day, when you asked how Lindy knew you'd been in the ER? Well . . . I'd been talking with Emilia outside school about how worried I was. About the vomiting and stuff . . . and, well, Lindy overheard me. I feel just awful about it. I should've been more careful."

I squeezed my friends' hands. "I'm not mad," I said. "But I do have one more confession."

The air in the room suddenly felt thick, my throat tight.

"You know that game we lost, in the summer?" I closed my eyes, forcing the tears not to fall. "I lied about rubbing my snow globe. And now . . ."

I envisioned my mother cradling the gift. Proudly handing it over, saying it represented a new beginning for me.

A new beginning that now felt very old, and very, very far away.

"Now," I continued, "it's gone. The snow globe's gone." My eyes scanned the floor. A single star, near the sink, reflected light from overhead.

"It broke." I nearly choked on the words. Emilia sucked in her breath.

Both my friends sat down on my tiny hospital bed, filling the space with love. They wrapped their arms around me and I clung to them, like I wished I could cling to my globe one more time.

Like I wished I could cling to my mother.

"Twy," Emilia said, "I'm so sorry you've been feeling guilty this whole time. And I'm so, so sorry your snow globe broke." She leaned her forehead against mine.

"We know how much it meant to you," Anna added.

Emilia's mouth curved into a small, sad grin. "Maybe almost as much as you mean to us."

As my friends and I embraced, I thought back on our years together. The shared sandwiches, secrets, and sleepovers. The stuffed animals we still loved. The homework we'd done together. The way we always supported one another, no matter what.

My hand touched my hair, and I thought of the battle I was about to face. The brain surgery on Monday morning. The chemo they'd have to give me through a port, which they'd soon place in my chest. The nausea, vomiting, and fatigue they said I'd probably experience with every infusion.

The hair loss. Oh, the hair loss.

I knew it would suck. All of it. But as my friends breathed with me in one big hug, all of us grieving together, I felt stronger. Like I could face this beast.

And I didn't have to do it alone.

Anna leaned back, snatching her backpack from the floor. "I know what we could use," she said. She unzipped it and pulled out an array of nail polishes. "Mani-pedis, anyone?"

For once, I was the one grateful for a distraction.

As we brushed the color on our toes, Emilia and Anna agreed that, if necessary, we would postpone our Thanksgiving sleepover this year—but we would absolutely have it. We talked about Christmas, and field hockey, and school. We even talked about boys a little.

I wiggled my toes, now streaked with purplish-blue and silver glitter. They shimmered in the light, like stars in the night sky. And that's when I decided.

I liked nail polish. And it was time.

Time to start a new lucky ritual.

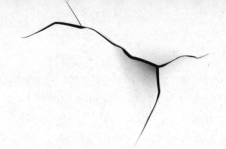

Chapter 44

ENOUGH

Once Emilia and Anna left, I read cards from my field hockey teammates.

You're so strong. I know you're going to get through this! Love, Erin.

I hope you heal quickly, Twyla. We need your energy! Love, Caise.

Hey, Bestie . . . I've been a butthead. I'm sorry. I love you tons. I'll be here for you every step of the way while you fight this stupid tumor. Mom and I are going to light a candle for you every night. Then, when you get better, we will do ALL the sleepovers. Love you, Twy. -Emilia

A knock on the door made me jump.

"Come in," I said. I tucked the cards back into the envelope.

Elliott pushed his way into the room, holding a vase filled with chrysanthemums, pansies, some sort of purple flowers I couldn't identify, and a couple sunflowers.

"My mom made me bring these," he teased.

"Well, tell her I said thank you," I joked back.

He looked confused for a moment, so I pointed to an empty spot on a table by the phone in my room. He set them down and stuffed his hands into his pockets.

"So . . . sorry I'm not there to help you fail genetics," I said.

Elliott grinned and flipped his head to the side, swinging his bangs out of his eyes. "The table's gonna be quiet without you." He looked at his feet. "Will you be back soon?"

"I hope so. I'll be out a while for brain surgery. After that, I'll have a port placed—this thing they'll put in my chest to give me meds and take blood draws—and when I heal from that, I'll miss a day or two every week for chemo."

Elliott winced. "How long will that last?"

"They won't be sure until they know exactly what the tumor is, but they expect ten weeks," I said. "Then it should go to once a month for a year."

Elliott puffed his cheeks and blew out slowly. "That's a long time," he said. He kicked the wheel on my bed. "It sucks."

I nodded. "Yeah. It sucks. But I'm glad they found it when they did, you know? They say they think it's a slow-growing type, so we just need to use chemo to kind of put it to sleep for good."

Elliott's eyes stayed glued to the floor. "So . . . so you're gonna be . . . okay?"

For a minute, I didn't know what to say. "Okay" suddenly felt like a weird, nebulous thing. I mean, I had Emilia and Anna back. *We* were okay. And Elliott was here—that felt okay. But the next day, I needed brain surgery for a tumor I'd have for the rest of my life. That part didn't feel so okay.

I also knew the question he *wasn't* asking.

I took a deep breath, filling my lungs with the flowers' sweetness, before answering the best way I knew how.

"I feel pretty well right now," I said. "I don't know, Elliott. They say I should live a long life. But this whole thing . . . it's scary, you know?" It felt good to say the words out loud. To admit that I didn't know something.

To admit that I was scared.

Elliott's gaze finally lifted from the floor, and for the first time, I could tell that he'd been crying.

His eyes looked faraway for a moment, and then they locked with mine. "Do you remember that day, when we were little, and Felix got hit by the car?" Sadness tugged at the edges of his mouth.

"Yeah," I said. "I do."

Elliott's chest rose and fell under heavy breaths. "I never said thanks for being there."

"Well, that's what friends are for," I said.

For a moment, Elliott stood, frozen. But then, slowly, he pulled his hands from his pockets and leaned on the rail of the bed, wrapping my left hand in both of his. His thumbs stroked the back of my hand for a few moments. Then he threaded his fingers between mine, pressing our palms together.

My heart fluttered.

"Is that what we are?" he asked. He glanced down for a moment, then lifted his face so his eyes were only inches from mine. "You know those pictures you talked about—the ones you saw at Anna's house? I asked her if I could see them."

My eyes widened. "And?"

"And," he said, "I was *not* holding her hand. She was covered in juice, and I couldn't exactly follow you to the girl's bathroom, so I initially tried to help . . . but then she said something about how that never would've happened if *my girlfriend* hadn't been such a klutz."

I stopped breathing.

"So I handed her a napkin, and then I whispered in her ear that she could clean her own damned dress."

The corners of my mouth lifted into a grin. And then, Elliott leaned forward and gently touched his lips to mine.

"Don't take too long to heal," he whispered. "Okay?"

"Okay," I whispered back.

Then he kissed me once more, and he left.

For the first time in way too long, I didn't feel like I needed answers. I didn't know why I had a tumor. I didn't know how long it would take me to heal, or how I'd get through week after week after week of chemotherapy. But in my heart, I knew I'd get through tomorrow.

And for now, that felt like enough.

Chapter 45

MAKING PEACE

After rereading all my notes from my field hockey team, I stuffed them back into the envelope and made a mental note to ask Dad to bring more books to the hospital. A sweet lady from Child Life had brought me a wooden box and a pouch to paint, but I didn't feel like doing either one of those things. Maybe after surgery.

Sigh. Surgery.

Dad poked his head into the room. "Hey, Twy, you have another visitor here. I'm gonna run down to the cafeteria for a coffee. You want anything?"

I nodded. "Yeah . . . a ginger ale, please? And who is it?" I asked.

"The girl who found you," he said. My heart skipped a beat.

"Oh, great! Send her in! Tell her I'll be right out—I have to go to the bathroom first."

I pulled on my slippers and checked the clock on the wall: 7:39. Visiting hours would be over soon. So much had happened and I felt exhausted, but I doubted I'd get much sleep that night. Maybe the nurses would take pity on me and let Angela stay after-hours.

I wheeled the IV pole behind me into the bathroom. The room was decent-sized, but nowhere near as comfortable as the one in my house. Yellowish tiles angled toward two drains on the floor, and silver bars lined three walls in a tiny stand-up shower that had no curtain. One-third of the bathroom was occupied by what appeared to be a large, lidded laundry basket. There were also two garbage cans; an open black one, and a red one with an orange biohazard sticker. I peed, washed my hands, and tossed my used paper towel into the black bin. I wrinkled my nose, thinking about what kind of stuff was supposed to go in the red one.

I expected to see my friend Angela when I re-entered my room. I did not expect to see *her*.

"What are *you* doing here?" I didn't mean for my tone to sound accusatory, but honestly, Lindy was the last person I wanted to see right then. She shifted in the chair, crossing and uncrossing her designer-clad legs, and furrowed her perfectly manicured brow.

"I thought your dad told you I was coming?" she said.

"Uh, *no*. He definitely did not. He said my friend, Ang . . ." My voice trailed off as I realized Dad had never actually mentioned Angela by name. In fact, he'd said he hadn't known her name.

"Wait." I squinted at Lindy, who looked at her feet. "Did . . . did *you* find me in the bathroom?" I asked.

Lindy nodded, tentatively. She rested the heel of her right Burberry boot on the left one. "Yeah. I followed you there."

I scowled, confused. "Why?"

My IV pole squeaked as I wheeled it back toward my bed. I climbed in, wrapping myself in the warmth of my blanket.

Lindy shrugged, twisting her curls over one shoulder. "Honestly? I was pretty pissed at what you said at the game. Part of me wanted to tell you off. But . . ." She shook her head, confusion stitched across her face too. "But something told me you weren't okay. Like, I'm not gonna make any sense here, but somehow, I just knew something was wrong. So I followed you." She shrugged again.

I squinted at her, still trying to process the fact that she was sitting in my room. "So . . . why are you here now?"

Lindy sighed. "Listen, Twyla, I'm not gonna lie. I don't think we've liked each other very much. But . . ." Lindy's eyes trailed to the window. Her face softened, and suddenly, she didn't look like the same angry field hockey player. She just looked like another lost high school freshman.

Albeit a really well-dressed one.

"You probably don't remember this," she said, "but I came to your mom's funeral. We were in the same class, though you never talked to me. You were always with Emilia and Anna." Lindy waved at the air. "Anyway, I told my mom we were friends, so we went to the funeral. Then, when the service was over and we were waiting in that long line, you, Emilia, and Anna came barreling out of nowhere and ran straight into me. You knocked me over, right in front of my mother, and you didn't say anything. No apology, nothing. You just got up and ran away, like I was trash to be left on the floor." Lindy picked at her French manicure, peeling white polish from the tip of her pointer finger.

"My mom's not exactly the most . . . forgiving person on the planet," she continued. "She decided right then and there that you guys were bad news. And as for me . . ." Lindy gazed out the window again, sighing. "I guess I was jealous."

My jaw dropped. "*Jealous?* Jealous of what, exactly?"

When Lindy turned back to look at me, she chewed her lip like Anna did when she felt guilty about something.

"Everyone is always so nice to you," she said. "I think . . . ugh. I always thought everyone was being so nice to you because your mom died. And to make it worse, everyone talked about how wonderful your mom was. And then there's *my* mom . . ."

For a minute, we both sat there, staring at the floor.

"Your mom's not that bad . . ." I started to say. But as soon as the words came out of my mouth, Lindy's head jerked up to meet my gaze. She lifted her eyebrows in a question.

"Well . . . maybe she can be a little . . . loud sometimes," I said.

Lindy laughed. "*Fireworks* are loud. My mother is the PTA villain."

I caught myself just after a quick burst of laughter, wondering if

I was being insensitive. But then our eyes met, and Lindy laughed too. Before I knew it, we were both clutching our sides. Me and this enemy I'd had for so many years. This girl I thought I knew, who thought she knew me—but really, we'd been strangers the whole time.

And it struck me . . . Lindy was right. My mom *was* pretty great. And I'd been lucky to have her. I hadn't been acting crazy, going through her stuff in the attic, looking for information. Questioning genetics or visiting her tree.

All this time, I'd just been looking for ways to stay connected to my mom.

Maybe, in her own weird way, by being mean to me . . . Lindy had been doing the same thing. She was just trying to find a way to relate to her own mother.

However villainous she might be.

Lindy fished a note out of her bag. "I know everyone on the team already gave you theirs, but I wanted to give you this myself," she said. She handed me the note, pushed herself to her feet, and walked to the door. When she turned back to face me, she smiled.

"You're a fighter," she said. "You've got this."

I grinned. "Thanks, Lindy."

She nodded, flipped her hair once more, and the door closed behind her.

Gingerly, I pulled Lindy's note from the envelope. As I read her words, my heart soared.

Twyla,
I'm sorry for not passing to you. You're a really great player. I also understand why you missed the ball now, and I feel really bad about all those things I said.
Anyway, I want you to know that you're going to be okay, and I know we're going to

play field hockey again soon. I don't know how . . . but I'm sure of it. I wish I knew why you were going through all this in the first place, but I don't.

I just know that everything happens for a reason.

Love, Lindy

Chapter 46

GODSPEED

Dad's soft snores filled the room, joining the symphony of beeps and buzzes from the machines around my bed. The halls stood dark and quiet now, except for the occasional nurse shuffling by. Sara Bareilles crooned "Brave" from Dad's portable speaker, and I felt as if she were singing directly to me.

I reached deep into my backpack to find my journal, but my hand landed on a baggie filled with tiny, crumpled boxes instead.

Nerds. And in the baggie, a note.

Twyla,
I'm sorry you missed Halloween. I saved these for you. I know they're your favorite.
　　Did you know that a dentist invented cotton candy? Weird, huh?
　　I love you. You're the best big sister ever.
Wolfie

For once, I just let the tears fall. I felt bad for yelling at him about the snow globe. No, he shouldn't have brought it . . . but he meant well. He always meant well. My heart sank, thinking of how scared he must be about this. I felt grateful that Ms. Givens would be bringing him by in the morning before surgery.

My stomach churned, so I stuffed the Nerds into the bottom of my backpack. My nurse had given me something for nausea after Lindy left, but so far, it wasn't doing much more than making me dizzy and tired. I wiped my eyes with my hospital gown. My chest tightened with fear as I thought about the last couple of days. There were so many unknowns. So many questions—none of them, seemingly, with answers.

Familiar, slow guitar chords strummed from the speaker, stealing my breath. Then the door to my room creaked open.

Angela.

Relief washed over me, and she wrapped me in a hug before joining me on the edge of my bed. A halo of light reflected off her dark hair. For a few moments we just sat together, her arm protectively around my shoulders, and listened to The Chicks sing about dragon tails, lost boys, and moonbeams. I studied her, for the first time noticing the curve of her nose, her slight build, the graceful way she moved. It was all so . . . familiar.

Angela sighed, glancing at the couch. Dad's frame rose and fell slowly with deep, tranquil breaths. She motioned to him with her chin.

"You're worried about him." It wasn't a question.

I nodded.

"*He* will be okay, Twyla. *He* has flipped himself back over hundreds of times, hasn't he? Thousands, maybe. *You*, however . . ."

"I'm still upside down," I said.

Angela shrugged a little with one shoulder. "You're getting there."

A question burned in my mind, and I inhaled deeply. She tilted her head as she watched me. Waiting.

"I used to believe there's a reason for everything," I said. "Do you think that's true?"

She stood and wandered toward the sink, picking up one lone star from the floor. "What do *you* think?" she asked.

I sighed. "I don't know anymore."

Angela cupped my hand and placed the star in my palm. Then she wrapped my fingers closed, holding my fist in her hands.

"Just because we don't *know* a reason, doesn't mean there isn't one," she said.

I sat up taller, leaning toward her, fighting the effects of the medicine. "But when? When will I know? When will I know why this is happening to me?" A familiar burning filled my throat, and I knew tears were close again. Angela released my hand, and I pulled my fist against my heart, afraid that if I didn't, I'd lose the last star. Angela tilted my chin up, meeting my gaze.

"You might never know why you're upside down," she said. "The important thing is that you stretch your neck out and *try* to flip yourself back over."

As she spoke the words, I leaned back against my pillow. My limbs felt like sandbags.

"No one expects you to fight this battle alone," Angela said.

Another question lingered on my tongue, but I didn't want to ask it. I didn't want to know the answer. But I had to.

"Are you going away?" I breathed.

Angela brushed my bangs aside with long, tender fingers. My eyelids drooped as The Chicks sang in hushed tones. I felt cocooned in love, the machines around me pulsing like wings in the wind.

"No, Twyla . . ." Angela's soothing voice coaxed my eyelids to close. "My love will be there beside you, protecting you, every day. You'll see."

Tears wet the pillow by my ear as I watched her reach into my backpack and pull out my journal. She set it beside me on the bed and leaned down to kiss my forehead.

I barely heard her as I drifted off to sleep.

"Godspeed, Twilight," she whispered. "Sweet dreams."

Chapter 47

MUSIC RETURNS

I woke to a nurse fiddling with my IV. Early morning sun shone through the blinds by the couch, where Dad buried his nose in a book. I blinked the fog from my eyes and stretched.

"Don't mind me," the nurse said. "I just had to draw some blood through your IV. You can go back to sleep if you'd like."

Dad put his book down. I yawned. The nurse made a few notes on her computer and headed toward the door.

"Don't forget, you can't eat or drink anything before surgery," she said.

I frowned as the door closed behind her. Surgery.

Dad shifted on the couch. "Do you want to listen to music?" he asked.

I started to agree, then suddenly remembered the night before.

I flipped my pillow and threw my sheets aside, frantic . . . but the star was nowhere to be found. My heart sank. Had I imagined the whole thing? Was none of it real?

"What are you looking for?" Dad asked.

Slowly, my eyes scanned the floor around the bed one last time. First, I had a brain tumor, and now I was losing my mind.

"Twy?"

I gave Dad a weak smile. "Nothing," I said. Maybe I'd been losing my mind for months.

Dad squinted. "Hang on," he said. He got up, then reached toward my face. "Hold still," he commanded.

255

He peeled something off my cheek, and then lifted my hand with his. He placed the item in my palm.

A tiny, silver star, reflecting light like a diamond in a sifting pan.

As I stared at it, I considered telling him. But . . . tell him what? I didn't know what to say. There was so much I couldn't explain.

So I just squeezed his hand and smiled.

"Thanks," I said.

My eyes landed on the journal beside me. I stuck the star inside the front cover, then leaned back against my pillow and cradled the book to my chest. My temples throbbed. Dad's brow crinkled as I rubbed them.

"Does your head hurt?" he asked.

"A little, yeah," I said. I kicked the covers partially off, sweeping one foot up and on top of my sheets. Dad laughed.

"What's so funny?" I said.

Dad smiled, shaking his head. "Your mom used to do that all the time. She'd keep one foot under the covers and put one foot on top. She said it was the only way she didn't overheat or get too cold." He leaned toward me, elbows on his knees. "You may not have her allergy. But you're a lot like her, you know."

I grinned. "Yeah? How so?"

Dad tapped me so I'd move over and make room for him. He leaned against the pillow beside me.

"Your mother had a way about her, just like you do," he said.

"A way?" I settled back against him, like he was about to read me a story.

"Well, you hold a pencil wrong, between your thumb and middle finger, just like she did . . ."

"I do not hold it wrong!" We both laughed.

"And you have her laugh." Dad smiled. "And no one ever loved critters like your mother . . . not even me. That is, until you came along." He elbowed me, and I grinned.

"Did you know that when your mom was in college, no one could touch her in an audition? And she always got every job she ever interviewed for. When she walked into a room, she absolutely sparkled. Everyone noticed her." Dad grinned. "Just like everyone notices you."

"You think people notice me?" I asked. Dad laughed.

"You shine, Twyla," he said. "It's impossible *not* to notice you." Dad ambled back to the couch. He leaned over to pull something out from behind it, and my heart fluttered.

His guitar.

I wanted to say so many things, but the only thing that I could muster was a breathless, "Dad!"

He sat down on the couch and tuned a couple of flat strings. I dangled my feet and bounced my calves on the side of the bed. He strummed a chord dramatically.

"The . . ."

I pretend-scowled at him. "Dad . . ."

"Wheels on the bus go round and round . . ."

"DAD! Come ON! Be serious!"

But we both laughed.

Dad strummed another chord, less dramatically this time, and started to sing. And for just a minute, I forgot about everything else in the world.

"You've got a friend in me. You've got a friend in me . . ."

Dad's eyes twinkled, and my chest filled with warmth realizing that he was back. Dad was back.

I'd missed him so much. His sweetness and his sense of humor, sure, but his music more than anything. With Mom gone, and then when he stopped playing, it was like all the color had disappeared from our world.

But now, here he sat . . . singing. All flipped over and right side up again.

I sang along with him until the song ended, and then we sang it again. Finally, fingers and voice tired, Dad tucked his guitar back into its case.

"Hey," he said, "why did the farmer try a career in music?"

"Oh no . . ."

"Because it had a bunch of sick beets," he said.

I groaned.

For a minute, we were both quiet.

"Dad?"

"Yeah?"

"I've missed you," I said. Dad nodded.

"Yeah, I've missed me too, Twilight."

I cocked my head at him. "Do you know what the name Dustin means?"

Dad shook his head. "You know, I don't think I do," he said.

"It means 'Brave Fighter.'" I crossed my arms over my chest, nodding. "It suits you." Even as the words came out of my mouth, I realized that sometimes, things do make sense. Like names. When Felix got hurt, for example, I knew he'd live because his name meant "lucky." I should've known Dad wouldn't be distant for long, with a name like Dustin. And Mom . . . I'd looked that one up ages ago.

Celeste meant "heavenly."

The hairs on my arm suddenly stood on end.

"Hey, Dad, can I borrow your phone for a minute?" I asked. He handed it to me, and I typed in my question.

What does the name Angela mean?

As the answer popped up, I smiled.

Of course.

I should've known.

Chapter 48

PICKING UP THE PIECES

"Knock, knock!" Coach Givens waved from the door. Wolfie squeezed past her in a rush, then froze. His face fell at the tangle of cords, and machines, and the surgical cap on my head. For the first time in a long time—maybe ever—Wolfie fell silent.

I thought about the Nerds and his note, and affection flooded through me. I wanted to scoop him up in my arms and hold him.

Dad knelt in front of Wolfie.

"Would you like some alone time with your sister?" he asked.

Wolfie nodded, face ashen. Dad turned to me.

"I'll let you know when the doctor comes by. Okay?"

"Okay. Thanks, Dad," I said.

When the door closed, I scooched over in my bed and motioned for my brother. Slowly, as if walking on a frozen lake, Wolfie inched toward the bed. He climbed up next to me, holding a gift bag, and perched himself awkwardly on the side. I put my arm around him, and he fell into me, exhaling a gigantic breath. Then he popped back up as if infused by a sudden burst of sugar.

"I brought you a present," he said. Then he shoved the bag into my hands.

"Okay, but first, I want to tell you something."

Wolfie's eyes widened. "What did I do?"

"Nothing bad!" I laughed, squeezing him around the shoulders. Then I let go and took his hand in mine.

"I found the Nerds, Wolfie. In my backpack. It was really sweet of you to save those for me."

Wolfie smiled, then started bouncing on the bed. "Open it," he said.

"Did you hear me?" I asked.

"Yeah." He made fast, tiny circles with his hands. "Open it."

I sighed. Wolfie and his one-track mind. I plucked the puffs of tissue paper sticking out of the bag and removed a heavy box, about the size of a large mug.

"What is it . . . ?"

"Just open it! Open it!"

Bounce, bounce, bounce.

"Okay, I'm opening it," I said with a laugh.

After two minutes of scraping a dozen pieces of tape with my thumbnail, I finally lifted the lid.

I gasped.

"Wolfie . . . I . . . how did you . . .?"

Gently, I lifted a glass snow globe from the box.

My snow globe.

Complete with engraved plate, a crescent moon, and tiny silver stars instead of snow. I twisted the key on the side, and the same gentle melody rang from the base.

"But . . . I don't understand. It broke. How did you find another one?"

Wolfie shook his head. "I didn't," he said. "This is yours." As if that explained everything.

"But it shattered," I said, pointing to the floor where it had broken.

"Yeah, but Ms. Givens took me to a store for a new glass part. We found one that fit, and I fixed it."

"But . . . but the stars, and the moon, and the plate, and everything . . . it all got thrown away! How did you replace it all?"

"Oh, that part was easy. Daddy swept it up and gave it all to Ms. Givens. Then she picked out the sharp parts!"

I combed my memory. I never actually *saw* anyone throw anything away. Dad must've saved it all after I'd fallen asleep.

"Wolfie . . ." I shook my head in disbelief. "How did you know what to do?"

Wolfie snorted. "You can find anything on YouTube."

I threw my arms around my brother. "This is the nicest thing you've ever done," I said. "Thank you."

"Well, maybe not the nicest . . ." he said.

I pulled back and squinted at him in question. "What d'you mean?"

Wolfie fiddled with his fingers. "I kept your secret," he said.

My heart skipped a beat. My secret? Had he somehow seen Angela too?

"I knew you were pouring that medicine in your napkin all the time," he said.

My jaw dropped. Never in a million years would I have guessed Wolfie could keep a secret like that. "You did? Why didn't you tell on me?"

Wolfie shrugged. "You're my sister," he said, as if I'd just asked him the dumbest question ever.

I hugged him hard, and he tucked his head into my shoulder, like he did when he was a baby. I thought Wolfie never paid attention to anything but weird facts . . . but I'd been wrong.

I'd been wrong about so many things.

"Twyla?"

I leaned my forehead against my brother's. "Yeah?"

Wolfie sighed and rolled himself out of the bed. He walked over to the couch and rested his chin on the windowsill. I sat on the edge of my bed, watching him.

"I'm scared," he whispered. His voice sounded younger than a fifth grader's. "Why is this happening?"

When he turned back to face me, tears welled in his eyes. I opened my arms and he ran to me, squeezing me with every muscle in his body. Like he was scared that if he didn't hold me tightly enough, I would fade away.

"You know, Wolfie, I think you were right. Sometimes, we *don't* know the reasons . . . but you know what?" I pulled away so I could look directly into his eyes, with my hands on his shoulders.

"I still believe there *is* always a reason. Even if I don't know it yet. Maybe I'm going through this to help someone else later. Maybe we're gonna start a YouTube channel about our experience, and it'll change the world! Or maybe . . ." I kissed his forehead. "Maybe we're supposed to figure it out together," I whispered.

Wolfie picked up my snow globe and shook it. "I'm sorry there aren't as many stars in it anymore," he sniffed. "I don't think we got 'em all."

"It's perfect," I said. "Just the way it is."

Wolfie gazed back out the window, and for a few minutes we watched the wind blow the last few leaves off a nearby tree. A flock of waterfowl flew by in the distance, heading south for the winter.

"You know the thing that's amazing about fall?" Wolfie asked.

"Hm-mm," I said.

"The trees and animals . . . they just know it's time."

I nodded. I knew exactly what he meant.

The door swung open. Dad and Ms. Givens inched in. "The doctor's in the hall, Twyla. It's about time to go down to pre-op. Wolfie, you're not allowed down there. Give your sister a kiss. You'll see her soon."

Wolfie's lip quivered.

"Hey . . ." A burst of strength filled my chest, and I hugged my brother hard. "Buddy . . . I'm gonna be fine. I promise. I'll see you soon."

"But . . . how do you know?" Wolfie's voice cracked.

I tousled his hair. "Because I'm your sister."

Wolfie nodded, as if that answer was good enough. Ms. Givens took his hand and guided him to the door. He turned back, a huge smile suddenly splitting his face.

"Oh! I forgot! Did Dad tell you about the puppy?" Wolfie bounced up and down.

My heart stopped. "Puppy?" I asked. "What puppy?"

"The puppy on our doorstep!" Wolfie said.

Dad sighed and began scrolling through his phone. "I didn't want to say anything until we knew for sure that she's a stray," he said. "But this puppy has been sleeping on our front stoop ever since you were admitted to the hospital. She won't leave."

When Dad turned his phone so I could see the photo, my heart stopped.

It was Sophie.

"She doesn't have a chip and we've put posters up everywhere," Dad said. "But if no one claims her . . . well, she seems really smart, and the vet says her demeanor is perfect for a service dog."

Tears burned my throat as I remembered Angela's words.

My love will be there beside you, protecting you, every day. You will see.

Ms. Givens took Wolfie's hand. He turned one last time, blew me a kiss, and left.

"You ready?" Dad asked. A team of people came into the room, tending to the machines that beeped and hummed around me. I slid my snow globe onto the table beside the flowers, and accidentally swept my journal onto the floor in the process. When I reached down to pick it up, my kintsugi leaf peeked between the pages . . . and I knew.

I was going to be okay.

No, I was going to be *more* than okay.

I was going to be stronger at the seams.

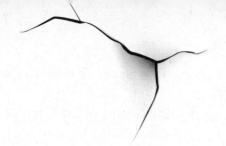

EPILOGUE

"You sure you're strong enough to play?"

I rolled my eyes at Coach Givens. The varsity score was tied, three to three, against the Eagles. "Put me in, Coach. I promise to flag you if I need to come out."

Even though chemo had ended six months prior, people still treated me like a china teacup. And really, I sort of understood . . . treatment had been tough. I'd missed a lot of my freshman and sophomore years, and I'd been so nauseous that we'd talked about changing treatment plans a dozen times.

But we hadn't.

On my last day of chemo, all the doctors and nurses sang a song, then cheered while I rang the treatment completion bell with Sophie by my side. I'd heard other kids ring that bell before, and it always filled me with a weird mix of jealousy, sadness, happiness, and hope. When my day came, I wished I could run from room to room, telling every kid, "Hang in there. It'll be your turn soon."

Now, with three minutes left in the final tournament game, I finally felt like it was my turn to be on the field again.

Samantha, the redhead who'd been Lindy's science partner, had taken my place at forward over the last year. Now, as she limped off the field with an injury, Coach Givens studied me.

"Okay, Twyla . . . but if you get hurt, your dad's gonna kill me," she said.

Samantha and I clicked our sticks together as I ran onto the field. Adrenaline pulsed through my veins as everyone in the stands jumped to their feet, cheering . . . and I realized they were cheering for *me.*

Twy-la! Twy-la! Twy-la!

Wolfie and Sophie bounced like kangaroos, and Mama Rose, Anna, Coach Givens, Emilia, and the rest of the Dragons—even the players on the other team—screamed and clapped as I took my old position. I blew Dad a kiss as he dabbed his eyes with his sleeve. Then I tapped my stick on the turf and glanced sideways at Emilia.

She grinned at me with fire in her eyes. My heart thumped against my ribs, a drumroll welcoming me home.

The whistle blew. I dug my cleats into the grass, and wind whipped my short, downy hair as I flew downfield, across from the action. The ball immediately raced toward our goal, where a couple of new girls played strong defense against larger opponents. Finally, Erin got a stick on the ball and shot it to Caise, who dribbled it through the legs of a quick defender. Another Eagle saw her chance, but Emilia was faster. She crossed midfield and brought the ball close to the shooting circle. With two defenders closing in, she looked for me. I wasn't open.

But Lindy was.

"Go to Lindy!" I shouted. Emilia whacked it straight toward her.

"GOOOO, LINDY! YOU HAVE THIRTY SECONDS! SCORE, LINDY, SCORE!"

I'd missed a lot of things over the last two years, but Lindy's mom had not been one of them.

Lindy took a shot, but the ball ricocheted off a defender's stick and Lindy managed to recover it again near the edge of the pitch. Now double-teamed, I thought she'd lose the ball . . . but instead, she scooped it with her stick, bouncing it in the air right over and past both defenders.

The move was perfection.

I mirrored Lindy's pace, but a defender stuck to me like glue.

Our bench started screaming a countdown backward from ten, indicating that the game was almost over. It was now or never.

And that's when I saw my chance. I spiraled, suddenly changing direction and running away from Lindy . . . then sprinted straight toward the goal.

I was open.

Seven, six, five . . .

"SHOOT, LINDY! SHOOOOOOOT!"

Lindy's eyes met mine for a split second. She pulled her stick back, and I waited for the ball to hit the net. But it didn't.

It came straight to me.

Three, two . . .

CRACK!

My stick vibrated as the ball whooshed into the net . . . just before the final buzzer.

There was one second of silence, and then the world erupted around me. I lifted my stick high, and felt my feet leave the ground as first Emilia and then my entire team hoisted me up into the air. Lindy ran to the circle, and I let my stick dangle down so we could click them together. On the sidelines, Dad, Wolfie, Anna, and Mama Rose hugged and bounced in circles while Sophie yipped at their heels. When the team finally set me back down, Lindy approached.

"Nice shot," she said.

"Nice pass." We grinned at each other almost shyly, like we were meeting for the first time. "And when did you learn to scoop so well? You need to teach me that sometime."

"LINDY! COME HERE THIS INSTANT!"

Lindy's face fell. "I'd like that," she said. Then she turned and ran back to her mother.

"Kind of makes you feel sorry for her, doesn't it?" Emilia leaned her elbow on my shoulder. I'd pretty much stopped growing while on chemo, so she now towered nearly a foot above me. Anna ran onto the pitch to join us.

"YOU GUYS ARE AMAAAAAAZING!" she shouted.

"Sleepover tonight?" Emilia asked.

"Ooh! I'm in!" Anna said.

I nodded. "Whose house this time?"

"My turn!" Emilia said, hand held high. "Mom bought stuff for us to make dream catchers!"

Anna suddenly cleared her throat, and Emilia looked just over my head. "Oh, I, uh, I think Anna and I have to . . . go to the bathroom. Right, Anna?"

Anna nodded. "Yup! Gotta pee! Byeeee!"

For a moment, I wondered if my friends were hiding a secret again.

"Hi, Twyla."

Elliott's voice made me jump.

"Hey!" I said. "I thought you were coming home from camp next week!"

His long, signature bangs were now gone, replaced by a stylish cut that showed off his eyes.

His remarkably bright, blue-green eyes.

He wrapped his arms around my waist and kissed me.

"I missed you. Nice widow's peak, by the way," he said. My hand flew up to my head, now covered in a super short pixie-style hairdo. I didn't look like the Ancient One from Dr. Strange anymore, thank God, but it was still much shorter than I would've been wearing it if not for chemo.

I smirked. "What can I say? Genetics."

"You gonna keep it short?"

I shook my head. "No way," I said. "I like it long."

He shrugged. "I don't know. You rock the bald pretty well."

My stomach fluttered.

Elliott took my hand, and we walked the long way around the field. "Did you get your results yet?"

Throughout chemo, my tumor had remained stable—which

they'd always said was the goal—but I still needed MRIs every three months for a year. Then, hopefully, they'd start spacing them out farther and farther, until they were eventually twelve months apart . . . for the rest of my life.

I grinned. "Just this morning," I said. "Stable!"

Elliott bent down and picked a dandelion. He stared at it for a minute, then blew the seeds into the wind.

"I know it's still summer," he said. "But do you think you might want to go to Homecoming with me?"

"I mean . . . that's better than asking me same day," I said.

Elliott tilted his head. "So . . . that's a yes?"

I nodded. "Well, I *am* your girlfriend," I said.

"Glad you remember that."

Oh, that lopsided grin.

Coach Givens called to Elliott, who trotted back to his mom in the parking lot. I headed toward the stands, where Emilia and Anna were pretending—poorly—not to watch.

I hated to admit it, but Emilia was right. Elliott *was* a geode.

A light gust blew, and the scent of jasmine filled the air. A pack of perfect, fluffy cumulus clouds passed, shading the pitch, and I turned my face toward the sky. I closed my eyes, soaking in the summer sounds: songbirds, the distant chatter of the dispersing crowd, and the whisper of the wind. Different from my woods, but still beautiful.

Kind of like my life now.

So much had changed.

Maybe that's all life was, really. A series of unpredictable changes. Two years ago, I never would've guessed that I was about to battle cancer or go through chemo. But I also never would've guessed that Elliott would be asking me to our second high school dance together, or that Lindy would pass and let me score the tournament's winning goal.

I didn't know why these things were happening. But maybe that was okay. Maybe it was enough to just go with the flow.

Something in the grass caught my eye.

A turtle.

Slowly, methodically, he crawled toward the woods in the distance. I wondered what he might find there. Maybe another turtle. Or a plethora of juicy worms. Or maybe, unsuspecting, he'd tumble down a hill and land upside down . . . belly to the sky.

"Good luck on your journey, little fella," I said. "Remember to stretch your neck out."

Then I ran toward my friends, excited about whatever the future might bring.

A Letter from the Author

Dearest Reader,

If you've happened upon this author's note before reading the book (or if you don't know my family's personal story), and if you're the kind of person who prefers to avoid spoilers (like me), then stop reading here. I've tried, but I can't explain why I wrote this book without giving away the ending. October 2, 2020, changed our lives in a way that cannot be told halfway. Truthfully, though, everything started changing long before then. We just didn't know why . . . and now we do.

You've been warned.

It was late afternoon. Leaves were starting to turn shades of oranges, yellows, and reds, and the air was thin and chilly. I remember wearing stretch pants and a running top, still clinging to the hope that I might have time to do a Pilates workout that evening if the hospital didn't take too long. I fiddled with my fingers, unable to focus on my book, and glanced repeatedly at the doors my daughter had walked through—too long ago. She was only supposed to be gone thirty minutes.

Why was it taking so long?

Deep in my gut, I knew. Just one day prior, I'd texted my friend, a pediatric neurologist, who'd seen Cassidy when all the other doctors had turned us away with questions unanswered. I'd told him that everyone was missing something. I knew my kid, and I knew something was wrong. Yet over the course of the last two years, she'd been dismissed by countless physicians, including gastroenterologists, immunologists, allergists, infectious disease specialists, internists, and neurologists. They'd all seen her for nausea and vomiting, strange afternoon fevers that always spiked around 100.6 between one and four p.m., fatigue, and even dizziness. And they'd all misdiagnosed her.

"This is just the way her body works. Those aren't really fevers."

"All her tests are normal."

"Does she have a therapist?"

No one had suggested a brain MRI yet, and I hadn't thought to request one. She had headaches, but it seemed natural for her head to hurt when her temperature was high. She'd been diagnosed with gastroparesis, anxiety, situational depression, and abdominal migraines. But medications didn't work and therapy didn't help. Her weight plummeted to forty-eight pounds—way too low for her twelve-year-old frame. Doctors repeatedly punted her back to gastroenterology, who was tiring of our insistence that they were missing something. But when she'd woken suddenly with horrific headaches two nights in a row, I texted my friend, who agreed to schedule the MRI immediately.

Why was it taking so long?

The moment the nurse entered the waiting room, clipboard in hand, asking me to sign my approval for contrast, my stomach dropped. I insisted on speaking with the radiologist and expected pushback. Pandemic rules restricted parents to the waiting room, without exception.

"Sure, come on back," she'd soothed.

It wasn't normal. But denial is a powerful force.

We all hear the horror stories, of lives changed in the blink of an eye with an unexpected diagnosis. But you never think it'll happen to you.

Until it does.

From the moment I first heard the words *brain tumor*, every memory in my life fell on one side of the timeline or the other. When I look at pictures of her, my brain fights itself like a warped game of tug-of-war. Was it there back then? Should I have known?

Could I have done anything differently?

Cancer, like other serious diseases, changes everyone it touches. It changes your priorities. Your routine. Your circle of friends. Even with the word *stable* or *remission* in your vocabulary, you're never free of its grasp. It's omnipresent. There is always another scan. There is always doubt. And there is always, always, always the feeling of brokenness.

I wrote *Stronger at the Seams* largely from the fold-out couch by my daughter's hospital bed during twenty-one rounds of chemotherapy. The process was therapeutic for me. Since the story is fictionalized, I could write what I needed—what *she* needed—while still honoring our truth. *Stronger* was born from pain, but also from the deepest, purest, most unconditional love I believe any human can feel.

The love between a parent and a child.

Cassidy rang the bell, symbolizing the end of chemo, on December 30, 2021. But her journey is not over. Her tumor sits in the middle of her brain, surrounding the hypothalamus. It cannot be removed, even in part. But to date, it has not grown since chemo began. In June 2024, she will return for her next MRI. And if that one shows stability—*when* that one shows stability—she will move to annual scans. And if it grows again, at any time, she would have to start chemo all over again.

That's a heavy weight to carry. But we know how lucky we are. Comparatively.

Brain cancer is the number one cancer killer in kids. One of five children will not survive.

There are types of brain tumors, like DIPG, that currently have less than a 2 percent five-year survival rate.

Only 4 percent of all federal cancer research funding goes toward kids.

Approximately 1 out of every 285 children will be diagnosed with cancer in their lifetime.

Most chemotherapy regimens given to kids are decades old. One of the drugs Cassidy required was patented over fifty years ago. The other one? Over sixty years ago.

Over 95 percent of children who go through chemo will suffer significant treatment-related side effects by the age of forty-five.

The statistics are terrifying.

If I could pray for any one thing that a reader might take away from this book, it's the strength to self-advocate. It's not easy to fight for a truth you don't fully understand, and it's even harder when people—older, supposedly wiser people—are telling you you're wrong about yourself. It's intimidating for anyone to fight against an established system.

But no one will ever fight for you the way *you* can. No one knows you the way *you* do.

We may not always be in control of our stories.

But that doesn't mean we are powerless.

Sometimes, dear reader, we all feel broken. Irreparably, eternally broken. But if we keep putting one foot in front of the other, eventually, we *will* make our way through the muck. We will be changed by it, of course—sometimes in gut-wrenching ways. But I truly believe there's beauty to be found in that. No one gets through life unscathed. We all have scars. And every scar has a story.

That's what makes us . . . *us*.

I cannot change the cracks in my life or in my children's lives. I've learned that the best I can do is hold their hands, validate their pain, and stand beside them as they try to piece themselves back together.

Maybe with glue.

Maybe with gold.

But back together, regardless.

Writing this book helped me find hope during the darkest days of my life.

May reading it do the same for you.

With love,

SHANNON

If you or someone you know has a child in their lives who has recently been diagnosed with cancer, please visit Cassidy's YouTube channel, "Candid with Cassidy: Fireside Cancer Chats," at https://www.youtube.com/@CandidwithCassidy.

No one has to fight alone.

STATISTICS BIBLIOGRAPHY

American Cancer Society. "Key Statistics for Childhood Cancers." www.cancer.org, 12 Jan. 2023, www.cancer.org /cancer/types/cancer-in-children/key-statistics.html.

American Childhood Cancer Organization. "US Childhood Cancer Statistics." ACCO, www.acco.org/us-childhood -cancer-statistics/.

"Kami." Web.kamihq.com, 2022. Accessed March 31, 2024.

National Cancer Institute. "Cancer in Children and Adolescents." National Cancer Institute, Cancer.gov, 2017, www.cancer.gov /types/childhood-cancers/child-adolescent-cancers–fact-sheet.

"Prognosis for Diffuse Midline Gliomas (Previously Called DIPGs)." The Brain Tumour Charity, www.thebraintumourcharity.org /brain-tumour-diagnosis-treatment/types-brain-tumour -children/dipg-diffuse-intrinsic-pontine-glioma/dipg-prognosis/.

Acknowledgments

If I've written this section as I hope I have, then it will be a collection of tiny tales. Windows into not only my life, but the lives of Twyla, Wolfie, Dustin, and all the other characters in *Stronger at the Seams*. Because pieces of *them* live and breathe around *me*, every single day.

I couldn't have written this book if my daughter had not been diagnosed with brain cancer. And I couldn't have gotten through her diagnosis without a slew of people who sat with me in my sadness and gently prodded me to keep going when everything felt impossible. When I felt irreparably broken.

So, with all my kintsugi heart, I'd like to thank . . .

Greg. When you said, "For better or worse," you had no idea what you were getting yourself into. Yet here you are . . . twenty-four years and countless tragedies later, by my side. You held my hand during seven terrifying years, thinking I was dying. You never left, and you never stopped believing. When Cassidy was diagnosed, I'll never forget how you crumpled in the kitchen and said, "I can't do this again." Do you remember my response?

"You *can* do this again. Because you're not alone this time."

See? I was right.

Cassidy. One day, when you're a mother, you'll watch your child breathe as they sleep, and you'll wonder how we did it. How *you* did it. Sometimes, there are no answers. All I know is that I marvel at your strength and determination, while simultaneously being heartbroken that you had to be so strong and determined, so young. But on those days when you feel the cracks opening, just know I will always be one song away.

Tye. My sweet, funny, weird-fact-loving, sensitive mini me. You have a heart of gold (and yes, I mean that with all the symbolism). This may mean that you'll someday feel more brokenhearted than others, but it'll also mean that you'll love with every cell in your body. Your highs will be high, and your lows will be low. Thank you for giving me Wolfie. You are beautiful, even when you feel broken.

My in-laws, Pat and Bert. You are the "parents" I always prayed for. Thank you for loving me, always, unconditionally. For isolating, which I know was a lose-lose scenario. You sacrificed so much to be there for us, and I'm sorry you had to make that choice. But I'm thankful you did. I know where Greg gets it from.

Our Covid-cancer crew: Bob and Debi—for giving us a safe haven during the worst of storms. The farm was our weeping willow for twenty-one chemo infusions. "Thank you" will forever feel insufficient. Ruscoe-Rocker peeps—for that trip to Florida, right after brain surgery. For all the karaoke nights, and for being our safety net. I can't listen to "Last Call" without tears. Worthen family—thank you for all the smoothies and hugs and sleepovers and board meeting mask battles. Kristin, you're stuck with me now. Wes—for unwavering, love-filled meals. Lee family—no one gets it like you do. I hate *how* we met. I love *that* we met. May "stable" be the only word we ever hear again. To Sam and Teresa—who also felt our pain too personally. Your positive mantras still sit on our mantel. May we never find mountain lion cub prints in our butter. To the Shoemakers—for the soul-filling stew. To Shannon, Dave, and Zanne—for the place in the woods that brings comfort, and for raining Wind River angels on families in need. For loving my Cassidy as your own. Zanne . . . thank you for giving my baby your heart on your final birthday.

The family that is so much more than family: Shawn—thank you for the perfect hug on that hospital floor on that awful day. For being someone I can trust, no matter what. And for taking the blame when I was a turd. Dominique and Courtney—I always wanted a sister. The universe gave me you two, who are unrelated and yet still friends, and I'll never understand how we all turned out sane (and, dare I say, pretty friggin' awesome?). Thank you, Melissa, Jon, and Ross, for loving my amazing siblings and supporting us through our years of hell. Jeff and Janet—I barely know where to start. For giving me courage, as a teen and young adult and older adult, every time the weight's been too heavy. For being the constant in a chaotic pool of genes. To Joerg and Katrin—for not letting us sink. To Abbey and Kathy—for all the walks on opposite sides of the street. To Mark—for knowing when we didn't have it in us to mow the lawn. To Paul and Linda—for always remembering birthdays, no matter how long it's been. And to everyone in the Stocker, Gnau, Barritt, Otto, and other descended family groups who prayed for us when I could barely breathe—you will never know the strength you gave.

Caise, Erin, and Steve—for the teen spunk, sweetness, decades-long friendships, and unconditional love that entered this book. You live in these characters.

Sarah Dewberry, Jenny Whitley, Elaine Dillard, and Lisa Huckaby—for being so much more than teachers. Thank you for being safe spaces.

My Crafties: Lauren, Michal, Joana, and Katie—this book would not be this book without you guys. Good Lord, I love you ladies. Thank you for the group FaceTime call the night I thought I'd lose my baby. For telling me I wouldn't, until I had no choice but to believe you. For not letting me drown in my sadness and encouraging me to build this book on heartbreak's back. And for reading endless revisions. And thank you to Amy, Lynne, Heidi, Caroline, Zainab, Jamie, Donna, Zack, and every other critique partner/writing buddy who believed in me.

EVERYONE—too many to list—who sent Cassidy and Tye gifts during treatment. Those were priceless moments of joy. Mega shout-out to Julie, Kelli, and the 12x12 crew; Shade (and everyone at church); Jillian and Creating New Tails; the Seltzers; the Balls;

the Waldrums; the Ritters; the Schwartzes; the Volks; SVG and the Sports Broadcasting Fund; For Those Who Would; the sports venue technology community for your beautiful support of my husband and our family; and everyone else who donated so Cassidy could get/train a service dog.

Pediatric Brain Tumor Foundation, Gilda's Club, and Make-a-Wish, for all you do.

Everyone at Cincinnati Children's Hospital—Dr. de Blank, Dr. Smiley, Margot, Dr. Lawson, Dr. Shah, Dr. Carina Braeutigam (crystals!), Julie, Bekah, Jobi, Stephanie, Heather, everyone in audiology and PT, every Child Life worker, every nurse, pharmacist, nutritionist, and oncologist who took too many late-night calls about yet another fever, and everyone whose path crossed ours … you are ranked #1 for a reason, and I love you all to pieces. To Dr. Farber—for finding the tumor. For saving her life. I know it wasn't easy to give me that news. To Dr. Gump—for your skilled hands during brain surgery. Jacklyn, JJ, Leigh, Sanethia, and everyone who ever accessed Cassidy at Norton's—thank you for making the sticks as painless as possible.

And last, but definitely not least . . . thank you to those who actually turned this story into a book. Allison, you never wavered. You've been my champion, my cheerleader, and my friend. Thank you for all the brainstorming sessions and late-night texts that told me when it was time to close the laptop. Julie—photographer extraordinaire . . . thanks for not letting me look bad! To everyone "behind the scenes" at Blink/HarperCollins—Sara, Megan, Kate, Ruthie, Cindy, Abby, Jessica, and Denise—thank you for working so hard to get this book into the world. To Ellen Duda, for the gorgeous cover. And thank you, thank you, THANK YOU, Katherine and Jacque. Patient, thorough, brilliant, comforting, and kind . . . you are *dream* editors. Thank you for believing in this story, and in me. I've learned so much and loved every moment. It's been an absolute privilege working with you.